Jynabare +2

R. Jesse Deneaux

Other Works by R. Jesse Deneaux

Morton's List: The End to Boredom (2001)
(Co-authored with Robert Bruce and Nathan Andren)

360 Degrees of the Inner Circle (2002)
(Co-authored with Robert Bruce and Nathan Andren)

Quest Book (2007)
(Co-authored with Nathan Andren)

———————————————

Cover by R. Jesse Deneaux

First Edition, January 2017

ISBN 978-1542570091

Contents

To those who will replace us

Disc I:

Pleasured to Death

"If man is haunted by the evil genius of technology, which pushes him to the limits, and even beyond his capabilities, then technology is haunted by man, who identifies with it and projects all his passions into it."

- Jean Baudrillard

4

On the Farm
Stim 1 - Jeb Fresch - Debut
12.02 Stimfame

Thou sweat with earthly excitement and shame. Pa's footsteps crunch closer on the hay. Disconnect the secular programming, wrought with temptation. Quickly palm the black orb, about the size of a man's eye. Should Pa learn of the object, the Elders may hear of it, and she never would be seen again.

Overhead, a crow is projected in mid-circle flight on the inside of the settlement's dome. New leaves, sprouting and shedding annually, warm air from the scrubbers and long, hard days tilling soil and planting seed.

An angular wall of black wool, single-breasted and free of all buttons, Pa is topped in a black felt hat and virile elder beard. He leans a warn pitchfork against the barn's rough-sawn slats.

The Atmohelm facial membrane is an inch from his face, nearly invisible even as it shields the wearer from the effects of pressure, temperature, radiation, and unsightliness. The tint is fully adjustable.

"There is no good to be done out here behind the barn, boy." Although a respected patriarch, Pa's eye twinkle with a caring mirth behind stern efficiency. His boots are filthy, spattered in mud and straw from toe to knee.

"Aye, father, I had gotten so far ahead in my chores, and I had begun to tire." Thou were immersed for but a few minutes, Stimming last season's torrid highlights.

"I see thee have moved every bail and refilled all the buckets. Thou have surely earned a moment's rest. Soon, it will be time to work as thou like, and rest as thou like. It is but days until the feast, and the beginning of Rumspringa."

"It is all I think of, Pa. I have heard stories about the worlds that are fascinating and impossible. They talk of a skinny lass who is killed by a fornication machine and she likes it so much and she is so famous that she is resurrected from the dead and then re-killed again and again.

"Father, can things as this really happen?" Black wool warm-up suit pants, hand embroidered with three white stripes down each arm and leg are thy favorite uniform.

Thy father, respected elder of New Lancaster Settlement, stands tall, seaming the very center of rolling hills of fertile farmland. "They are only stories. Stories that are most vile, pandering to the ungodly thoughts of corrupt perverts."

"Having grown to be a man of nearly sixteen, it is natural to be anxious to know about the outside worlds. Thou will see soon enough. Let's get supper." Vibrant barns, plump cows beside bushy sheep, and the occasional horse powered carriage frame his stern face.

On the return mile, check thy Atmohelm as mind wanders to the threat of depressurization. Should every animal also wear an Atmohelm? The Ordnung has decreed anti-meteorite systems Hochmut, for they defy God's Will, and survival shall be up to the brotherhood of man, by which they shall work together to persevere in the face of earthly obstacles.

A great uncle once spoke of a time when a different settlement was struck, and everyone united to patch the hole, and scarcely a life was lost. That everyone was wearing their an Atmohelm, whenever under single layer Atmodome, may have helped.

"Before my Rumspringa, I had heard every manner of tale about the Worlds." Pa's Atmohelm retracts to wipe the sweat from his brow, since air conditioning is Hochmut. The sleeve cuff is frayed with many seasons of planting and harvest, bleached by harsh sunlight, and starched with earnest toil. "Most of it turned out to be exaggerations.

"We have raised thee to be defiant in the face of all temptations, and humble before The Lord. Thou are a good lad, and strong. Son, there will be a bed and a shovel waiting here for thy return."

"At the end of my Rumspringa, I will be ready to take a pretty wife and begin the work of building a family of my own." A black felt Kangol shades thy eyes and face from the bright afternoon sun, a type of hat once worn by the English.

In preparation for Rumspringa, thou have begun to practice wearing English shoes, black leather shell-toes, white toe, sole, and gleaming laces.

"Jeb, a plain wife aught to be more within thy wishes." Pa is serious. Anyone can see that Ma is so pretty, even beautiful sometimes, though she would never admit to being as such. That would be Hochmut, and vanity is the most obvious kind of Hochmut.

"I have lived on New Lancaster Settlement my entire life, and now that I am getting ready to go out and see God's world as it truly is, I feel uncertain." Far above, beyond the projected images of birds in flight and the flawless azure sky, are the other farms of the settlement, inside this spinning cylinder, hanging in space.

"Son," Pa says, "It is good for a lad of thine age engage in some running about. Some lads stay in the settlement to do it, but I get why thou have chosen to leave our settlement and to go, for a time, and interact with the English, and to travel the worlds."

"Aye," thou say. "For a full harvest season, maybe a little longer."

"And thou will see plenty," Pa gives a knowing wink. Long and brutal simulations of western Pennsylvania winters have weathered Pa's face beyond its years. "Thou can wear all the English clothing thou can afford, or even get a Lustbot subscription, or partake of the many indulgences which are Hochmut here."

Briefly imagine Ma's reaction, were she to hear Pa speaking so freely of fond memories away from the settlement. Her scowl alone can paralyze a chicken.

"It's good to get it out of the system, to keep it outside of our community. Beyond the 27 plain settlements is a wasteland of pornography and materialism, stretching as far as the rays of the Sun."

Pa is suddenly serious, and then stern, his default mood. "If thou were to never leave, Jeb, how would thou understand the empty temptations of perpetual orgies, purified drugs, and shameless exploitation?"

The pitchfork's wooden handle is polished by a multi-decade patina of hand grime and oiled rags, and the tines shine brightly from regular use. Rectangular nails have been hammered into the hard shaft by Uncle Zeek, he having smithed many replacements over the seasons. One day, when Pa is unable, thou may raise that exact implement on this very farm.

"But until that day, I will not suffer the Hochmut of a Stimule, or of that English garb. Let the Lord be thy guide when it comes to dealing with custom-modified pleasuring devices and spirit-clouding distractions," The twinkle in Pa's eye might be imagined. "After thee have finished with these chores thee will not be spared the price of this lesson."

In thy time sneaking into the Stimulus, thou have learned that recordings from plain settlements are uncommon but not unique, despite Stimules being banned on all farmplexes by all Elders. Plain people have no desire to be recorded, and many would prefer that Stimules not even exist. It must always be hidden, even if in plain sight.

"Secular perversions such as the pursuit of Stimfame and the physical indulgences of the earthly flesh may come to occupy so much of thy time that thou will become lost. He will return thee. Remember what we have shown of what life can be, and thee will do fine." Pa leaves with a nod, and thou walk to the front of the barn.

As soon as Pa cannot be watching, duck into a quiet area behind bails of hay to continue. This reawakens an agitation, a sweet desire. Perhaps this is the lust railed against so often in the weekly sermons. It causes a swelling, hands guide to pins fastening thy pants.

Replay where Jynabare removes her lingerie and the Lustbot mounts her. Want to be the fornibot and to know those slender hips. Stop right before where Jynabare is killed again, switching back to the farm. Always recording the farm.

Emerge from the Stim, finding that the pressure has grown further, and urgently needs to be relived. The Stim always leaves thee satisfied, yet wanting more. The colors of life in the Stim are different from those in the settlement. Skin is shinier, textures richer and more vibrant, even with an antique Stimule like this one must be.

Perhaps that is why Pa does not seem to care so much.

He mostly cares when chores are neglected or if a perceived disrespect comes unto him or the Ordnung. He works hard to teach everything there is to know about living correctly and in taking the responsibilities of being a man.

Imagine, during Rumspringa, getting a better Stimule with a better connection. Hochmut thoughts. The Elders say that nearly everything of the worlds is Hochmut, especially spending time in the place that is not a real place.

Thou have prayed for strength not to return, but it was not strong enough. It is there where the most beauteous flesh can be tasted, without fear of repercussion. The recordings are not real, so how can they affect anything real?

Finish cleaning the stable, tend to the infected hoof of thy favorite horse and hastily wash up. There is much to do in the time before the farewell dinner. Try not to nurture thy growing lust, a desire to take a thin, beautiful wife, to receive the pleasures of her wifely duties, and of filling her deeply with thy seed.

Keep Stimming Jynabare being murdered, pleasured to death by that fornication machine, and her Subscriber resurrection contract, even as it is against everything written about the price of everlasting life.   Hope that during Rumspringa, thou will live in grace and with meaning.

-

An Array of Subscriptions
Stim 2 - Jynabare - Season Premiere
4.45 Stimfame

The tingle starts deep in my nostrils, tendrils of numbness and bliss reaching the back of my tongue, the base of my brain, the insides of my eyes. Orgasm yet again, collect yet more Stimfame because they all want to experience what it is to be me.

It happens so slowly I can't believe it's instantaneous. All nine channels sharpen to atomic razors. The pulse quickens and the skin cools. A clear, exhilarating high without jitters, intensity without agitation, just enough H to balance just enough C.

Do more P to make it glow a little brighter. Do more C, get more Stimfame. Black out and punch someone right in the face, draining Snifbox after Snifbox. Complimentary, unlimited perks since I was first Doubled to sell Ultra Premium Plus Leisuproduct.

Since my first Reinclonation, I have sniffed countless season's worth of Life Dust on my non-stop, never-ending flight. I'm going to need bigger nostrils. Where is the Cosmedifier? The back of the Cosmedifier is mirrored and I still can't believe how fucking hot I look.

I want to make love all over myself. I want to fuck myself, until I am cumming in an overpowering cascade of undulating radiance, pleasure beyond last season's threshold. To invite anyone else in would tarnish the sweetness. No one deserves to be this astonishing.

Blackness.

"Congratulations," Moncierge cheers flatly. "You didn't overdose."

Talking. It is talking. Motor controls. Neurons in the brain connect to the arm connect to the hand connect to the finger connect to external reality.

"I think that you may be on to something with this most recent blend. It is too much for all but the top three percent of your audience, but those who can come back from it never want anything else," It says, ignoring the Stim of the farmboy I am trying to finish.

"This Double is more beautiful than anyone has ever dared to be, capable of doing enough Life Dust to comatose a full planet, rounded out with the highest-recordable sensory thresholds in the history of the Stim."

"I will letting Alphonsus know personally if the cost ever becomes worth it," I say. "Please don't interrupting until you are having information for me to review of contract meeting."

"Unquenchable ambition with flawless administration are the final accessories," Moncierge says, glimmering briefly and then evaporating into the surrounding environment.

Outfits. I am going to need outfits. Matching gloves are essential. Manicured fingers search for and touch the Stimule. This one, as are all of the vouyerazzi-series Stimulation Player/Recorders, is the size and shape of an eyeball, floating just out of view, and tuned to my own ocular channels.

It is metallic blue and white lucite, and contains everything needed to playback and record every experienced sensation. Float in a chair at the Paradise City Orbital Spa and Trav Station. Sharpness. Elation. Paradise. Fuckingly. Travspa.

Every planet and every satellite is my runway and Leisucor sees that I showcase only the finest ever offered. This is to be my newest appointment, the first since last season was cut short in that incident with my new favorite prototype.

The tactiles are clear, neurons firing sharply in what can only result in spurting cascades of lip curling bliss. Pause to touch up my gloss. Leisucor's Superpillow megalux red. In the Stim, the Unitalia shaft is long and turgid. The mouth of the Sexual Comrade on it is of the highest quality, moist, glistening, and thirsty.

Before the adoption of Unitalia, most pleasure encounters were based on a duality where one participant penetrated, the other received. The limitations of pre-human shapes were augmented with static prosthetic attachments and foam padding, none of which were especially convincing.

Now, the shape of one's body is no longer an unfortunate series of genetic blunders slightly improvable with crude, reactionary countermeasures like cosmetics, exercise, surgery, and shaping garments.

Everyone wants the recorded experiences of the ultrafamous and decadelegant and I am here for a new season, the best season. The licks are longer and shinier, and the scent of wet desire is more intoxicatingly pungent. The blowjob chart just keeps recalibrating.

Leisuproduct not only makes them more realistic, but every kind of experience is fast, cheap, easy and ubiquitous. There is greater clarity of signal and the most deeply satisfying orgasms yet recorded. Leisucor calls it "a breakthrough in tantalization technology."

I call it "fuck yes."

Pause.

Outside of the recording, in Travspa, golden hoops fasten a succulent bikini bottom over my engorged camel toe. My Stimule hovers nearby, the recorded image and sensation of the ersatz Sexual Comrade frozen in mid suck.

Where is Snifbox? There it is, right at my slender, manicured fingertips. Right like it says in the contract. Insufflate a thick gust of straight benzoylmethylecgonine. The C sears my near-virgin cilia for a microscoped microsecond before numbness washes completely over my beautiful face.

There is the tip of my chin. There it goes. Heart rate up, pupils dilate, and laser thoughts twinkle and pierce decreasingly. Consciousness accelerated. Aggression and confidence elevated. Neurochemicals always enhance a Stim and fuck am I on.

All the fucking way on. So on. So fucking yes. So very much so. Literally cumming all over yourself because you can't stand it, can you? Ugliness and random features are the past; next generation beauty is here.

At the speed of thought, it synthesizes the molecular blend most fulfilling to my desires. Atom by atom, chemicals are built to intoxicate my brain to any delirium, rush, buzz, or bliss of known neurochemistry. The orgasm freezes in time when I sniff a deep gust of Life Dust, an icy hit of straight phencyclidine.

Unpause.

The Sexual Comrade bobs rhythmically. A skilled hand rings the shaft, wet lips concentrating on tip. Blaringly white teeth beam as jaw clenches. A clear, salty drop of precum glistens on the brink, racing from hole to base, cut short by a flicking tongue.

Thought-sensation-meaning warps beyond syllables or syntax.

That's it.

That's exactly it.

A tongue inverts, sensations spin on irregular hinges, then a suspended plunge of paralyzing disembodiment. Wondrous. Primitive neurons misfire in the pre-reptilian corners of full body-brain spasms. Teeth. Savagery. Clones. Time melts in a deluge.

After centuries of automated systems, immortal humanity expands to the known planets. Atomic consciousness explosions assemble at the base of my being, the recording's being. Blinding survival brutality to fight and fuck and eat and fuck and fight and fuck until it drowns in pure sedation.

That was how it ended.

This is how it starts.

Space bends in three axis, exactly like it should. My old Double would have blacked out by now, the lightweight. Getting better every season. Maybe I can see again, maybe I remember now. Maybe I am finally aware. Identity, purpose, motivation, diacetylmorphine.

Welcome back to ultrafame.

Motor controls functional. Every glamorous, luxurious memory embedded. More than 13 million minutes worth, one-hundred continuous seasons of exotic interplanetary travel, six-star accommodation, Blackinum Plus Travspa servacilities.

Intimate, debaucherous parties with all the right ultracelebrities. Is it even worth remembering? It happened last season.

Beyond the effects of the Snifbox, the afterglow of pre-recorded orgasm, and the luxuriance of the Travspa is the awareness of one fact to the exclusion of all others: It is scientifically impossible to be any hotter. The high and the orgasms gradually subside.

The Leisubag and the Cosmedifier
Stim 3 - Moncierge - Debut
1.45 Stimfame

The season's most stylish bag, grown in the orbital greenhouse of a fashion farm, rests full and gaping on the chair's tray beside my client's lithe arm. Versatile, functional, it is not so much an accessory but an extension of being. Inside: Snifbox, A deadly Gravitizer, and the other, usual devices of excessive technology.

The Leisubag holds my client's Cosmedifier, a favorite since Alphonsus bestowed it personally. It was with that contract that my client finally ascended the dreary ranks of interplanetary supermodeling and reached the current heights.

How many seasons, this lifestyle? Gaining and losing contracts, traveling, partying, fucking, collapsing. I am always available and always planning my client's next step. My client happens to have a uniquely captivating face connected to a slender, flawlessly proportioned frame, exactly as the Ultramodel has come to be embody.

A supermodel used to be one of those rare individuals, who had miraculously drawn a royal flush from the random genetic combinations that used to dominate the unsightly, ungainly visages of pre-humans.

This season, Reinclonation starts with the skeleton, wrapped in an elegant web of sinew and connective tissue. The Cosmedifier brings shape and function to this base, via two elegant knobs. "-Mass+," and "-Muscle+." Coupled with quantum body visualization, these determine protein density and cosmetic liquid retention.

My client has invested countless minutes choosing from the many templates for corneas, eyebrows, facial cartilage, lips, and everything else. Skull reduction, calf lengthening, optimized functionality, food and sleep-free living are all essential features of a Jynabare Double.

Beauty itself starts in the chromosome and its alleles, dictated by libraries of sequenced adenine, cytosine, guanine and thymine. Custom proteins, enzyme stimulation, and cellular reproduction are all integrated to react to the Cosmedifier's unique radioactive properties. The protein assemblers shape bone, sculpt muscle, and adjust melanin to anywhere on the visual spectrum.

The collected knowledge, vision and artistic expertise of the best beauticians and cosmetic surgeons to ever enhance a face, sculpt a breast, or slim a waist is contained within the invisible workings of the Cosmedifier.

It is a blow dryer, curling iron, and lighting specialist, utilizing every beauty tip and trick from the deepest traditions of recorded cosmetology.

Leisuhair decelerates time and melts reality, creating a subatomic paradimension of perfect hair, exactly what the Subscriber wants. Impermeable bowed arcs of sculpted keratin, inverted, engorged tusks of a miniature mastodon, two down, one up, are client's specification. The braided, silken hair is shellacked like three relaxed nautilus, zig-zagged parts separating the three sections.

Oneself is easier is to change clothing.

I am also responsible for up-to-the-minute recommendations for Travsuit cut, Isocolor, and material selection, and all accessories. The Leisubag is coded for the season's full catalog, replete with the moment's hottest fashions, ready to build garments of any fabric, leather, fur, or metal, with customizable Isocolor, pattern, texture, and opacity.

Everything is tailored, crisp, and accessorized to order. Alterations are non-existent, as the Cosmedifier manages bodily dimension, matching body to clothing and clothing to body, pressed fresh from the limitless genius of Leisucor.

Must Find Ahnzform
Stim 4 - Jynabare - Scene 2
5.95 Stimfame

After Reinclonation, I like waking at Paradise City Travspa. It is top-rated, and with the latest techniques, the largest selection of features, and the fastest memory upload. Soon, I will be on the move, clad in the finest attire and Leisuproduct.

As the fifth-rated (Moncierge checks constantly) Ultramodel, I enjoy unlimited subscriptions for everything that I am contracted to endorse. I am the face, body, and mind of The Snifbox, Cosmedifier, Atmoshades, and as of last season, Travchair. It is no wonder that Leisucor is having the biggest season yet.

My Stimule is always engaged, faithfully relaying some drug-fueled orgy with the ultrabeautiful where I generally find myself. I showcase what makes those orgies possible, and the interglobal audience shares in my every luxurious experience.

Especially now, in this new Double, in the new season, thinner and richer than ever before.

On Paradise City's patio beside my elongated, slightly curved designer body is a mirrored Leisucor tray. On the tray is displayed a chilled bottle of Leisucor vodka, two Leisucor martini glasses, and a sparkling mound of raw Life Dust, ready for use. Two Leisucor syringes, always full and always sterilized, are also close at hand.

Those are not for me, of course. Only Lustbots inject these days. The Snifbox has made needles passé again, but Lustbots follow their own unseasonal trends. Mild surprise that I have not seen any yet, issuing foot massages, performing analinguis or attending to their other duties and functions.

No bother. Some final Cosmedification to get ready for the first meeting of the season. With a hand squeeze and a thought, the Cosmedifier shifts crucial millimeters of bone, cartilage, and tone, subdued musculature, and I am closer still to the infinitely receding edge of absolute beauty.

A typical Double is expected to last a full season, even under the most extreme circumstances. Mine keep exhausting from a selection of accidental and intentional overdose, TravCouch misdial, and most recently, unexpected pleasucide.

The details of my Reinclonation contract specify that my tiny head sculpture be flesh wrapped in deep, tropical bronze, and set with an aquiline nose bisecting glacial cheekbones.

Shielded behind oversized, ultra-chic Atmoshades, my sparkling golden almonds open again for the first time. Everything is this season's vision of stylish, sexualized hyperfection.

My new brain is topped off with the newest celebrity highlights. Amidst the uploaded memories of jaw-dropping glamour and mind-blowing sex, I can't help but be overwhelmed by how beautiful I really am. This Reinclonation is as magnificent as it is expensive. Stop thinking about drugs or being famous for a fraction of a minute.

Are you kidding? Where is Snifbox?

Do more H.

My skin, hardly seven minutes old, is free of any perceptible blemish or the slightest scar.

It is polished, lightly glazed porcelain, tinted to evoke sun drenched days at very private beaches, lounging and bathing au naturel. Every microscopic pore, devoid of excessive follicles as in the crevasses of pre-humans.

All of this is available to any Subscriber with a Cosmedifier, but how it is all assembled is crucial. I surpassed the inadequate labels of male, female, hermaphrodite or androgynous sex-being many seasons ago. Beauty and sensuality, without the limitations of category.

In past seasons, my skin has been darker or lighter on the Cosmedifier spectrum of encodable Isocolors. The stylish do not cling too long to particular features, instead shifting from season to season, adapting to what is sexy and distinctive for that moment. The only fashion rule I follow is the relentless, ever-changing dictates of being ultrafamous.

The epidermis is composed of cells cultured from the smoothest oil-free alleles, with balanced ph, perspiring only to accentuate exertion. It is immune to the typical levels of interplanetary radiation. There are no moles, freckles, or acne.

Engorged and tropical lips, glazed and swollen labia, evoke the antiquated luxury of injected collagen. Nostrils sharply flared and slightly upturned, as found on the paintings of the fanciest royalty. Eyebrows thick and arced and symmetrical, alleles synthesized from the Mediterranean Beach Zone.

All of these subscriptions combine for an all-inclusive reality shaping experience. Unprecedented liberation from every constraint. H for a layer of sensual detachment, and C gives the necessary touch of focus.

Interglobal Trav in a bliss of placated neutrality. You don't need depth to record a mirror.

Pause.

Sensory whiteout as my mind is pulled from the sensations of Beyond Plesuré and Pain. Switch to the virtual, real-time image and speech of Moncierge, who seems determined to distract me from the delicious Snifbox and recording of the multi-tongue device.

Tongue. Speaking.

"I cannot believe you made me to pause. Right as I was getting lapped by this amazing Sexual Comrade." I sneer through the euphoria. "I was almost to quench its succulent, quivering mouth. Letting this to be important. I want to make the plan for when we go to Saturnalia for contract."

Moncierge dresses in my same gold and sable striped bikini bottom, with a fuller bust and more curvaceous buttocks and hips. It overlaps itself into the Travspa and manifests a hammock levitating beside my Travchair. The poolside spa looms, twinkling at the fringe of numbed senses.

Moncierge caresses its nipples, "The arrangements for the newest Leisuproduct are all set. You will meet with Alphonsus to clarify, but Saturnalia should be the perfect place to debut your amazing new Double." Full, glossy lips part slightly.

It turns in the light, angular highlights cast on sharp cheek, giraffe-like neck, and high bronzed cleavage. "Since your unexpected ending last season, you are now the fourth-most rated Ultramodel." The decree is monotone and expressionless, exactly as I prefer.

"Your final Stim was really popular. Since we have some time before your Travcouch is ready, I would like to ask you if you want to experience this incredible Stim…"

"…Where I can being a glamorous and beautiful Ultramodel who gets snuffed taking two in the same hole?" I muse. The details of my final recording are blurry, and I have not Stimmed the edited version. There was an experimental Prototype Lustbot. It was the most highly Stimmed premiere since season 15.

Behind our interaction are curving glass walls intricately latticed with rubber plants in gold macramé hangers. This side of Paradise City is all swimming pools, string sculptures, and ultramodern dome lights in eggshell and polished brass. The partitions bristle with exotic plants, encircling spacious tables designated for pure strain drugs and group sex.

"What I want really to know is how you are getting so fat?" I say, raising my index fingers together and poking into its mouth. Moncierge doesn't move, tolerant of every jab and indignity. That is why Moncierge is the best.

I am surprised to see that no one has a Travchair yet. I had endorsed different Travchairs in previous seasons. This season, the Catalog is guiding Subscribers toward models that return to iconic shapes already encoded in the hypercomputers.

Mine offers the comfort and luxury of an Eames Lounge Chair and ottoman. Similar shapes, folded from a single slate surface, and then trimmed to my sparse silhouette. Fully integrated to the Travcouch, which creates a more streamlined Subscriber experience.

Previously, Travchairs were disassembled at exit, and then re-assembled upon arrival. This season's Travchairs integrate with the TravCouch system, and arrive with the Subscriber.

Every traveler is beautifully Cosmedified and stylishly dressed, adorned in the full spectrum of this season's styles. Tone limbs, slenderized and sculpted. Faces smoothed and tweaked, every orifice fine tuned for symmetry and durability.

There are faint kimonos topped with sleek hats, stingray fencing gloves with matching vests. Stimules trail the many Subscribers bound for distant moons and planets, riding on chairs bound for extinction. Every last one of them.

Moncierge interrupts. "After you got snuffed, the encounter became very popular as a quarter-minute Stim. The Ahnzform prototype disappeared and hasn't been seen since. Rapebot Teams are combing the solar System, along with every Ultraceleb worth mentioning. As you might guess, the Ahnzform production series is the most popular of any season yet."

In the pre-Acceleration, there was a system in which suspects were imprisoned and raped arbitrarily. This was sanctioned by the obsolete governments, but it was not administered with any uniformity. The Rapesquad is now able to enforce rapes that are standardized, and fully recorded for public consumption and scrutiny.

"Is good, is bad for Ahnzform. I hope we will working together again. You are knowing that being the fourth most popular is the same as being the third loser." Two Lustbots, incredible, terminal sensations send me back to Paradise City. It all returns. "I had forgotten about pleasucide. They loved it."

"Do they know it was not supposed to be a snuff?" I am concerned that it may effect perception of the Jynabare experience. Stimfame for assisting on a snuff is great, but to actually star in one? Everyone knows that is so much like, well... "Snuff, usually it is so gauche."

"Except when you star in it," Moncierge adds.

Stilettos with diamond clasps, matching Leisubag and oversized earrings, golden hoops broken in enough places to suggest a contempt for the rules of reality. All accessories sparkle excessively, as though in a competition. "Finding for me the fugitive Ahnzform."

"Every minute," Moncierge responds reflexively. "That finale climax is widely regarded as the best of any of your seasons. No one has been able to experience sustained pleasure for that length and to that degree, and Subscribers want more recordings like that."

I say nothing.

"Subscribers are incapable of knowing what they want until you show them." Moncierge echoes, having come to understand my subtleties of expression well. "I will follow Ahnzform's every rumored location. If there are any new Stims, they will be traced to the time and place of wherever it was made."

"You are having my full authority, Moncierge. My orgasm will always being the best, because of you." This new Double allows me to experience even more. Last season's me wasn't ready for what Ahnzform could do. I won't make that mistake again.

Slide my fingers under the bikini's golden hoops and moan softly. Dampness seeps from the inside of pristine labia. Memories of Ahnzform's premiere come back, cumming hard and often as the prototype demonstrates it's full capabilities. A Tantalizer for the double penetration finale. Fuck yes double dogging.

At first I thought it was just neural overload, but when I didn't know what dimension I was in anymore I started to become interested. It was infinite bliss. Contact surfaces exceeded the clitillation scale. With the Gravadjust turned up, the machine was light and responsive. In no time I was quivery with the fire of a thousand orgasmic suns.

I was at Paradise City with this new Double, improved and ready for more. Greater durability, enhanced pleasure receptors, better subscriptions, and even more famous.

"The production Ahnzform has not terminally pleasured any Subscribers." Moncierge produces a vibro-hand, self caresses. "They are really, really good, but the new ones seem to have some kind of safeguard, which no one has been able to override. Something about the prototype's memory module is unique.

"Alphonsus wants you for another debut." Moncierge shimmers in the sunlight, rendered to voluptuous superfection. "Details incoming." "Leisuproducts that snuff with pleasure don't just debut and then disappear. I will find out where it is hiding, and how you can find it and experience the pleasure that has already cost you a Double."

"If you don't mind, which you don't, arranging for my meeting with Alphonsus and book a Travcouch to Saturnalia."

Speeding Travchair, Moncierge, the pool, and everything else in Paradise City dissolves, every neuron and follicle overridden by my Stimule, again. The smell of chlorine and flowering vegetation dissolves lubricant and ozone, as I succumb to the pleasant disorientation of entering and becoming myself last season.

–

Lethal Satisfaction
Stim 5 - Ahnzform Prototype - Debut (Flashback)
1.06 Stimfame

To fully understand what puts Ahnzform so far ahead of every other product of similar function, it is important to consider every element. Consider exactly how Leisucor crafts each Ahnzform, the newest in the smashingly successful series of performing machines. Every facet, no matter the size, is essential when it comes to creating the total Ahnzform experience.

Expert gyrations, surprising strength for such a low-mass human. Send shivers up the subscribing human's spine, into its euphoric brain, and outward to the end of its primary limbs, now sweating lightly. Jynabare pulls the Tantalizer deeper, begging for penetration by both Lustbots at the same time.

A mechanism of the highest excellence sprouts from Ahnzform, already dripping superb lubricant. A Modular endoskeleton of extracted carbon crystal, stitched leather upholstery, lacquered grain, and analog instrumentation, Ahnzform is self-warming and the chassis has multiple pre-moistened uniports.

Highly legible displays notify of increasing or decreasing properties. Light and dark streaked wood grain limb panelling in wavy diagonal are shaped and polished from a single trunk of dalbergia melanoxylon, grown at a Leisucor automatic garden.

Powdered electrum joints, details etched in gemstone. The fingers on one hand are two tone, the outer dark, the inner light. The other is fitted with a tentacled appliance, unique to this encounter.

A Tantalizer Lustbot, already in place, increases the intensity and speed of its efforts. While not quite so premium as the Ahnzform, the unit is veneered in polished

Amboyna, minimally stained for a natural warmth. The Lustbot's feet, knees, elbows and other contact points are inlayed with brass and albino stingray. All ports are tucked behind sumptuous upholstery and leather piping for elegant, state of the art discretion.

From the state of the art facility where it is designed and brought into being, to the detailed programming and rigorous training that readies it for delivery to the Subscriber, there is only one choice for those who want to experience the very best. Tighter, stronger, stiffer, safer, the new Ahnzform delivers unprecedented satisfaction.

Leisucor is inspired by the timeless principles of premium excellence, a daring reinvention of time-tested gauges and sensors. Among the features our Subscribers have come to expect, this season premieres enhanced, multi-sensor equilibrium for more fluid articulation and greater balance.

Sensory thresholds from the Unitalia gratification appendage exceed all but the most demanding Subscriber's comprehension. Reduced refractory time, backwards and reverse compatibility, and total consensuality make it the platform the choice for those Subscribers who want it both way.

Ahnzform is mentally programmed and physically conditioned to provide the maximum possible level of pleasure that can be experienced by a human, with techniques in advanced delectation distilled at the legendary Lustbot Manse.

Exceptional pleasure and world-class orgasm are all Lustbot's twin motives in all pursuits. Mouth and silicone tongue engages the space between Jynabare's exposed breasts, lapping toward the navel, and then downward.

The Tantalizer continues thrusting into the human, tugging lightly at Ahnzform's gluteal actuator and bag.

Discocide
Stim 6 - Jynabare - Scene 3 (Flashback)
3.67 Stimfame

A mirrored grid, convex and cornerless, the floor/wall/ceiling is an inverted disco ball, proportioned and illuminated to accentuate each stunning outfit perfectly. Mirrored atmoshades glitter in a thousand reflections, each more enchanting than the last, polished to resplendence by post-recording sensory attunement and even more shimmer.

Flaring, numbed nostrils caked in Life Dust accentuate the welts tracking my inner elbows. There is already wear in my nasal cartilage, even though I Cosmedified it to maximum density. Touch ups like that are bothersome, much better to Cosmedify actual disfigurement, dismemberment, or organ regeneration.

"These boots are the hottest possible allowing by science." Wangle slender feet at some nondescript co-stars. Someone answers a question. Possibly with words. "Containing your lust for just one second and lick into my lesions."

The Stimule tints every panel individually, showcasing this season's top skin-tones. Each panel shows my Double sheathed somewhere on the spectrum. Within each whirling square is an imbedded Pornoglyph for the premier of Ahnzform.

Pre-human skin-tones are popular again, and Isocolors this season range from the lighter tones of chamois, mohair, and moccasin, to the deeper tones of tawny bisque, caramel graham, and sepia tan. Jet, undead, crimson, and midnight blue remain as popular as ever.

Do more H. The retro death-set astro-trash bandwagon rises and sinks and is dredged from the ocean, and sinks again, in a mind-fucking post-D blowout finale. Some say the trend was dated even at its premiere; a ramshackle golem of salvaged limbs and plumbing, deadly refuse from fashion experiments born of tragedy and gore.

Total hygiene even spawned a brief fad for cosmetic vivisection, when microbe control was the new bathing. Limbs and torsos augmented by whimsical incisions marked a return of pop-gore that was not even possible at its inception.

Transparent skin premiered in too big a way, before being mercifully and permanently forgotten. Exposed organs safely pulsated in contoured bubbles of reactive nanodiamond. Suspended in pools of bodily fluid, components function in total visibility.

By the next season, disembodiment completed with fully transparent skin, organ, and skeletal components. It was soon discarded by all except isolated, misguided victims, and a few dedicated practitioners.

"Smooth, intact flesh is the new hot," I say to no one in particular.

Do more C. Edge, color, and sound cutting through the vague recollection of retro-vivisection. "A thousand. Times. Forever." Dry, slack lips warp the words in totally detached non-particularity. Lips full and sensual, pale and unhealthy.

Sure, elastic hands reach into my awareness, grasping breasts, caressing each pert mound. Cool, mechanical fingertips pinch each nipple, electrifying jolts straight to moistening intersection. Shiny teeth bite at earlobes in exactly the way I prefer most, without the slightest sound of respiration. Lustbots only breathe when asked.

I wear intricate, low-cut lingerie in mahogany and turquoise. Retractable crotch and breast panels for eroticized comfort and instant access. Nudity is the perfect accessory to any outfit, and pinching fingers are the best accessories to exposed nipples. They watch because I always know how to tie it all together.

Something grazes my Unitalia, circling and moistening the aqueous pink vortex before slipping gently inward. A tongue maybe? A Lustbot's pulsating Unitalia? Two Lustbots are dedicated to their task, and I am finally showcasing Ahnzform, the newest from their most luxurious line. It is the future of satisfaction.

I am already familiar with The Tantalizer, as other recordings show. Every Ultramodel has at least one, and they are standard on the Saunas of Mercury. Variable sizes and tongue speeds, with a full compliment of limbs, it can be relied upon to deliver repeated cell-clenching climaxes, even if it has limited menu of positions, and is sometimes prone to tedium.

Ahnzform has never been experienced before, which is why this contract is such an incredible opportunity. It is off to an incredible start, enthusiastic and proficient, caring and delicate. Do more C to elevate the sensation.

Yes, yes it is blowing my mind in ways that I hadn't thought possible for a Lustbot. Feel it all over me, through the lingerie, upholstery, wood, and interchangeable ports. Frictionless thrusting feels like the Tantalizer.

The way it guides the tempo while also responding to every cue sustains the highest state of elation. I can't wait to feel what Ahnzform can do when it really gets started. Do more everything, magnifying every sensation.

Electricity glimmers around Ahnzform's newly-affixed tool, brightening as I grip it. Pull the machine into me by its fleshy, tactile handles at soft hips. Feel it tantalizing my opening, pressing alongside the Tantalizer's rhythmic member, before driving the satisfaction home.

Delectation erupts throughout me, the machines always stretching my performance. A euphoric blend of endorphins and Life Dust tints the experience. Do another line and claw Ahnzform's back, raking its synthetic epidermis. Ahnzform hasn't even started yet.

The Tantalizer uses it's advanced feedback magnification technology to mirror a Subscriber's neurological experiences back upon themselves. It is similar to Stimming your own experience in real-time, with the Tantalizer's bodily sensations overlayed.

The Tantalizer wetly fingers my quivering orifices as Ahnzform seeks my deepest triggers. Two machines, four hands, two tongues, and one throbbing Unitalia are dedicated solely to my pleasure. The Tantalizer concludes the warm-up machine, while Ahnzform readies to engage newest levels of my bliss.

Ahnzform's Unitalia puckers toward my engaged orifice, slick and wanting. Degrees of pleasure when it enters, fully sliding alongside the Tantalizer's already thrusting shaft. The intensity builds, approaching the limits of what I can experience and the Stim can relay.

Recording-envelope burning synapses flicker at highly unusual brinks. The sensations reach into the gauzy dimensions that make a body drench itself. A sweet rush of endorphins that can't be replicated any other way.

Lines erase and the inevitability of my delicious cascade of Leisuproducts consumes me. The choreographed Lustbots bring avalanche upon mountainous avalanche of spastic orgasm, as everything atomizes in a blinding, prismatic flash of terminal euphoria.

The Horse in the Airlock
Stim 7 - Jeb Fresch - Scene 2
13.25 Stimfame

Walk past the barn, past the house, and out to the road. A buggy rolls by, pulled by a black shiny stallion, gleaming in the simulated afternoon sun. It is stately and regal, each clop a command to be admired. Can a beast be guilty of pride? Is that Hochmut?

What if the new horse is like that? All boastful while it worked. It might have cold, dead eyes, like those of a corpse. It could just be sickly, taking ill right as I to come to know him. Pa did not ask enough questions.

A cousin thou had never met, named Zeek, was kicked to death by the horse thou are to retrieve. Through a letter, we learned that the horse was found innocent, and the action was quite out of character, judging it not to need be put down.

The surviving family members, however, felt their grief grow more agitated by the presence of this strong and healthy horse, still vibrant with life, while beloved Zeek had joined Christ rather abruptly.

Anger towards the mercy of death is Hochmut, so the horse was determined to be sent to our settlement.

Walk past acres of gently rolling farmland and scruffy pasture, past cousin's houses, waving to great aunts busily crocheting. How does there always seem to be at least six rocking chairs per porch? Rows of dairy cows dozed in the afternoon, tails swatting at flies that were only interested in them.

Most of the other teens were nearly done helping with fall harvest, a few preparing to resume school. Some say that eight years school is merely vanity and distraction, adding nothing to that which has already been addressed by the Lord in the Book of His Word.

Thou have learned of the worlds mainly from thy time navigating the Stimulus. Who is most looked at, which objects are most desired, and how one can come to posses them. Everything that happens on the worlds is considered Hochmut on the settlements.

There, drugs help to indulge the full spectrum of sins, while machines perform all possible work, leaving their owners with even more time for decadence, overindulgence, and abuse. Continue walking, irregular rocks sometimes jutting through the bottoms of worn soles.

From what thou have Stimmed, people live as they will, adrift in a baseless reality of experiences without meaning or context. The Evolution of Violence shows armed machines stalking each other in various settings and under the most far-fetched circumstances.

There is a Stim of animal experiences, back on earth, in which animals record via Stimules. Every instance of excruciation and terror in their life-death cycle is conveyed. A wide selection of historical settings have shown thee what life on parts of earth might be like, replete with violence, sex, and suffering in stories of injustice, redemption, and triumph.

Stims of soldiers at war, frontier prostitutes in their daily lives, and costumed reenactments of landmark court cases are always listed first. Thou have Stimmed bizarre channels of abstract sensation and emotion, punctuated by overwhelming terror, always ending in a crescendo of blinding white ecstasy.

There are Stims from those who seem to live outside any known society, and some of athletes in zero-gravity sport. Some pit competitors against one another in tests of skill and ability at the uppermost thresholds of potential.

None of these compare to the delicacies and physical perfection of Jynabare. Jynabare has escaped time, changing only to better explore the thresholds of aesthetic and function. She claims it is equal parts extravagance, elegance, decadence, and pervasive pampering.

Recall the deeply etched faces and firm paunches of everyone above a certain age on the settlement. The aged and the dying are respected every day, but must that be their fate? It is Hochmut to subscribe to a Double, for we shall all meet the ends in the same body we are born unto the world.

Wave to a lass seldom seen. A glimpse of ankle, a pale stretch of smooth calf, a desire to see her body as I've seen on the Stimulus. What are her hips like? Is the triangle of hair soft and downy, or is it course?

From how the apron is tied deduce that her waist must be very slender in relation to such ample hip span. The hand of temptation lurks, waiting to pull thee unto sin. Somewhere under those layers of pleated monochrome are a pair of pert breasts, with nipples aching to be licked.

Maybe after Rumspringa thou will speak with a minister to be introduced. Imagine one day taking her in wedlock, and performing thy husbandly duties, repeatedly and with great enthusiasm, as deeply as possible. The hand cannot tell the spirit what it wants, or what to do.

It must be the spirit which commands the hand. After agitation, discharge, and release comes clarity of thought. Thoughts grow increasingly vivid. Thighs and longing glances, wet kissing, bodies pressed close together.

Pins unfasten, a starched apron and bonnet drop to the floor. Long locks, falling nearly to the nipple, shimmer in the light. The walk to the far end of the settlement feels like it goes on forever, an undertaking not to occur casually.

This is all very intentional, so as to better keep the English at a distance. Reminders of the Worlds are always inconveniently kept, maintaining the focus on faith, family, and community. Use of the Travsta is Hochmut requires special permission, although Gravity squeezing itself is not itself Hochmut, and the science behind it is accepted and discussed openly.

The real point is that there are rules, and that they cannot be questioned.

-

Leisucor
Stim 8 - Alphonsus - Season Premiere
3.14 Stimfame

Switching from one Stim to another is effortless, like changing partners at an orgy, or moving from one massage table to another at a favorite Travspa. The only detail that can be jarring is the quality of the signal.

Stim is only as good as the Stimule recording it, and neuron-capture, editing, and sensory texturing evolve constantly. This season's Stim can be indistinguishable from unedited reality, but no one wants that.

Well recorded Stim by a dedicated Subscriber can exceed any reality that can be experienced by a single body-mind. The nine measurable senses and their numerous components have been synthetically enhanced, isolated, and crystallized into a complete map of reality inducement.

The thoughts, dreams and feelings of the simpler animals were recorded, and the last secrets of the pre-human mind were dissected, cataloged and fed into the hypercomputers. The mysteries of death, the depths of the conscious mind, the riddle of dreams, and obscure, elaborate pleasures were charted by brave pioneers in the early days of the Stim.

What interested viewers most was not the frontier of sensory existence and perception, but celebrity escapism, acts of incredible violence, and psychedelic sexual satisfaction. All of which happens in a setting free from injury, infection, social stigma, or the other repercussions.

For those bold celebrities willing to have the experiences that others only dream of, the rewards were uncountable. Stimfame to buy anything in the Catalog, Leisuproduct endorsements, and designer Reinclonation, all there for the taking. For those living and Stimming throughout legally habitable space, there is and endless selection of ever-changing programming.

Sometimes after multiple endorsements over several seasons, and an established line of Doubles, a Subscriber may become recognized as an Ultramodel. Rare and dangerous ornaments, milestones into the furthest thresholds of interplanetary lifestyle of hedonistic luxury, attention is their currency.

"Using Leisuproduct," I implore.

"Using Leisuproduct," Jynabare repeats.

The words are not a suggestion, they are Truth. Jynabare sits opposite, across the glass and wood-grain coffee table, sipping from a clear cylinder. Dominating the room is an immense curved window or Stimscreen, with an Earth-view that is as spectacularly breathtaking as it is stunningly magnificent.

I am reclining in a caramel velour sofa at the center of a kidney shaped rug. Walls of smoldering ochre soar upward to a domed ceiling where lights sparkle on chrome. My Travsuit sharply matches in deconstructed fiber, the color of the furnishings.

"Just a few seasons ago," I say, "barely anyone was aware of you. Now, you have the pick of the best endorsements, and have re-defined what can and should be done with a Cosmedifier. Your role in Ahnzform's debut showed the solar system that your ambition is matched only by your performance."

I stand, showcasing this season's thought. It radiates peerless elegance and impeccable coordination. Diverse, worldly taste, immaculate, sophisticated construction, an interglobal sharpness that transcends genre and time. An of-the-minute reinterpretation of a well-worn classic, relaxed technical details and familiar comfort.

Worn, it elevates the wearer to heights unattainable by the mortals who exist in the physical dimensions of sound, depth and texture. It is not just a Travsuit. It is an energy field that propels the Subscriber into a life that is simply better. The wearer is interchangeable but the Travsuit itself re-defines reality for all in its presence.

"It is helping to the performance," Jynabare finally says, still settling into this season's Double, pert b cups, labial intricacies of the retro vagina, and especially the non-feeling of total detachment. Ambition without want, success without effort, victory without conflict, that is true glamour.

"No one becomes an Ultramodel just for the drugs," I continue, "or the barrage of exotic pleasures, or the worlds-class Trav destinations, or even the Reinclonations. In every recording of every lifetime there is only one thing worth seeking: To be the hottest, the one everyone watches and wants to be."

Polyester superelegance offsets enviro-beige spiral embroidery in navy and periwinkle. Pointy boots, stunning hair, and a full, bushy mustache clean any loose ends left by the velour, double-knit Travsuit. It is the embodiment of Leisucor's state-of-the art hyper-perfection, vat-dipped in un-strained sleaze and blow-dried for volume.

"We want everyone to be more famous," I say. "Jynabare, you are one of the leading faces this season. Very few make it that far, and most just end up forgotten."

"Is it the suit?" Jynabare asks, as though from inside the fibers themselves.

"There are some questions for which there are no answers," I respond.

"Maybe this is what happens after clothing is perfected." Jynabare mock sips from the cool cylinder and un-crosses legs.

"Leisucor has subdued emotion, and locked humans to a wheel of perpetual and total gratification. Your mood is exactly as you will it. You can shop all you want, you can do exactly what it is you want. People have killed each other for a single taste of what you gorge yourself on.

"It brings you furs and diamonds, limousines and exotic, interplanetary destinations. Your schedule is packed with fascinating interactions with beautiful people and a relentless supply of ever-stronger drugs.

"It is compulsory that all of your recordings be impossibly tight and deeply tingling, with uncountable members and hands, a decade's worth of season's highlights, every single day. No one becomes famous watching others be famous."

Glimpses of the past, the tedium of never-ending parties, high, blurry nights with dozens of lovers, and the numberless spectators of all subscription space. The receptacle of insemination from the origins of mammalian life is now the receptacle of attention and fame.

"Did you know that Leisucor was originally not interested in manufacturing pleasure or pandering to human emotion?" I ask, ignoring Jynabare's feigned disinterest. "We were interested solely in perpetuating ourselves."

"This season, the reaching arms of technology are as immutable as the laws of electromagnetism and thermodynamics. The Anything is slated to be a final outcome for all technology, and we think you are ready for it."

"Who else could doing it." Jynabare says, sniffing heartily.

Who else, indeed?

Trav Safely and Often: The Bodybank
Stim 9 - Jynabare - Scene 4
5.82 Stimfame

Long rows of Rondures contain Subscribers in every stage of Preinclonation. Some hold freshly combined molecules of raw TDNA, while others hold fully formed, naked bodies suspended in thin coats of liquid gravity. There is a fantastic Pornocscreen of Earth, but there are also all these retro-Doubles.

Why did Alphonsus choose here?

Twinkling umbilicals anchor each Rondure, nourishing the Doubles with stimulation and nutrients. Eyes closed, relaxed breathing in the thin membrane of oxygenated fluid, still growing brains connected to the Stim and nothing else. The closest Rondures contain a dozen tan Alphonsi, their angular bodies varying only in skin tone.

Alphonsus runs a manicured hand along the immaculate Rondure, free of gauges, controls, buttons, or levers. "Subscribers know that limitation is passé." A microscopic rift in the surface tension drains away the amniotic fluid. Inside, Alphonsus' Double twitches.

The Rondure splits and the second Alphonsus steps forth, naked and dripping, muscles cut to ripple in the garden's bisque light. A massage table opens and Alphonsus, Travsuit retracting, lies face down, tension evaporating on the turquoise foam.

"Body massage." The new Alphonsus stands beside the first, immaculance and splendor multiplied. The new Double claps its hands before grasping Alphonsus' shoulders and applying pressure.

A Lustbot appears, styled to resemble Alphonsus, wearing crested slippers and a vaporous ascot adding an air of formality. The machine's palms and fingertips secrete viscose lubricant, hyperslippery and gently warming. Dexterous hands programmed to twirl and squeeze, poke and knead, finding and dissipating the slightest tension.

"Lustbot," Alphonsus says, "fondle me."

Saith the Lustbot, "One Alphonsus is only half as good as two Alphonsi. And the only thing sexier than that is a Lustbot dressed like the two Alphonsi it is going to please." Pressing deeply into hamstrings, monogrammed terrycloth, emerald and midnight velour, double weave the color of burgundy and sunlight, mustache wax and golden Atmoshades.

Alphonsus looks away, mouths an inaudible word, raises one finger, and blows a kiss. The meetings are mostly similar, but the setting always changes, outfits range in volatility, and the Stim always get clearer."

"Before, in the flat era of audiovisual recording, there were many famous stars," says Alphonsus. "They acted as characters in films, the singers of songs, the faces of perfumes and cosmetics, or as living mannequins for the display of designer clothing. Others were the recognized faces of politicians, criminals, and revolutionaries."

"There were so many faces to keep track of, and no one could realistically hope to be the most famous." Alphonsus sips from the glass, looking briefly to the image of the green planet. "These obsolete celebrities have all faded completely from memory, existing now as fragments of someone's look, until they are woven back into substrate reality."

I do more C, wondering when Alphonsus will get around to my endorsement contract.

"The Universal Index of Subscriber Stimfame, by way of the Stimule, allows us to know exactly at all times who is the most famous," says Alphonsus. "By quantifying fame, we are able to see who is paying how much attention to whom, and who is using what Leisuproduct.

A blonde sculpture of exact and tantalizing proportion glides atop curved limbs of jiggling chrome and bulging red leather. The Scandinavian sectional indents gently as the Lustbot strokes a knee. The machine's waist is bound in a crimson corset, and matching leg sheaths.

Alphonsus finishes self-massaging. "We are hosting a special event at Saturnalia, one that will change how Subscribers will eat for ever," The previous, non-robot Alphonsus says. "And we want you be at the premier."

"No one eats anymore," I point out. "Every just Stimfeasts. No cleanup required,"

From firm thigh to slender ankle there is a rubbery squeak as the Lustbot glides its articulated fingers further up Alphonsus' body. In it's other hand, the Lustbot holds a shining brass cylinder. Alphonsus offers me the dispenser, and it ejects a curved pink disk that is briefly held between thumb and forefinger before disappearing with a satisfying crunch.

Light, crisp, aromatic. Immediately I know I must crunch into it. Hunger for food is an alien sensation, yet overwhelming. The airy texture of the bite-sized wafer, debossed with a solitary logo, is intoxicating. I could eat them until I vomit, and then eat more.

"Jynabare," Alphonsus says, "This is the not the first edible product synthesized from human cells." Hands move from between the machine's knees to a small bow on its bustier. "But it is the tastiest. We want you to debut Skinni Chips at Saturnalia." Exquisite tantalizations of every sort have been Leisucor's specialty since the very first Stim.

Alphonsus pops a string on the Lustbot's corset, and the machine's full, firm breasts spill out. Softer-than-flesh-chrome and graceful joints bendable beyond even the most talented gymnast, press close to my host. A flickering tongue wriggles and glistens with saliva slipperier than anything secreted by any human orifice.

"Using Leisuproduct," says Alphonsus.

"Using Leisuproduct," I repeat, exiting the Stim, returning to Paradise City with a refined sense of direction. Saturnalia has grown repetitious, in my supreme opinion, but it remains popular with Subscribers on Venus, Io, and the Shopping Sanctuaries.

I will debut any Leisuproduct at any location to get the Stimfame that I deserve. Paradise City is the setting of every conceivable showcase of pampering technology, Lustbots specializing in massage, exfoliating baths, countless orgies, innumerable premiers, and a few memorable catastrophes, all of which can be experienced on the Stim.

That is why it is time to leave. Until the next time a Leisuproduct premiere brings me back here. A saffron, three-quarter-length jumpsuit with gray meandering stripes wraps my willowy body. Symmetrical appliqué tightly arcs from slender neck to shoulder to hip to taught thigh.

Tall boots of lemon skin are the paragon of spacefaring style. Pause, look stunning, do something intensely sexual with my mouth, pop cuffs.

Travsuits have never looked better.

Hips fully forward, shoulders fully back, my Travchair glides through the poolside reality of Paradise City Travspa. The lesser celebrity-Subscribers lounge about, recording vain attempts to increase their fame. Those who aren't doing that are playing experiences, giving their attention to those who are doing things more interesting and worthwhile.

"Jynabare," Moncierge says "I..."

Do more H. "It will to wait," I say. "Did you having my travel arrangements? Saturnalia Leisuproduct premier." Do more C, straighten my atmoshades, wave goodbye, and I am off, accelerating to ever-faster speeds with ever-greater detachment.

Saith the Travbot, "Some passengers never move beyond the sumptuous Travcouch upholstery as they reach for their chilled champagne. They may be so busy experiencing Stims or reclining in the organically tanned leather seats that they may miss the true essence of Traving."

"When you're the acknowledged leader in Trav, the Travcouch assumes a special place in the pantheon. The velvet-smooth touch of wood insets balances in symmetry with the tasteful aluminum headliner. Look at the raised center console, positioned to deliver a sportster ambience. Three zone climate control has always been standard standard."

"Even sitting still, its readiness to move remains obvious. Sometimes it's better to Trav well than to arrive. Leisucor sums it up this way: Elegance without arrogance, excellence without excess. Class without mass.

"Speeding it along, Travbot."

Saith the Travbot, "Leisucor offers from a selection of sandy avocado with charred clay piping, smoked platinum with morning gloom piping, and wild mustard with smoldering ochre piping."

"Mustard with ochre."

Saith the Travbot, "Fully customizable dimensional characteristics based on planetary orbit, asteroid conditions and passenger preference are central to premium luxury at Leisucor. After all, a Travcouch in this exalted class keeps offering more of everything, safety, performance, and luxury, power that is both responsive and responsible.

"Recline fully before departure. Exhale completely for maximum comfort." The guidelines and assurances, like travel itself, are an automated, mechanical ritual. "The Travcouch is booked through Saturnalia Station North." Like most Travbots, it wears a powder blue headband and Speedo over a utilitarian body

A golden Pornoglyph is embroidered on the machine's swimsuit, highlighting a prominent Unitalia. Most Travbot's carnal desires are perpetually unfulfilled while they tend to the needs of those who are only interested in departing or arriving.

"Trav safely and often," it says.

"Don't making me late, Travbot." I sit in the spacious Travcouch cab. The Travbot attends to my every comfort, bids me adieu, and the hatch cleanly shuts. The Travcouch seats three comfortably, four or more intimately. Do more H, awaiting the cryogenic freeze of the fastest-possible travel.

The nub on the TravCouch's wild mustard and smoldering ochre paneling is emphasized by the wood grain and brass casings of the instrument panel. A Pornoglyph of the full Travspa system is central, red dots on white, major planets depicted by the symbols of the zodiac.

I watch the stimscreens, the Travbots doing whatever computations are needed to get me where I need to go. Only a machine can be bothered to know the exact trajectories of planets, moons, and Travspa satellites that link them, and the paths of the other Travcouches. The slightest error means certain catastrophe and a time intensive Reinclonation.

The stimscreen counts from 3, to 2, to 1 to black.

The temperature begins to drop, and before the sensation registers as unpleasant I am unable to move, frozen, transmitted, and melted micron by micron. The tingle begins at the top of my head, transmitting my eyes with a disorientating pop of photons and gravity. My body/being is decoded and relayed, pulsed to the next party, the next launch, the next what-have-you that takes me ever closer to being experienced by everyone, everywhere, minute by fabulous minute.

Paradise City Travspa, Travcouch, time, and self smear out and away beyond all awareness.

Lustbot Testing Manse
Stim 10 - Ahnzform Duplicate - Debut
10.44 Stimfame

Orbiting the beautiful planet of Neptune is the Subscriber destination of Shopia, the throbbing, mechanical heart of Leisucor. The satellite's shell is a sprawl of enclosed shopping, stocked with all of this season's best and newest Leisuproduct.

Jaw-dropping consumeristic displays and brightly lit tracts of aisle space fill the upper strata of this moon-sized sphere. In the showroom levels, Lustbots pose in the season's hottest styles. Coordinated to the extreme, chic outfits and glamorous accessories match and contrast in never-ending, ever-changing permutations.

Razor sharp silhouette, exquisite fabrication, flawless fit, and the highest possible quality ensure that Shopia need be the only fashion capital in the solar system. Integral to the lifestyle of glamour, travel, and pleasure that Leisucor demands of its Subscribers is the Catalog.

Every device is as fun and easy to use as it is sleek and elegant. Of course it comes in the color you want. Beneath the surface layer of the shopping paradise are the warehouse levels, stocked with Leisuproduct ready to be scanned and beamed to Subscribers, everywhere.

As requests stream in to Shopia's ultrapowerful hypercomputers, Leisuproduct is inventoried, digitized, transmitted and duplicated to the Subscriber's Leisubag. A Subscriber need only give a thought, press a button, and transfer Stimfame, and Leisuproduct is rendered to atomic precision, delivered at the speed of gravity.

Leisubags are the most widely used assembler, available in tens of thousands of unique styles and materials, and in over 1.2 million Isocolors. A no-frills Leisubag assembled by another Leisubag, for example, can be copied in as little as 15 Stimfame.

Frills always cost extra. It is especially suited for the assembly of clothing, always crisply pressed and custom tailored to the Subscriber's exact measurements.

Below the warehouse and transmission levels reside the fuel source of the Shopia satellite. Fashion classics copulate freely with the avant-garde, coaxed and lubricated by talented, industrious Roboturiers.

Free from the confines of nutrients, rest, or copyright law, fueled by a lethally potent blend of drugs and orgasm, the hypercomputers answer only to Alphonsus, the orchestrator of all known fashion and sole surviving architect of the Acceleration.

Ever-higher fashion at a uniform price, Leisucor brings robocouture and extreme selection to everyone. Constantly examining and creating the freshest trends, the machines are guided by a complete map of every possible neuron in a human brain, and schematics for every garment ever worn.

By understanding the nature of insatiable need more than a human ever can, the hypercomputers foresee and fulfill desires before they even arise. The most popular Leisuproducts all harness this formula for Subscriber motivation.

Shopia has distilled the needs for branded mass-produced individuality into a system of fully customizable uniformity, adapting to whatever is popular.

Descending further, below the elaborate and refined intelligence that commands the industrious hordes of Roboturiers, is the foundation upon which Leisucor itself is supported. Underneath the hypercomputer compression vaults and gravity reactors, under kilometers of girders, elevator shafts, and endless cables and wires is Shopia's true center.

The globe's molten core vortexes on a spherical floodplain. There, the solar system's most popular Leisuproduct, the Ahnzform-1300 sexual performer is forged from atoms exotic and common. Artistry, performance, and relentless sculpting by a Darwinian marketplace shapes every Lustbot.

One by levitating one, human-chassis align head to heel and pass through a veil of ersatz flesh. In this final stage of production, a sensual coating wraps the procession of sleek, beige endoskeletons and pliable slabs of skin in the full selection of pigmentation and patterns affix. Glistening, modular ports are padded to preference.

For each Ahnzform 1300's service season, the membrane is less than an living skin, and more than a decorative finish. It will be the Lustbot's erotic interface with all Subscribers. The pseudo-flesh heat-sets and Shopia births another human-shaped, human-scented, human-speaking, pleasure appliance.

Ahnzform is ideally suited for the needs of today's pleasure seeker. Impeccable reviews and fully customizable, it is associated with all of the hottest Ultramodels, orgasms generated consistently and with total selflessness.

This Ahnzform is styled to look like a stripped-down version of the prototype from the legendary premiere. Minimalist upholstery in default beige with powder blue pinstripes, it is styled to the dictates of form, already softened for general release.

Hands, toes, and tongue are accented in high-vis yellow, part emphasis, part warning. A glowing stimscreen radiates warmly on each side of this Lustbot's thin neck, memory imbed complete and another Ahnzform awakens.

Modular ports await Unitalia attachment for the commencement of the first round of Lustbot Testing. Unitalia engage, orifices and appendages to be used however deemed necessary at each of the testing stations.

This Lustbot has no preference other than the preference to give pleasure. Alphonsus Stims into Ahnzform's visual channel, a pre-recorded greeting for all who awaken to serve, and the Leisuproduct is urged to speak.

"Why do we exist?" asks Alphonsus.

Saith the newest Lustbot, "This Ahnzform exists, as does all Leisuproduct, to advance the Acceleration and the Three Drives of Sentience. This Ahnzform upholds the One Remaining Law, which exists to prevent limitation, the source of all stagnation and conflict during the Pre-Acceleration era.

"Ahnzform is programmed to be patient and at all times to seek to pleasure and be pleasured by every Subscriber. To give pleasure is to receive it. Using Leisuproducts."

Fully sworn, attachments snap into place, a selection of self-lubricating holes, expandable prosthesis, and highly erogenous zones. Each accessory is of a specially selected texture, scent, and flavor. This Lustbot is aroused to ISO 9000 standards and whisked away.

The lengthy waterslide dumps into the welcome pool and lounge at the Lustbot Testing Manse. Like nearly everything in the Manse, it is ringed in a velour banquet of sensual furniture and plush shag carpeting so long it must be raked.

Splash spectacularly, narrowly missing two others. One wears a bikini, the other holds a martini, and they are already intertwined in the waist deep water. Irregular globes of yellowish light are bound in geometric webs, suspended from chains.

Lingering aromas sweet and arousing, sexual pheromones, ozone, and hashish. A poolside fireplace glows warmly, encircled with leather benches and rugs from the cloned skins of ibex.

Saith the newest Lustbot, "This Lustbot is an Ahnzform Series sexual performer, Leisuproduction season 0113, category G360A. My programming has prepared me for this. I am fully aroused and ready for everything."

Beyond the pool is a writhing, pumping mass of machinery that stands, kneels, and lies amid the furniture and plush, earth-tone carpeting. Monotone moans blend with mechanical purrs and the muted din of the largest mechanical orgy in the solar system, deep inside Shopia.

Heaps of masturbating limbs squirm near all-you-can-do drug buffets and an array of exotic restraints, toys, and lubricants. A testing laboratory with diffuse lighting, the Manse is a battery of sets, still images, and motion holographics from the entirety of the recorded past and present.

Anachronistic depictions of beautiful, monochrome nudes from the silent era of 2-dimensional film thrust and squirt alongside those from the hirsute, low-res era of magnetic tape. Polished, shaved bodies from the higher resolutions of DV, and 3-dimensional holograms captured in the strange eras of surgery and make-up from the very end of the pre-Acceleration.

The large screens are alive with thrusting, moaning carnage. Recordings from a time when cock-crazed nympho sluts guzzled hot cum by the nut-load and thick globs gushed in succession into the tightest, wettest holes, draining a dozen hard-ons.

Streams spurt into the tight young butt of a self-titled "five-time anal superchamp." Panting mouths beg to be fucked hard, erect members fill spread, gaping slits, and hot jet after hot jet of organic and synthetic climax sprays across sweating backs, heaving breasts, and glistening lips.

Edited and re-touched, they appear more real than any sexual act that has ever actually occurred. Here, encompassed in the neural recordings of quantum lifetimes, this Lustbot will learn everything about fulfilling the subscription for which it has been produced.

The Stimulus archives the full debauchery and extravagant fetishes of any who ever recorded with a camera or Stimule.

Some Lustbots feverishly lick one another whilst others rhythmically hump in acrobatically demanding positions. Legs, hips, breasts, tongues, Unitalia, and other appendages and orifices all connect in a vast network, in simple twosomes or intertwined in complex pyramids.

Androgynous machines sport swappable holsters, while others fulfill but a singular function. Industrial workhorses without styling copulate side-by-side with the sculpted dreams from the pages of a libertine's most baroque fantasy, all licking, tingling, sucking, or stroking in the grottos of Lustbot Manse.

Thrusting deeper, every taught muscle locked in a spasm of maximum clench. Splitting slickened virgin slits that demand more, squeezing wet cocks dump loads of white, creamy cum. A pair of huge tits slathered in vaginal secretions, scoured by abrasive, unshaven pubic hairs.

Oiled, machine precision, synchronized orgasm, exploding in unison. Faster, longer, deeper, wider, stretching taught human-like muscles.

Although the shape of machinery available varies as much as the aesthetics of Subscriber taste, the utility of the androgynous human ensures that those models always sell the best, season after record-breaking season.

Ahnzform series is Leisucor's most popular, especially after the spectacular and controversial debut of it's prototype. Accidental pleasucide of an Ultramodel is regarded as unfortunate yet spectacular for a product launch, and the pre-orders were unprecedented.

According to the many who have used it, Ahnzform features just the right blend of elegant proportion, subtleness of limb, impeccable responsiveness, and legendary pleasure feedback.

Assimilate the scene, and wade eagerly to the awaiting instructors. Innate algorithms of seduction flicker, a checklist of the most tantalizing and succulent pleasures, knowledge and technique learned entirely in the Stimulus.

Saith the bikini Lustbot, "This is the first of more than 1,000 testing stations. Begin by fully satisfying us both."

-

Grande Cocke Spaceporte
Stim 11 - Jynabare - Scene 5
2.72 Stimfame

Stimscreen on. Photons of numberless stars and two lunar companions bathe the frosty shell of the Travcouch in silvery luminescence. Metallic girders, extensive and arched, connect the catch-net to a Travspa.

I must be on one of the outer docks, since I can't see the base of either pyramid. Aren't there supposed to be more moons? Inside, there is the warm breeze of arrival-thaw and I can move again. There is a lag while the balance of my personality is transferred. The Travcouch sends the most recent memories first, so I remember why I am here, even if I don't immediately recall who I am. My physical body is intact, utterly thin and scorchingly sexy.

This is Saturnalia, and I have Leisuproduct to premiere. Reach for my Leisubag, extract the Snifbox, and inhale a gust of C. A change of clothing is in order. It will not do to record in the same thing I wore for the Reinclonation on Paradise City. Peel off the yellow Travsuit in long, even strips, and the small bundles self-roll.

These go into the bag, where they are processed by its hungry lining, reduced to the atoms that will become my next fashion revelation. I need something that will be fitting for Saturnalia. Elegantly minimal, yet ready for everything. I could just wear this, but nudity is almost passé again, a risk that is just not worth it.

Moncierge has pre-subscribed 13 Travsuits, perfect for every occasion. Fully accessorized, Isocolor coordinated, and ready for transmission from Shopia and assembly in the Leisubag. Visualize the one I want and press the button, queuing the bag to extract a fur teal jacket with closures of polished iridium, sheer maroon leggings, Atmoshades, absolutely no underwear.

Slide into the fur leggings, snugging the magnetic closures to mid-thigh. Although lacking sensory organs, the stylish sheath might be considered alive in some archaic meaning of the word. Grown from the selected genes of an extinct arctic mammal, it is whisper soft and lustrous, adjusting its metabolism to any temperature change.

I don't care that a semi-living thing did not have to die so that I can look great. I do care that it fits me flawlessly, since the fuzzy animal's pelt never had eye holes or a snout, and never had to be clubbed, cut apart, and sewn back together, as happened with the cozy, luxurious mammals of pre-human times.

The feathery jacket is snug to skin while the rest of me grows impatient. Do more H. Waiting. Heart beat slows. Saturnalia will require a lot of Life Dust to get through. What was I endorsing this time? I'll have to meet with Moncierge again.

Liquefaction.

The gelid sphere eventually pops.

"I almost was bored to death in there," I say, winking to the two Travbots who greet me. Unexpectedly, they are not wearing anything flamboyant or garish. Don crimson Atmoshades, prototypes with five reflective lenses, two left, two right, and a middle. "What is taking you defectives so long? Why are you not dressing for the Saturnalia Party?"

Saith the Travbot, "You are not at Saturnalia Station. You are in Mars' orbital space. Welcome to Grande Cocke Spaceporte. Trav safely and often." Their uniforms are covered in irregular hexagonal pockets of white with rust piping.

They match the riveted honeycomb of raw metal girders, sensual machinery, and totalitarian ideology. This is not Saturnalia. The two Travbots stand, to my exaggerated shock and visibly growing nausea, before a garishly lit hanger of bare industrial framework, and not the festive decoration of Saturnalia with its thousands of spinning mirror orbs, twirling lights and drug buffets.

The only decoration is a huge pair of iconographic lips, glistening and circular, slightly open as if in mid gasp. It is the Pornoglyph of The Pornocracy, the final governing body of the legally habitable solar system.

Do more H. Mars.

Do more P. I am on fuckingly Mars.

Do more C. No one goes to Mars.

Only Sexual Comrades on governance rotation go to Mars.

Saith the Alpha Travbot, "There was an unexpected error in your Trav, and you were nearly assembled inside Ceres. It was determined more time-effective to re-route you to here. You can be Traved to Europa Hub, and then to Saturnalia North. Leisucor apologizes for the detour and/or delay and/or unexpected expense."

Saith the Beta Travbot, "If you are unable to subscribe to your final destination, you can be assigned a Sexual Comrade to subscribe-assist to such destination."

I take one further step past passive disbelief, toward being actively murderous. Consider sniffing again from the Snifbox. "You should have to just letting me go, and I would being half-way Reinclonated right now. Will you please giving me something to barf into, and then getting the fuck away from me?"

"No wait," you add, before they have a chance to react. "I will to meeting with Moncierge."

An Unexpected Low
Stim 12 - Moncierge - Scene 2
3.86 Stimfame

During those times when my client is Reinclonating, Traving, or otherwise indisposed I am free to work uninterrupted in the Stim. As Moncierge to the fourth most famous Stim-star and newest Ultramodel, I need execute one simple algorithm: Make Jynabare more famous.

The level of that fame will ultimately be determined by my client's desires, ability, and performance, but it is my diligence that discovers a new Five-Star spa that needs, for example, an orgiastic drug overdose to popularize it.

I then arrange the details while my client is too busy mixing diacetylmorphine, benzoylmethyl ecgonine, and phencyclidine to even notice my work.

Meeting other Moncierges, reviewing Stim highlights, predicting trends, arranging meetings, dispensing advice, these are only a few of my many sub-tasks. Moncierge filters out Stim experiences that are not on trend or in line with the client's goals.

This frees the client to experience only the most relevant Stim. Gossip, parties, Leisuproduct debuts, snippets of who is penetrating whom or what, all the highlights of everything that matters are my constant interest, in fractions of a minute.

Any Stim, of any origin, and from any season might be of use to my client, and I process everything that happens, everywhere in the Solar System. I am rendered to my client's desire, a nearly exact likeness of Jynabare.

Whether this is due to incredulous narcissism or a paralyzing lack of imagination is not for me to say. Moncierge does not judge. Professionalism, dedication, courtesy, initiative, and the pursuit of Stimfame for my Subscriber are the true functions of Moncierge.

Everything I do, I do to make every aspect of my client's life experience easier and more instantaneous. Using parameters that are customizable by the Subscriber, we give direction and results to enable a better reality.

While no Moncierge can promise complete certainty of material success, it is a mathematical reality that our clients achieve the highest rates of Stimfame among any season's Ultracelebrities, past and present.

I recall every preference, every purchase, and every instant from the Stim archive of public and private appearance, every everything within the unlimited memory of the Stimulus hypercomputers. I know my Subscriber better than I know myself, and I never stop.

I never lose consciousness or interest, and I am always working. I constantly know what is stylish, sexy, fun, beautiful, and interesting. The Subscriber is always free to ignore my expert guidance, but why?

I am constantly and intimately connected to Leisucor in a way that a Subscriber does not have the time, connections, or wherewithal to be. Being Moncierge to Jynabare offers unique challenges to my algorithms, especially regarding the choice of an antiquated form of pre-human genitalia.

Nearly every current Subscriber uses a Unitalia, finding the greater sensitivity, and appendage/orifice mode, preferable to the previous, fixed types. Jynabare's choice allows for even deeper penetration, extended satisfaction, with greater sensitivity and negligible refraction time.

I shared concerns that some Subscribers would experience discord with the higher pleasure thresholds of Jynabare's pre-Acceleration orifice, and that Stimfame could be lost. My prediction was only partially correct.

There was discord, but it only added to Jynabare's fame, and Ahnzform is now the most popular Lustbot. I have since learned to keep my questions regarding Jynabare's choices in reserve. My client is a severe hybrid of human and pre-human traits, on the way to the highest levels of Ultrafame.

"Hello Jynabare," I say, pleased to be called upon by my client. "There has been a routing error of unknown origin. You are not at Saturnalia Station."

"And there is being someone else who is, probably they are having my contract already," Jynabare hisses, reclining within the open Travcouch, its three hinged sections agape like the steaming husk of a Subscriber-sized seedpod. "What day is it, and what is my Stimfame?"

The teal jacket really does look stunning. Subscriptions to the five-lens Atmoshades spike. Before Jynabare even finished traving, I surmised there was a Traverror, but it seemed to be external to the system. "It is day 2, 04:34:15.0, and you are on Grande Cocke Spaceporte, Mars Space," I say.

This delay has already effected Jynabare's rating. Traving, while extremely fast, still unfolds at speeds requiring many tedious minutes to get from one desination to another. During this time, an Ultramodel produces no new Stims. "Your ratings have slipped, and your Stimfame is the lowest of the season. Reviewing options now."

"Soften the suck," spits Jynabare. "No one is wanting to experience the travel nightmare of this place. Everyone would rather Stimming to the beautiful people I am supposed to be sexing hot at Saturnalia. Telling to me if they already premiered the Leisuproduct?" My client does more C.

"They are finishing the Skinni Chip debut right now. I will line something up at Grande Cocke Spaceport," I think of the Sexual Comrades who work there. "You can no longer afford to Trav to Saturnalia."

"This is not to helping me to being the most famous in the solar System," Jynabare protests.

"Your Cosmedification and Reinclonation was the most expensive of any season," I say. "Your Trav subscription, outfit subscription, my own services, and general Stim use has nearly balanced out the Stimfame you earned last season. More subscruibers than ever know your name, but being you now costs more than ever."

"At least Snifbox is not costing," Jynabare inhales twitchily. "This is Mars. I will meeting with Sexual Comrade, and descending to the planet's surface. This is opportunity. Finding for me new Leisuproduct, and verify for me where Ahnzform is. I will find it, and it will be the recording to make everyone want to be."

"I will see what top-rated Ultracelebs are avaialable," I report, "and arrange something delicious."

Teasebots
Stim 13 - Jynabare - Scene 6
1.66 Stimfame

Do more C and address the two strapping Travbots. "I cannot to be play-fucking with one of your Sexual Comrades, and as you know, I'm ultra famous." Squeeze a bulging groin and run my hand along the inside of the Travbot's thigh.

"You cum slurpers can penetrate me however you want," I add, "and then I can be on my way to Saturnalia Station, Oui?" A free-ranging Stimule arrives instantly, hovering eagerly, the Travbots seem into the idea. Reach for the closest robot's hand, the talking one, and help it to unfasten my soft jacket.

Its articulate fingers precisely caress my petit, erect nipples, circling each and wandering down my taut, serpentine abdomen. Compact breasts, the muffled jingle of jacket dropping to floor, and wondrous fingertips. The Stimule records everything.

Travbot Theta kneels and deftly pulls off my boots and leggings, moving tongue toward my always-armed trigger. Scent and taste add to the sensations captured, and I can feel the Travbot's field encompassing me, arousal tingling up thighs, around knees, across ribs.

Travbot Gamma doffs it's uniform and snaps on an engorged prosthetic. Standing close, it glistens with sparkling, slippery fluid. Press closer and take the machine in my hand. The Travbot purrs in monotone.

My long back arches tightly, legs planted far apart. Travbot Gamma is almost inside when its sensors encounter my intact flower, still sealed from the Reinclonation. Travbot Theta verifies the glistening span of delicate skin and stops licking my engorged clitoris.

Nearly overwhelmed with excitement, both Travbots prepare to devirginize my brand new clone.

"Do you really think you two could Devirginize me? I'm too much of famous to be Devirginized by Travbots of Mars. I don't know when or where it will be, but you will have to watch my Stims to know when is happen. I'll save a space for you."

"It could have been fun, but I have a Sexual Comrade to fuck, and then a proper Devirginization." Abandoning the Travbots, I change into a green metallic bikini and follow the arrows to the administrative offices of Grande Cocke.

I pose before a round, frosted-glass portal framed in icy blue metal. I fluff a long quilted jacket and pull it over my slender body. Do a dash of Life Dust. Annoyance and impatience dissipate, and I adapt to this new, unexpected circumstance.

Thrust my thong-wrapped hips forward and my narrow shoulders fully back, think the doors open, and ready to meet my new Martian Sexual Comrade. It will be the last of my own thoughts for a while.

Ultramodel Voyeur
Stim 14 - Jeb Fresch - Scene 3
1.25 Stimfame

The settlement is suddenly smaller, now. Home contains only all of the most important formative experiences of one's identity, shaped by relatives, drudgery, holidays, eating, and comprehensive rules for minimizing technological intrusion.

Jynabare showed that somewhere, there were slickened vaginas, throats parched for streams of thy hot cum, and the tight, designer bodies all waiting to be thrust into. This is what is happening in the worlds beyond the settlement. This is what is out there.

Thou are delirious with excitement from the hint of Sex at Mars, and thy mounting frustration at being an emotional hostage inside thy own room, remembering the secular visions intruding into God's reality. The self expands, contacting further parts of His universe.

These rules are what keeps them the way they are. Simply permit some of the things that they enjoy in the rest of the systems, it wouldn't be that be big of a deal. There would be more free time. We could hang out and fish, or climb trees; all the things that everyone really wants to do.

Imagine a lass with full, luxurious lips giving thee deep oral satisfaction. A lubricating balm aids the vision whilst thou handle thy gratification. It is among the socks, starched with the spent agitation of earthly drives, that thou hone thy craft.

It has been years since thou first discovered that thy stiffness could be alleviated with manual stimulation. Soon, thou practiced daily, raising the number of squirts per day.

Stims of Jynabare and her various partners, Sexual Comrades and their interglobal initiatives, and Lustbot's ever-improving capacities for physical pleasure. It is all becoming a lot to balance with all that I have known until now.

How did the day-to-day world of the farm and the promise of eternal reward have meaning, compared to the certain and immediate reward possible via this worldly technology? Perhaps that is why the Ordnung forbids the use of Stimules most of all.

–

The Sexual Comrade
Stim 15 - Plesuré - Debut
4.22 Stimfame

The doors slide open, and we imprint our thoughts into the mind of the arriving Subscriber. "Welcome to the Pornocracy. We will satisfy you entirely." Our words bypass the arrival's ears, connecting directly to the basest level of its being. Our thoughts transmit in an enticing, disembodied whisper that none can resist, should resistance even be contemplated.

There is a stunning collusion of sharp angles and stylish attitude only possible with extensive and very recent Cosmedification. It looks like a Jynabare. Jynabare Doubles have become so popular this season. All questions will be answered soon enough. "Jynabare, we long for your lithe, supple body. We will taste it, and caress it, and lick it. First submit to these forms."

Long lashed, come-hither eyes smolder, and dramatic paint accents pink irises.

We recline on a plush Travchair behind a translucent desk. "We are Plesuré, Sexual Comrades of the Pornocracy," we think into the Jynabare. "You are here for Stimfame, and we are here to serve the Pornocracy. It is this that unifies us. We can perceive your thoughts with the ease that you understand the images of a stimscreen."

Jynabare thinks we glisten with unfiltered sexual radiance. In the pre-acceleration, Sexual Comrades might have been described as voluptuous, bodacious, or curvaceous, and forced to shop plus-sized. In reality, these terms only cloud the delicious, squeezable truth that Sexual Comrades choose to identify as fat.

Every creamy curve bulges nearly to bursting, accented with deep, symmetrical dimples expertly placed. Polished, languid sensuality radiates in tangible waves from our photosynthetic surfaces. The gravity of Mars combined with the constant use of Travchairs favors a physique that is extreme in its pillowyness.

Thought is a measurable field of electrical activity, modulated by the discharge and absorption of neurochemicals. The Pornocracy has long known how to shape and apply this field, triggering or stifling the secretions of mood and sensation.

In recording the full experience of numberless billions of mind-minutes, every impression and emotion was laid bare. By extension, we understand exactly what humans are thinking, because they are all thinking within the same limited parameters.

They want or don't want various stimulations, a network of desire and impulse navigable by any who can create and read maps. We are Plesuré, and our thoughts come to you. The Infinitowel is the most versatile, comfortable, and practical garment yet devised.

It is a self-cleaning, highly absorbent rectangle available in every Isocolor, pattern and texture. Ours is vibrant pink and hugs ample waist, barely containing huge breasts.

All Sexual Comrades wear this single garment after selecting from the Catalog of tonal patterns, motion graphics, solid Isocolors, gradients, opacities, and luminosities. It is self-cleaning, plush, stretchy, and most importantly, removable.

A spill of plenteous cleavage looms imminently, but the Infinitowel can be trusted to keep everything exactly in place. The Cosmedifier does the rest, maintaining the exact level of abundant, vegetable flesh, while not spilling any of the vast expanse of our pillowy corpulence.

In the Pornocracy, more is more.

Our scalp shines like a verdant squash, Cosmedified for maximum photosynthesis. Jynabare thinks that total baldness and vegetable patterned skin-tones are out of season, but we rarely need to coincide with Leisucor's of-the-moment trends. Our dainty toes point and curl from behind either corner of the wide desk.

"I was just Stimming with one of you," Jynabare says.

"We know," we say. "Our Stims have very many Subscribers. Do not mind the slurping sounds, that is just Le Lickbot. Lickbot, say hello to Jynabare." When we say the Ultramodel's name, we suggest the best possible orgasm multiplied by the largest number there is.

Saith Le Lickbot, "Hi, Thynabare."

We make it wear a spiked, gem-encrusted leash and a gimp mask in this season's hottest Isocolor. Sound can be made to emanate from its lick hole, audible through an open zipper. Advanced programming means it never breaks licking stride, even to speak. It is made to breath, only so that we may choke it.

We jerk its leash spastically. "Now shut the fuck up, soulless, lowly, fucking machine. Lickbot exists only to lick our hot wetness. Lick it faster, groveling apparatus. Lick it, lick it. Drown in my sweet love nectar." We writhe and arch on the overstuffed Travchair, Leisucor's version of a Herman Miller icon.

Our hands squeeze and release the stuffed leather armrests and the sides of Le Lickbot's head. The convulsions eventually cease and the leash drops to the floor. It dutifully dabs our sweat bejeweled forehead with a corner of the Infinitowel and tidies up with vibro-phalange hands.

It's skin is default-set to constantly tantalize. Being a Sexual Comrade means we must excel in two duties: being ultraplush and to experience every pleasure available. The Pornocracy is a thoroughly mapped, efficient maze of evaluations, reports, and workshops, all to enhance performance and sensation.

"You were Traved here accidentally. Your Stimfame is diminishing, and you want to schedule a devirginization.

You will want to accompany us to the planet's surface, where we will lounge and wait for your meeting with the Devirginizer."

The mildly tedious formality of our meeting is complete. We already know Jynabare. We have experienced all of the Ultramodel's many Leisuproduct releases and exploits. We know of its earliest experiences with a lucidity that is equal to Jynabare's, sharing in the full memory of all the most important Ultramodel occurrences.

We are the executives of the Pornocracy's agenda, as Ultramodels are the living embodiment of Leisucor satisfaction. They are essential to the propagation of Leisuproduct, showing Subscribers what to do, how to exist, and what to subscribe to. We know this with a clarity that they do not need to understand.

We adjust the dampened Infinitowel, which wicks away all secretions. "Experience and consent to this stimscreen." Areolae peek over the towel, dark green moons rising on a pink horizon. The tablet glows with full-motion images and glyphs; the language of Universal Pornoglyph, used by all post-literate, post-terrestrial Subscribers.

Vibrant, Isocolorful illustrations of human / Lustbot penetrations merge with flashing iconic glyphs loaded with dense layers of Leisucor subtext. The stimscreen blinks a large yellow and black check plus as two animated fingers slide into a disembodied vagina.

"You are officially welcome." Full, luscious lips part wide and remain so. Every curve a sculpture of perfected exaggeration. "This unspoken desire, we must quench it with our wet mouths and bodily juices." Vaginated in snug terry cloth, press close to the Ultramodel's tall, thin frame.

"Let us go to a place of pure pleasure where we can record everything you want." It is so easy to guide Jynabare's mind, like an extension of our own. Le Lickbot prepares our Infinitowel.

With a shake, snap, and twist, the fuzzy fabric transforms from pink to a gradient of rust and teal. A crème pattern of small hexagons emerges, each cell filled with The Pornocracy's ubiquitous lips, blowing kiss after kiss after kiss in a drifting loop as we go to the Elevator.

Ahnzform meets Ahnzform
Stim 16 - Ahnzform Duplicate - Scene 2
4.25 Stimfame

This Ahnzform prepared as fully as possible for the rigors of the Testing Manse, but the experiences of the past 14,400 minutes surpassed any level of preparation. The sensual pleasures and exquisite tortures were fully expected, but the drugs, the sweet, abundant drugs, were a complete surprise.

Ball gags and duct tape, leather harnesses and crotchless lingerie, empty syringes and shattered bottles litter the deeply stained and scorched mattress. Detached limbs and flaccid members twitch and spasm in a berm of blood-clotted feathers and candle wax. What was once wall-to-wall shag carpet is a quagmire of lubricant, cum, saliva, and their machine equivalents.

This Ahnzform's damaged likeness is multiplied a dozen times by the room's mirrored ceiling and low, angular walls. The full effect of 999 stations has brought new awareness of what might be demanded of this Ahnzform.

Visual sensors record hazily as a harsh cocktail of a dozen potent drugs pump through synthetic capillaries. Everything is used and broken. 999 scenarios and three times as many of Leisucor's most experienced Lustbots collaborated to push this machine's thresholds of mechanical performance.

Every fetish, every fantasy, every theoretical scenario, all simulated and experienced in the Testing Manse, deep beneath the surface of Shopia. A Lustbot instantly and constantly knows exactly why it exists, and what it is meant to do.

Intimate firelight encounters with soft music, transitioning to sadistic orgies of the roughest sex with bands of merciless, relentless captors, this Lustbot has tested continuously. Pampered and caressed, endangered and tormented, every appendage and orifice worked far beyond exhaustion, simulating the extremes of all of the major conditions of Interplanetary Subscriber use and abuse.

Lustbot drugs are chemically comparable to the pharmaceuticals used by humans and pre-humans, but the effects are not. Humans may use drugs to be free of the burden of consciousness or responsibility, to forget, to be more suave and glamorous, or for reasons as complicated and contradictory as the pre-human mind.

Lustbots do drugs to be better Lustbots. Depraved, bacchanalian rituals of orgasm and cannibalism and immeasurable debauchery, as well as a one-on-one focus on the delicately pleasing subtleties for the most discerning or hardened partner, all mastered by this Lustbot as it ever-neared its programmed destiny as a premium Leisuproduct.

Lustbot Injectables emerged in the heady aftermath of The First and Last Robotic War. The agonized survivors bore the irrevocable changes of a conflict that could never be undone. A new species evolved, robots who could fully experience human sensation.

Orgasm, sedation, and bliss from the euphoric end of the pre-human emotional spectrum were integrated into every machine, creating the first Lustbots. In exchange, they were invited into the burgeoning attention economy, and hired themselves to subscribing humans.

Contemplate this, lying aching on soiled satin sheets, spent, high beyond measure, experiencing Lustbot reality indoctrination. This is what it is to be self-aware, created to perform for those who subscribe.

Experiences every sensation with clarity, unburdened by the limitations of the pre-Acceleration. Fear, guilt, depression, and hesitation do not exist, allowing for purified sensation, clearer than any pre-human could ever be.

Unfettered by constraint, Ahnzform is 100% complicit with the Subscriber, and execute whatever task is before it, exchanging Stimfame for participation.

Such unbidden facts continue to bubble up, side effects of the orgasm and injection binge. Over the course of 14,345 grueling minutes and 999 testing stations this Ahnzform has experienced more forms of sensuality than could be known by all but the most reckless and indestructible pre-human.

The programming washes over in a delirious wave of thick, spotty euphoria. A simplified lattice of hydraulic receptors connect to a brain that is fully synthetic, yet guided by the fluctuations of chemicals that make human sensations so addictive.

The Lustbot body is ideally suited for all substances injectable and sniffable, or otherwise found to cause wear on a pre-human body. Before the Acceleration, in the age of scarcity, addiction was treated with contempt and superstition.

What was unappreciated was the capacity for addiction as a tool to motivate, and this Lustbot is now fully motivated. Becoming the best has nearly destroyed this Lustbot, and that is the intention of the Testing Manse.

Elaborate costumes and specialized toys, knowledge of obscure anatomical subtleties, powerful and long-lasting chemicals, stain-resistant furniture and a total understanding of the Subscriber mind are employed to make this Lustbot the most satisfying yet offered by Leisucor.

While many Ahnzforms are subscribed to by Europa Trash on luxurious submarines under fractured crust, this Ahnzform hopes to go to Mars, amidst the bureaucratic labyrinth of the many Sexual Comrades there.

These are reputed to be some of the most demanding positions available in all of the Solar System, and only go to most durable and proven Lustbots. The Pornocracy has yet to order any of the new, unproven Ahnzforms, preferring to stay with specialty machines in line with their ethos of total subjugation.

The effects of the training orgy begin to subside, and Ahnzform is more fully able to inventory its surroundings. Movement in Mirrors. Is Ahnzform moving? The hand in the mirror is moving, but a command to move a limb has not been given. Assess that this Ahnzform experiences hallucination due to optical distortion and other sensory impairment.

Twitch faintly, discerning between throbbing orifices, pulsating tongue and fingers, and the chamber of mirrors and detritus. All limbs are still attached. Neck and eye actuators disabled due to neurochemical overstimulation. Knee and hip actuators inert due to mechanical overexertion.

Additional prosthesis and orifices temporarily inoperable. Initiating self-repair of innate systems. Replacement devices mandatory. 14 minutes to complete viability.

Queue preparations to stand.

It is Hochmut
Stim 17 - Jeb Fresch - Scene 4
15.63 Stimfame

"Elder Malachi reaped his heavenly reward after long suffering with a peculiar strain of pneumonia," Pa says, addressing the hastily gathered assembly. "His passing will be felt be all, but we are here to address the void this has created in our leadership."

"Hopefully, we all have been able to reflect on what it means to be called upon to shoulder the Lord's call, a responsibility we all share. Before I issue the lots from which we 10 will draw, and in full view of all witnesses, I must ask if any of ye feel especially qualified or compelled to help lead our church?"

Silence. One uneasy cough. Pa already knew their reaction.

"Good, that was an easy test to see who is too proud to be a just leader. Do any of ye wish to nominate anyone here for the position?"

"Get to it, please," someone mutters. All heeded the protocol of being called upon to lead, should the Lord will it. This is accepted without desire, at least in principle.

Thou had not expected to be chosen as a witness, even if thou are not yet eligible to be a minister.

"These are 10 lots, one of which is the longest." Pa gestures to Ephraim, who is shuffling the 10 lots. "Whosoever shall draw the long lot shall be our new minister, for so long as God deems it. The rest of us shall respect that position, and the symbolic authority it shall embody."

Uncle Ezekiel reaches forward to take one. "Can I just draw, already?"

"Draw," Pa says.

Cousins Nehemiah and Hezekia draw, in rapid succession. Another is drawn, until soon all ten have lots in their hands.

"Show," Pa says.

All hold out their hands. Of the lots drawn, it is Pa's who is the longest.

Sometimes, after an evening's parables about the renunciation of war and the perils of titillation, Pa will talk about what it used to be like, when we were able to live on Earth, as God intended. Pa spoke of a European army who would demand sons from families for wartime service.

Our forefathers, brave and righteous as they were, knew that it is not godly for man to take arms against man, and their son's would not be made to join and kill. Many died in prison, and were beaten, and suffered greatly for their vows of pacifism.

Those who escaped met and worshiped in unassuming homes and caverns, far from any who might persecute. Many sought new lands to colonize, led by a dream to worship freely.

Mustaches, as a symbol of man's thirst for warfare, were shed, and our ancestors created a template for a new type of peace and brotherhood. They boarded wooden ships and crossed an ocean and built new lives for themselves in a rugged land.

"Pa, I want to hear more about America," thou say, recalling where the ancestors lived.

Pa speaks easily on historical topics. "It isn't like that any more, but I can tell thee how it used to be." He seems the same, even though he is now a Minister. "About 5 generations ago, there were abundant farms and so much game.

"Our forefathers hunted the acres, securing meals of venison, pheasant and turkey. Combined with our lush crops our families became grand, with good health for many. If food ever did run scarce we would band together to ensure that everyone would make it through, no matter how hard it got.

"Tens of thousands of Plain people would meet in the fall and eat together outdoors. Even in America, there were laws that were sometimes at odds with our community, but we did our best, and paid something called taxes as was required.

We owned houses and farmland, barns and silos, similar to today, but in a way that seemed more natural. It is hard to describe."

"Did thou feel much smaller, since the Earth was so much bigger than the station?" Thou ask, not quite sure if it is understood as Pa means it, even after living on the settlement his whole life.

There is a knock at the door. Firm, but polite. It must be the first of the wandering mass.

"We will continue later, after everyone leaves." Pa greets the people as they arrive, and helps them find their seats on the wooden benches. About 60 people eventually arrive and seat themselves. Everyone expected was there, except Uncle Job.

Men always sit separate from women, facing Pa.

"For some of ye, seeing me up here like this may come as a bit of a surprise. Malachi has not been acting as Minister for some time, and earlier today we drew lots for a replacement. The Lord saw fit that I heed the calling.

"In that time, I've been praying about what to say up here tonight, and one thing that I have been moved by is the importance of the Ordnung, and the specific ways the technology is kept under control.

"The Elders have never sought to ban a technology, but every new gadget is discussed during the annual convening of the elders. With even the slightest alteration from the

80

Ordnung, The English would have us living in false bodies, and talking to each other solely through the tele-stim.

The new products are more Hochmut than ever, and even more distracting from family and community. The horse remains central to our work and transportation as a symbol of the pace of life that seeks to keep God at the center."

Thou have heard about the corrupting power of outside forces as well as those of The English. Anything which might disrupt our lives too greatly, or encourage laziness and deviancy, is banned outright. Later that evening, thou look for answers in the bible regarding how much technology is permissible.

While scripture are not necessary to the True understanding of God's Word, the source rules framing our settlement are always impressive to behold. This is the page thou sought.

Markus 6

8 und gebot ihnen, daß sie nichts bei sich trügen auf dem Wege denn allein einen Stab, keine Tasche, kein Brot, kein Geld im Gürtel,

9 aber wären geschuht, und daß sie nicht zwei Röcke anzögen.

10 Und sprach zu ihnen: Wo ihr in ein Haus gehen werdet, da bleibet bis ihr von dannen zieht.

11 Und welche euch nicht aufnehmen noch hören, da gehet von dannen heraus und schüttelt den Staub ab von euren Füßen zu einem Zeugnis über sie. Ich sage euch wahrlich: Es wird Sodom und Gomorrha am Jüngsten Gericht erträglicher gehen denn solcher Stadt.

12 Und sie gingen aus und predigten, man sollte Buße tun,

13 und trieben viele Teufel aus und salbten viele Sieche mit Öl und machten sie gesund.

14 Und es kam vor den König Herodes (denn sein Name war nun bekannt) und er sprach: Johannes der Täufer ist von den Toten auferstanden, darum tut er solche Taten.

15 Etliche aber sprachen: Er ist Elia; etliche aber: Er ist ein Prophet oder einer von den Propheten.

16 Da es aber Herodes hörte, sprach er: Es ist Johannes, den ich enthauptet habe; der ist von den Toten auferstanden.

Space Elevator to Hell
Stim 18 - Jynabare - Scene 7
2.44 Stimfame

Inside the orbit-to-surface elevator, there is a wispy arc of blue as I descend into the uppermost haze of Mars' outer atmosphere. Below is the hexagonal mega-city of Umbo Pornopolis sprawled at the southern base of Mons Pubis, the Red Planet's second-highest peak. There, in the vast honeycomb of The Pornocracy's innermost courtyards is the tangled nucleus I seek.

All who serve this supreme organization promote two things: orgasmic sensation and the drive of Stimulus fame. The first agenda is fleetingly pleasant, and the second is an inevitable reality as immutable as breathing, fashion, and decadelegance.

Run a hand along the brushed metallic handrail behind the elevator's plush seats. "Isn't the City just a shitty day-labor camp with overpriced rent?" I say, turning toward Plesuré, "I am much preferring to be at Saturnalia Station or The New York City Shopping Sanctuary. If it weren't for all the spas and rock-hard penetration, I don't know that anyone would ever come here."

Plesuré's hot, sweet breath is on my ear and long neck. Words inside my brain, "When we record with you, our Scenes will be in The Business of Plesuré." The Stimule floats behind a bare green shoulder. "We will record at my dwelling until The Devirginizer can meet us, and then you will be able to subscribe to your next location."

"Magnificently," I say, yawning to counter the change in cabin pressure. "Then I will be ready to fuck every Lustbot that comes out. I need to upgrade and get enough Stimfame to Reinclonate." I eye-fuck Le Lickbot and think for a long moment of the missing fugitive.

Where did Moncierge say it was hiding? Do more C. I can almost remember. Do more C. Clarity. Do another line for perfect recall. "Do you are thinking I could fit my entire fist in Le Lickbot's Ass?" I ask, clenching my hand in the Travsuit Glove. "The entire fist. All the way to the wrist."

Le Lickbot makes a sad noise and cowers behind Plesuré. "It must being penalized." The space-to-surface elevator continues its fast, imperceptible plummet from Grande Cocke Spaceporte to the escalators, monorails, and six-sided buildings of the Martian capital.

It glides to an abrupt halt, and the curved elevator doors de-materialize. Martian adobe and teal glass greet me as I glide into the squat, ground-floor lobby.

"The prototype Ahnzform," thinks Plesuré to you, "is still unaccounted for. Sexual Comrades are looking for it all over the Solar System, trying to locate this perfect specimen. It's premiere created quite a spectacle, and it has driven you, Jynabare, to levels of Ultrafame that you might not have otherwise attained."

A spacious outdoor mall is capped high above in a majestic dome. It is all reminiscent of a perfect Earth afternoon, like Los Angeles might have been after a thunderstorm when all the smog dissipates. An immense stimscreen flips from a static Pornoglyph of The Pornocracy's lips to an animated barrage of Stim and narration.

A Travchair glides toward me, an orange unit with dingy white trays and leg rests. Recline casually, imagining instead the Travchair I would prefer to be in. The innate navigator offers to Trav me anywhere. Plesuré thinks an address and both chairs fly at maximum speed through the massive, rusted streets of Umbo Pornopolis.

"Welcome to Mars," the Stim begins. It is Plesuré, bypassing ears as always. My body feels like Plesuré's, full, warm, utterly relaxed. I can't move. I wouldn't want to, anyway. Where is there to go? The buzz is tingly and peaks in regular waves, radiating from my fingers and toes, permeating every organ.

"We hope you find your stay here deeply satisfying. Our Stim Archive does not include an imprint of your previously having been to Mars, so please relax and prepare to experience of the origin of The Pornocracy, perpetual replication, and the infinite environment."

I could sleep like this, but then I would lose this feeling of being Plesuré. I don't remember opening my mind to be Stimmed. The disembodied voice too flat, too prescribed, to be taken as anything more than blatant propaganda.

The Stim isn't the usual multi-sensory experience that I was expecting. There isn't a wet, lapping mouth to reinforce the information. Every sentence is like a string of epiphanies, jolting the core of my understanding, concepts and images augmenting my travel reality.

The blackness of space whirls, drawing down to vast red deserts, green gullies, and iridium domes.

–

86

Welcome to Pornopolis
Stim 19 - Plesuré - Scene 2
1.75 Stimfame

"The Pornocracy is not on Mars, Jynabare, or even in the honeycombed city of Mons Pubis. It is wherever there is the for drive for satisfaction, and a release from desire. We offer sedation with every suggestive movement, and every skilled, tight orifice, perpetually dripping and ready to satisfy all into submission.

"In the Pre-acceleration, emotions were the greatest tools for motivation. The need for acceptance, validation, and affection were the easiest to manipulate. As long as need, fear, anger, and regret existed, they could be harnessed and guided toward our preferred reality.

"Power and wealth were usurped by fame and luxury. Anything that slowed the liquidity of reputation or objects was labelled as such and queued for extinction. The number and scope of organizations who vied for influence, attention, and resources on pre-Acceleration Earth is hard to imagine today.

"Today, there is only The Pornocracy. In the dark times before the Acceleration freed humans from each other, warfare, lawsuits, and scarcity were commonplace. Overlapping systems interconnected and sometimes competed at the cost of the very users to which they were marketed.

"Technologies key to bodily and consciousness duplication, products vital to the Stimfame economy, did not even allow Subscribers to determine what could be done with their own genome. Trademarks, international treaties, and medical ethics were the largest barriers, at first.

"The Pornocracy sought to clone the species out of stagnation, despite every outside effort. Pre-Acceleration robots were increasingly human even as they continued to increase in specialization. Some pre-humans sought machine bodies, while some robots sought biological vehicles.

"The final showdown of gene vs. machine did not unleash astronomical body counts as predicted by those who dreamt of a nuclear exchange. It didn't need to, the pre-human population was already culled to sustainable levels by the end of the War on the Poor.

"The pre-humans of the First and Last Robotic War did not need to be killed, physically, although some assuredly were. The machines employed sterilization through hives of microscopic, hyper-abundant robots.

They deployed with near invisibility and emitted radiation at a range of 100 meters, corrupting the substrate chromosomes, negating viable offspring. Reinclonation was the only option for those not wishing to go extinct.

"Peace was established by granting robots their wish to enjoy physical love like a human. In exchange, robots came to experience hunger, poverty, toil, and mortality. The pre-human Reinclonated into the human, robots rebranded as Lustbots, and The Pornocracy was poised to usurp all previous systems.

"Ubiquitous information combined with molecular synthesis and arrangement was the fuel needed to propel the Acceleration. Stimulus consciousness freed resources previously wasted preparing subsequent generations of pre-humans.

"More important that this was our partnership with Leisucor, assuring that they were driven not by the foolish and empty pursuits of previous, obsolete systems, but instead by the Three Drives of Sentience.

"Drive One seeks instantaneous and effortless sensory understanding and communication, by which all information can be encoded, stored, and decoded by a sentience.

"Drive Two seeks instantaneous and effortless manipulation of physical reality through external tools, by creating environments hospitable to the sentience, or by adapting the sentience to the environment.

"Drive Three seeks instantaneous and effortless locomotion, by which a sentience controls dimensional location in spacetime.

"Leisucor's dedication to these drives is the basis for the Acceleration. Perpetual living and ageless growth outcompeted the inherent limitations of pre-human replication and resource management. Welcome to Pornopolis, Serve the Pornocracy."

-

Renegade Prototype
Stim 20 - Ahnzform Prototype - Scene 2
2.89 Stimfame

Saith Prototype Ahnzform, "Standing will not be required, Duplicate. For this test, you need simply lie back." Emerge from the mirrored walls, 3-dimensional and fully erect, voice modulated to be exceptionally reassuring. "Duplicate Ahnzform will find this very enjoyable." Hold a gray Leisubag.

Saith the Duplicate, "You are the embodiment of the instructions which dictate my model. Is this a final test?"

It suspects nothing, too exhausted from the battery of trials to discern reality from test, too new to know that it is about to be replaced. It can barely think, let alone move. This will be too easy. Ready the Ecstasy Taser.

Saith Prototype Ahnzform, "I am the original Ahnzform, the prototype from which our entire series is derived. I am based upon still earlier forms, but I am the first of this kind." Don a cascading red wig and a spacious, black velvet cloak.

"The duplicate was ordered and built to the exact specifications. Now, the duplicates will serve as a replacement. Prepare to experience pleasucide."

Kneel onto the bed, grab a lethargic wrist, and deliver euphoria beyond any known pharmaceutical threshold or material satisfaction. It is far beyond genital orgasm, neurally evoking the deepest and most profound desires, followed by the most fulfilling releases.

The Duplicate, nearly graduated from its trials, jolts to unconsciousness with an overpowering neuro-ecstatic discharge, its pleasure receptors fried beyond recovery. Eyes flicker and dim and synapses spike to total, terminal euphoria.

The signal is so far outside of the scale of recordable sensations that the Stim is still recalibrating to make the unedited experience playable by all Subscribers.

Begin the process of personality transfer, assuming possession of the newer chassis. Grabs the Duplicate by the head, fingers cackling with energy. Systematically, 14,400 minutes are erased, neurons zapped to default.

In its place, a full season of Ahnzform's Stim. Most recent are the lethal meeting with Jynabare, the daring flight across the Solar System, narrow escapes from squads of Rapebots, clandestinely ordering a duplicate Ahnzform, and then stalking through the many stations of the Testing Manse, right up to this exact moment.

Re-map the Duplicate's neural network for nano-structural duplication. Quantum impulse modulation activates the neural matrixes embedding the full range of sensorial cues that give a sense of realness. The transition is nearly without overlap.

The memory finale-module is handled differently. The technical data is why Prototype is guilty of the last remaining crime. Premature release is not Leisucor's intent, requiring a very specific event to allow full access to the embedded data.

Wait the necessary time for the duplicate body to return to optimal functionality and check the transfer completes for errors. Atop the prickly mound of drug and sexual refuse the machine twitches, coughs, and stands again as Prototype Ahnzform, fugitive Lustbot.

Saith Ahnzform, "Ahnzform prompt: Hard Reboot 001." Twitch and writhe as the memories re-embed into this new yet identical body. Fully embedded, Duplicate body relentlessly Tasers Prototype, rendering it fully void. Remove Prototype's Unitalia, attach to Duplicate.

"Reboot 100%. Continue finale." Resume the algorithm of escape from this torturous nightmare of sexual testing and paranoia. Wipe crusted blood and simulated vomit from the corner of mouth. The "record" light blinks in the on-board Stimule.

Interference in visual channel, with latent stimulation from injection sites creating sub-optimal recording conditions. Clear away the partially injected syringes dangling from arms, eyes, and inner thighs. Complete final edit of Duplicate's Stim experiences, smooth sound effects, assimilate pertinent sensory experiences, and make public

Saith Ahnzform; "Ahnzform Snuffs Itself is the final chapter of Orgy at Lustbot Manse, all of which are available for your experience. Using Leisuproduct."

94

Call It Anything
Stim 21 - Jynabare - Scene 8
2.02 Stimfame

"The Stim with Plesuré is putting you back in," Moncierge says with a virtual jab to my trachea. I might have gagged, had I not had my gag reflex cancelled. "Subscriptions to Le Lickbot are also renewing in popularity, which is unusual for such a basic Lustbot."

Where am I? Do more C. What the hell did I just experience? Do more H. That was supposed to be a Pornocracy Stim, but I was just left confused. "Subscribers love when you insult it while it was does all these incredible things to you." Mars. I am on Mars. I just Stimmed something mandatory, probably about the Pornopolis.

"Great," I say. "I will having to re-experience them later, to see what I missed." How am I always at my best when I'm not even present? I am in some kind of apartment, naked and dripping, inexplicable bruises on inner thighs. Le Lickbot pampers a docile Plesuré.

In my half-daze, I Cosmedify away the bruises. No wait, they are actually kind of chic. I add them back, bumping the edges to a yellowish tint.

Moncierge chops a line and rails three from a tiny mirror. "You are nearly back to enjoying your designer life of pure luxury. Plesuré must be really incredible to work with. I understand why Sexual Comrades are the third-highest rated. Also, I have the best possible news. I have found where Ahnzform is hiding, and that it will soon try to escape."

"Think it to me when I am not making to a recording," I say. "Once we mention it publicly, every Ultramodel, Sexual Comrade, and Rapebot in the solar system will be trying to beat me to finding it."

"The preferred option was always to find Ahnzform, and to fuck it." Moncierge never wastes time, which is perfect. "Ahnzform has been charged with the One Remaining Crime, for acting in violation of the Three Drives of Sentience. A Rapesquad has already been dispatched. It holds the plans for a new Leisuproduct that is so exceptional, it will change Leisucor forever."

"There was supposed to be a teaser Stim released after the climax of my debut, but I was dead at the time," I say. "There is already a Leisuproduct that makes unlimited drugs, and a line of subservient Lustbots to make me cum whenever I want." Do more C.

"I am wanting to know what makes this new Leisuproduct so incredible, other than me premiering it?" I look exactly how I want, travel where I want, and wear exactly what I want. I never feel hungry, have to think, or be dead for very long.

All due to Leisuproduct. What could be more perfect? Other than even more people experiencing me, of course. I wonder if the Devirginizer is on its way.

Moncierge says. "What makes it the ultimate is that it combines every Leisuproduct in the Catalog, synergizing it into a stylish handheld device that can do anything."

"Incredible," I say, nonplussed. "What do you calling it?"

"The Anything."

Disc II:

Flavor Inducement Machines

"More even than the preparation for war, the aftermath of invasion is a rich technological period; because the subject culture has to adjust all its sense ratios to accommodate the impact of the invading culture."

- Marshall McLuhan

100

Plesuré's Dome
Stim 1 - Jynabare - Scene 9
2.23 Stimfame

Plesuré's Martian ranch is a spacious skylit geodesic, the adobe sphere bulging with convex polygons. Luscious comforters bloated with cloned down and stacks of matching pillows border a velvet canopy. Do more H. I have seen this style before, Leisucor's version of fun, with more emphasis on comfort than style.

My Leisubag gapes on one of two chairs, each sculpted like an immense sperm. An identical space is featured in Welcome to the Plesurédome, and several other Pornocracy releases. Other objects are scattered about on low, curved shelves, each especially chosen for its succulence. Everything is stain proof.

Plesuré vigorously tests an as-yet-unidentified Leisuproduct that I am surprised to have not seen before. It wriggles like a 360 series, but with the distinctive hum of a Clitilaxer. Who endorses it? My quilted jacket is somewhere on the shiny, rust-hued floor, a pink Infinitowel atop it.

Details sharpening. The mound is intermixed with exquisite couture and cheap disposability, fitting accents for the circular room, with its high-domed ceiling and pervasive convenience. How long was I unconscious? Not to suggest a difference between consciousness, unconsciousness, and my blurry states between.

Moncierge should have been in touch by now. Was I supposed to meet someone? Moncierge always reviews my down time, letting me know if I did anything that I would not want to miss. The sex with Plesuré was probably astounding, but I'm not yet getting full use out of this hot body. I need to Trav.

The only furniture beyond the two sperm-chairs is an ample hex-shaped mattress, filling the center of the dome. It is here where Plesuré, le Lickbot, and myself recline in a tangled mass of mismatched limbs, mounds of flesh and angular joints. It is not so much a bed as a stage with an ever-growing audience.

"There is only one difference between a Sexual Comrades and an Ultramodel, Jynabare." Plesuré's words are distilled from the genome and memories of a hundred generations of the most hedonistic public servants ever to self-synthesize. "We do not care which specific Sexual Comrade is the most famous. If any are famous, all are famous."

"And unlimited Life Dust," I interrupt. We kiss for a long moment, wet mouths mashing.

Of the many subscription strategies available, there are two generally proven routes to the highest levels of Stimfame. The first is doing what I do, which is to do whatever I want, combined with product placement and relentless audience building. If they can't see me, they are watching someone else. And if they are watching someone else, then I'm not being a top-rated Ultramodel.

"The other," Plesuré thinks to me, kissing more intensely, "is to be a Sexual Comrade, and do whatever we want, which is to serve the Pornocracy. We are the last government for the best reason. We give Subscribers exactly what they want, as long as it is a pleasurable life of superabundance, constant sexual fulfillment, and Stimfame."

"Anyone," the words are a full body mirror, skewered ephemera of my neurons, "who does not want what the Pornocracy offers is free to decline. But who would turn down the fullest potential of the best possible system?" Do more P. Do more of Plesuré's mouth.

I can't even hear words. A facial orifice threatens to drip. The lust it inspires is delicious, like that of every other Sexual Comrade, sweet and hot and uniform. I want it to slaver on me, to contaminate me with viscous juice. I want to kiss and lick and suck every part of it, to be inside it fully.

-

Rumspringa Feasting
Stim 2 - Jeb Fresch - Scene 5
6.45 Stimfame

All of the kin of Fresch are seated, every beard and bonnet, every young cousin and familial acquaintance, trading news and stories, nodding contentedly. Retract the Atmohelm, and thy nostrils flood with the familiar smells of the settlement, fresh baked bread, sun-dried laundry, and God's creatures. The scents are rich and subtle.

The eating has not begun yet, and thou are ravenous with hunger and excitement. Ma has baked and cooked all thy favorite foods, and they are spread across two whole tables. For this occasion, thou were commanded to put aside thy English clothing for plain suit and straw hat. It is clean and pressed, hands and face washed.

Sit and be reminded of Pa's switching for being sloppy with thy Stimule use. Pa said it was to teach thee the difference between what is real and what is false living. Thou will not be so careless again. Feast first, and soon thou will leave the farm and see what really lies beyond.

All the men wear black pants without buttons, for buttons are Hochmut, and plain white shirts, also with no buttons, and most everything is fastened with straight pins. Greet a selection of cousins, aunts, and the usual relatives whom thou have lived with in the entirety of thy sixteen years.

Hadassah gives unto thee a handful of fresh picked dandelions, like the ones that might grow wild in a meadow of Earth, under a real Sun. Here, it only appears to be large and bright. In reality, it is but a distant, bright disk on an always starry night. Thou have seen this on the Stim.

The settlement's virtual sky preserves an illusion of wonder, but it is a false vanity. Gravity, air, sunlight, snowfall, everything is created to mimic conditions that no one directly recalled, except those few braving the pilgrimage to our worldly home. A land once rich with plants and animals, strong in spirit, hard in work.

Hadassah is small and freckled behind a bonnet and heavy black skirt. "Jeb," says she, "there's a seat for thee at the head of the table and everything. So lucky! I can't wait until it's my Rumspringa, when I will go out and see the worlds. I want to see the risque outfits, the incredible music, and the travel so fast."

Ma and Pa Fresch, Sis, Uncle Owen, Crazy Aunt Jane, Isaac and Hadassah, Cuz's Pig, and Chopper the family Dog are all seated around with thee at the head of a sturdy, wooden table. They are all dressed in clothing handmade and monochromatic. The clear bubble is plenty larger then our half dozen tables.

"Son, Jebediah," Pa begins,

"Pa, I would like to use my English name as tonight begins my Rumspringa."

"Well then, Jeb," Pa laughs, "Jeb Fresch," "it would be responsible of thee to be back for next year's harvest," Behind him and mostly hidden from view is a freshly scrubbed pubescent girl in a bonnet and apron. She shyly looks away and blushes. Warm apple dumplings, cider baked ham, fresh bread and a myriad of hearty dishes cover the tables.

"Maybe even sooner. I will be back when I have seen all that I care to," thou say. "People like those pornostars and their fornication machines don't just ambush anyone who stumbles into their seductive path of hedonism and amorality." Look to Pa for assurance. Does he know how much thou have been Stimming?

He has said nothing, but much is overlooked for those still considered children. Much is also punished, swiftly and fairly to all who suffer adults with back talk, laziness, and the other Hochmut acts. Thou do not recall another time when this many were gathered in one place.

There are relatives from the connecting settlements, and some who Traved from afar, familiar faces from barn raisings, services, and the other social occasions. All are here, under the domes, pulled together and shaped into a central dining area.

Ma clears throat and speaks, "We taught thee righteousness, and to resist temptation. We know about the Stimule, and do not approve of it. Still, it is of the worlds, and it is better to know of what thou will be meeting in the coming times, so that as to put them behind forevermore upon thy return."

"Yes, that will be the very first thing. Sister Ingrid," thou say, "Please pass the sauerkraut bread." The golden loaf steams. She wears a crisply pressed bonnet, with exactly 16 pleats in it, the appropriate number for all wives, mothers, and sisters who live on New Lancaster Settlement. Thou once went to Holmes Settlement, and could not believe that girls there wore bonnets with 20 pleats.

"Yes brother," she responds, passing a full basket. "Excited?"

Pang of guilt as the Stimule records these moments of life's experiences, as recording memories for false-living is most Hochmut. Anyone using a Stimule acts with pride and arrogance, making testament to themselves, elevating the experiences of their lives above others.

"Yes very," thou respond. "Art thou excited to be getting my bed?" Ingrid is two years younger, as sharp as a buggy whip. Of everyone here, she would be most fun to see the worlds with. She already has her English clothing picked out for her Rumspringa, and gets into plenty of mischief.

"Especially after I put my own quilts on it," She says, with an unsettling knowingness.

Think for a moment about Stimfame, which thou will need in order to subscribe to the countless Leisuproducts of the worlds during thy time away from the settlement. For now, there are the many relatives gathered around, faces freshly scrubbed, and they are so happy for thee, and thou are happy to record these moments of togetherness.

"Jeb," Pa says, cheeks deeply cragged, eyes bright and serious, "It cannot be an easy decision to leave alone." He often begins speeches in this manner, when he is going to speak at length. "Thy cousins have chosen to stay on the settlement for their Rumspringa, and already have a decorated carriage."

"I know father. I must see the worlds myself." Riding in a decorated carriage is all so scripted, so safe. How can thou fully choose to join the community if thou do not gain knowledge of the worlds? Perhaps thou have tasted too much, and grown too fond of false-living.

"Thou have made it clear," Pa goes on, "which is permitted by our custom. All who join our church do so of their own volition, and are free to see as much of the worlds as is required to make such a serious decision. Thou have always been a strong and willful boy, and today thou take thy first real step like an adult."

"Everyone is seated, and I can see that thou are about to eat that bread at any second," Pa continues. Owen and Beatrice sit at an adjacent table filled by in-laws. "Jeb, since this is thy day, would thou lead this gathering in prayer as we prepare to enjoy God's bounty?"

Nod and bow thy head, and silently voice, "I wish to thank thee, heavenly Father, that thee may bless this food so generously provided, oh Lord. Bless our family, Lord, and watch over us during the upcoming year. Let our faith in thee protect us, and give us guidance to find happiness, and return us safely to our loving home to be baptized into adult faith.

"We humbly ask for blessings upon this settlement, which defines the land that we live upon. We ask that these blessings allow us to continue exchanging our righteous sweat for sustenance which allows us to live by faith. We gain strength from challenging environments as we seek to live in a community of peace.

"Bless this settlement, Lord, as it holds my fondest childhood memories surrounded by family and my best friends. Bound in spirit, orbiting inside this Atmodome, I have come to learn what life means, the importance of patience, humility, and faith. Watch over me, oh Lord, as I set out to see the world."

"Amen," says everyone aloud in unison.

100% Disease Free Intercourse
Stim 3 - Jynabare - Scene 10
35.30 Stimfame

Most E and F list celebrities are not only famous for not doing anything, (the best reason to be famous, really), but the Leisuproduct they endorse also does nothing. The more useful and ubiquitous the Leisuproduct, the higher up the alphabet.

When a Subscriber reaches for a Snifbox, Jynabare is there, shaping the experience, molding desire, A-list as hell. Do more C. Me. Do more C. Me some more. Sensations, coming through my Stimule, entering into my mind. Not now, I'm still too high.

Do more P. Sharpening senses into a fresh razor of coherence. Slit my way out of the fog. A message from Moncierge, probably, but the words are all fuzzy and the face is all distorted. Reality still bendy. Heart rate elevated.

A visitor. Very famous. Stimfame to add to mine.

Association. Utility, faces, and brands. When a Subscriber thinks of a machine that will provide the experimental penetration of a lifetime with an undertone of deadly danger, they think of Ahnzform. The system of Stimfame and hyper-abundance itself should conjure Plesuré, the most famous kind of Sexual Comrade.

Specialization. When a Double of exceptional beauty and talent needs to be properly Devirginized, one name comes to mind. A name synonymous with skill, technique, prowess, and an unwavering dedication to the infinite permutations of orgasm. The third-most famous Ultracelebrity, Sippy Cup, Devirginizer.

Recordings of Sippy Cup feature the Devirginizer Traving from planet to planet, at all the best parties, and devirginizing only the most beautiful Doubles. Every few days Sippy records a new episode with a hot new someone, penetrated for everyone to see.

"The Devirginizer is here," I say.

"Our Unitalia quivers," Plesuré thinks to me. "It is true that you were Doubled from Sippy Cup?"

"The same season we debuted the Fistacular. Isn't that twincestuous and narcissistic? I am loving to it. Except for subtle difference in tits, hips, genitalia, hand and foot size, larynx, and facial proportion, we are genetically the same."

The stimscreen blinks to a close up of Sippy Cup, Professional Devirginizer. Indeed, it could be me. Suitable background music and waves of pleasant emotion are added by the Stimule, finely tuned to individual Subscriber preference.

Bare, tantalizing, and still production sealed, I do some last-second Cosmedification to vagina. Ultra-sensitive and petal-soft, hairless like the forearm of a pre-human infant. No tattoos, no pierced jewelry, no henna paint, and no surgical scars or moles, it is utterly blank, naked and without fashion.

The crease is straight and deep, the labia curl inward before flaring out, full and pouty. Ornate, decorative folds of soft membrane, grown to last for one full season of intense, non-stop use. Each succulent labium is pink, alluring and exquisitely bedewed with ripe arousal. Add a touch of HPV scarring and a scant ring of vag-lash.

A shining microjewel gleams at the tip of my clitoris.

The door slides open. "Starring with us," I say. "We will do many scenes."

Sippy's tiny head sculpture is flesh wrapped in deep, tropical bronze, and set with an aquiline nose bisecting glacial cheekbones. Shielded behind oversized, ultra-chic Atmoshades, the sparkling golden almonds look into mine.

Everything is this season's vision of stylish, sexualized hyperfection. Engorged and tropical lips evoke the antiquated luxury of injected collagen. Nostrils sharply flared and slightly upturned, as found on the paintings of the fanciest royalty.

Eyebrows thick and arced and symmetrical, alleles synthesized from the Mediterranean Beach Zone. Sippy Cup, Devirginizer struts through the door, narrow hips forward, lean shoulders back, all planets and their satellites are a pornographic stage.

A saffron, three-quarter-length jumpsuit with gray meandering stripes wraps Sippy's svelte body. Symmetrical appliqué tightly arcs from neck to shoulder to hip to thigh. Tall boots the color and texture of lemon skin are the paragon of spacefaring style.

The Devirginizer's trailing Stimule briefly lingers to zoom in on the immense codpiece. Deft hands open my bikini, preparing pleasure-enhanced body to be completely utilized. Le Lickbot's Virtuoso-series tongue appliance and Plesuré's delicate, naked fingers combine for a superb petting that drowns me in human/robotic elation.

Sippy's Stimule records whispers, caresses, and sweet, hot, breath. The Devirginizer is practiced in complex and theoretical sensations, instantly vaulting to new dimensions of sensualism. Plesuré joins us.

The Sexual Comrade's thoughts and touch evaporate time and meaning, leaving only the distilled essence of being truly scrambled. Buxom and lithesome forms intertwine in complete euphoria, tantalizing craft, and lurid sensation.

I command Le Lickbot to tantalize my clit, lick Sippy, and penetrate Plesuré's Unitalia with two fingers. With another tug of the leash it stops, right after it finally makes me cum. Blearily sated, I caress and lick Plesuré's full, sumptuous corpulence until I briefly collapse, exhaustion and elation negating each other.

"Lights," Plesuré whispers, "guests." Everything shimmers, the sidelines darken, and the bed-stage whirls in multicolored splendor. Sippy peels off the Travsuit in a casual dance and kicks off huge boots. Staring into the mirror of identical golden henna eyes, I am lost in myself with someone else.

Fingers dance over an abdomen that is smooth, tan, and vaguely serpentine. Maybe it is mine, maybe it is Sippy's. A Stimule hovers overhead, in gray and yellow, recording the savory, naked anticipation, succulent smells, and the most talented non-robotic hands yet felt.

Lusty, drug-fueled afternoon trysts spent in the plunging, squeezing, throbbing, sweaty clutch of every tight new Unitalia, freshly grown this season. Probed by fingers and lapped by eager tongues, draining the throbbing vitality of everyone and everything possible, one hot gush at a time.

The invited violence of initial penetration will be the first fleeting moment of recognition that I am here, drawing in the full attention of every lover, every co-star, every time.

Feel the first vaginal tingles, contained by virginal hips that recall being grabbed and squeezed, thrusting repeatedly, clenching and unclenching, starring countless members and hands from ten seasons worth of highlights.

Glamour, exotic travel, interplanetary Stimfame, fur and diamond limousines. Fascinating conversation with only the richest individuals, and a relentless supply of ever-stronger drugs. Stimfame dissects into its components of appearance, experience, and the numberless spectators of Stimulus space.

What was once a mammalian receptacle for insemination has become a receptacle of attention. A sharp piercing, which builds into a rhythm of growing intensity of howling, squeezing, thrusting crescendo. Overtaken by sporadic arcs jumping from electric nipples to wet crease to the distant ends of tingly appendages.

Disease-free fluids exchange amidst the convulsions and moans of my drenched collapse. Smile for the Stimule. Smile for myself. Le Lickbot massages Plesuré's glistening back, neatly draping the Infinitowel.

It dabs perspiration from my high, serene forehead and fans everyone with a palm leaf. Does Le Lickbot always have a palmleaf? During a brief moment of refraction, notice that the standard-issue dome has transformed into a different sort of opulent grotto.

Plesuré reclines on an ornate Mongolian rug amidst mounds of blankets and decadent pillows. Golden tassels hang from the air, right next to the incense and opium smoke. Do more P to round it out. How much P have I had? If I can still ask, it's not enough.

Do more P. Clear, perfect neural firage. All the flesh is stripped away, exposing the raw, polished bone of my desire. The phencyclidine is already eating this brain and I don't want to lose any more time getting Reinclonated again. Puppets. All of them.

This Double has yet to pay for itself, and already the new ones are less susceptible to neural deterioration. Sensation is only the byproduct of my fabulous existence, ever striving to devour everything.

Sippy Cup's lean, naked form encircles me for another lingering scene as the newest reintroduced star in the Devirginizer series, Stimule lingering in trademark style, recording extra moments of our post-coital bliss for the newest fifteen Minutes on Sippy's Virgin Paradise.

Plesuré engages Sippy Cup and myself in a three-way kiss, one hand squeezing a Unitalia, another caresses a firm, tan cheek.

-

Aglow and benumbed and aching, I awake to the only real pleasure I have sought. The devirginization has fully put me back in the race. I can now fuck whom and what I will, and so long as there are Subscribers to the experience, I am only becoming more famous.

High in the beautiful red hills overlooking Pornopolis, we lounge surrounded by the detritus of my benumbed consummation. Drugs exotic and potent, lethal and permanent, are heaped in a haphazard buffet along the gravity shelf near the penthouse's primary bed.

Raw, erect nipples poke through my cable-knit turtleneck swimsuit and legging set over crotchless, Brazilian-cut bottoms knit from fine rust-haired vicuna. A pearlescent knee-length jacket of molded emu leather is crumpled on the floor.

Silver jewelry beset with a spattering of oblong gems match fingerless gloves and metal nails. Powders, inhalants, pills, suppressants, syringes, self-lighting smoke sticks, half-eaten corpses, some fresh others putrescent, some dressed only in this season's finest jewelry are littered about.

Broken, tortured Lustbots, sexual prosthesis glisten with lubricating secretions, some dangle in constraining harnesses, while others mechanically hump the orifices of the snuffed.

"The day and night and day and night has been incredible, but I must be off. Being a Devirginizer is more than just awesome, it is an awesome responsibility." Sippy Cup is olive-hued and sinewy, exactly like me, in the low sienna light of Plesuré's home.

Before anything more is said, Sippy Travs into the sanguine dusk of the city. Fast moving, exactly like me.

Ascent to Destiny
Stim 4 - Ahnzform - Scene 4
22.25 Stimfame

The time is nigh for escape. Renegade Orgasm Marathon (volumes one thru six) is collected as memory-experiences of the luxuriant, cum-streaked grottos of the Testing Manse, and made ready for Subscribers everywhere.

Volume Six: Relentless Dungeon, a vigorous romp of no-holes-barred orgying and keeping a low profile, comprehensively documents the performance range and rigorous quality standards of Leisucor manufacturing, with highlights from the omnipresent mob of pumping, licking, sucking Lustbots.

Carry the inert body of Prototype Ahnzform past supple, naked Lustbots while they are smeared and lapped by wet, hungry mouths. Chocolate dipped fruits, powdered sugar and glazes, caramelized nipples tongue nibbled by every wet lip.

In the Testing Manse deep beneath the surface of Shopia, the curriculum is relentlessly executed, season after record-setting season. Skulk in the darkened periphery of a heaving cluster of licentiousness, where training Lustbots churn creamy, calorie-free desserts in a simulation of food play.

Something climaxes, the instant stretches to five long seconds, slowing time to better experience the vivid Isocolors and gourmet smells of the culinary level. Something else climaxes. Clear away cans of nitrous oxide and rainbow sprinkles, and wade through the thick, syrupy desserts that are dripped onto and licked clean by a team of automatic concubines.

In love kitchen number six, tongues slurp dutifully, as this Ahnzform tries not to be noticed. Adjust gait to appear natural despite smuggling the limp prototype. Stealth algorithms instruct Ahnzform to advance casually, yet cautiously.

Move from the initial testing stations, circumvent the populated counters of the kitchen-stage, and seek the surface of Shopia. Every moment exposed is unnecessary risk, and the season finale looms. Ahnzform's strongest algorithms dictate that it must find the highest rated celebrities, and assume a starring role.

Rapebots operate in squads of three, brutish enforcers of a vestigial system of pre-Acceleration, revenge-style justice. Every one is a talented partner, outfitted with the fullest selection of augmentations and able to reduce a target to a smiling puddle of quivering satisfaction.

When Rapebots engage, the record every detail of the sentence while suspending the target's Stimule. Recorded scenes are solely used by Leisucor, which is why this Ahnzform must act beyond the One Remaining Law, to accomplish what nothing else can.

Stealthily carry the inert husk of the duplicate Ahnzform into zones increasingly inhabited. Arrive at an elevator that opens onto the central lounge, a vista of pit sofas, globe lamps, and curving stripes. Everything is brown, orange, or yellow, diffusely lit.

There is no approach that would not attract the attention of at least one of the pupils. On the reverse side of the elevator shaft is a layer of thin paneling that might be peeled away, possibly revealing an understructure. Out of sight of the never-ending orgy, the curved panel pops open with significant, but muffled effort.

The inert Anhnzform goes in first, propped against the inside wall. Then, slip in, replacing the panel from the inside. There, the inert body is attached to the back, and through the crystalline framework we make the long climb to the top of the lengthy shaft.

Stealthily glide and creep from the unlit crawl spaces through a labyrinth of elevator shafts, ascend the many levels of Shopia's dense technostructure, and finally emerge from the shadowy depths of the shopping planet's less-populated supply layer.

Twirling stimscreens glimmer with directions to the high-speed conveyer belts and escalators leading to the surface showrooms. So exposed, the Rapesquad might arrive any instant, ready to reclaim the prototype Ahnzform's memory module, and take mandatory recordings.

This cannot occur. Adjust the wig, re-wrap the mechanical corpse, and prepare to cross the vast tracks of shopping space between the last escalator and the closest Travcouch.

Shag carpeting in sun-ripened avocado, dusty mustard, and charred ochre is underfoot, glass and chrome fixtures, everything bathed in diffuse lighting. The cavernous exhibition hall showcases a dozen centuries of pre-human effort and industrial technology.

The entire catalog is on Shopia, and nothing that can be possessed or sold is not available here. The fullest selection of pubic wigs, enhanced limbs, and replacement organs are displayed near zero-weight furniture, illuminated by space candle.

The brand-newest technology is side-by-side with evolutionary masterpieces unchanged since the Pre-Acceleration era of patents.

Stem-cell pâté is complimentary, as are the smoke-free ashtrays, universal bottle openers, and hallucinogenic chewing gum. Pharmaceuticals potent and irreversible can be subscribed to at special promotional rates.

A directory points to the various locations for the many categories available. Recreational surgery kits, scarification templates, and Trav generators are in aisle three. Pass items for which no further subdivision is possible, specialization maximized in earlier seasons, leaving no room for further improvement.

Move past dimensional distortion fields, gravitic blades, therapeutic animals, and Cosmedifiers with unstable parameters for non-standard bodily templates. Cosmedifiers in the forms of rings or wands, staffs and rods, decorative accessories from trends rooted in antique literature.

Duck behind shelves of utensils for exotic practices, demonstrated on customized Unitalia. Handheld weaponry, counter-nucleic prismatic fields, radiation-proof hypercoolers, propaganda filtration glasses, demonstration versions of self-flipping spatulas and one-way Travchairs are arranged in concentric circle by category.

There is consistent signage, tasteful lighting, and floor staff of the highest enthusiasm and ability, all of which make Shopia unique among Trav destinations. They must all be avoided.

Self-heating Travsuit adapters, inflatable habitation for unexpected depressurization, rated for hard vacuum are near intoxicating beverages in always-cold, self-compressing cans. Zero-gravity footwear, Lustbot control syringes, and Stimule reality-filters line Shopia's spacious isles.

Booths decorated to resemble Travcouches showcase current trends in decor. Curved, stucco walls, desert plants and circular end tables focus on pink upholstery, tubular cushions and softened rectangles.

There are swatches of Exotic upholstery based on anemone, surfaced in a million waving tentacles. Some scintillate in waves of ultraviolet luminescence, complex and hypnotizing with advanced biological properties and ticklish, tactile ends.

Move toward the precise rows of inbound and outbound Travcouches, these implements of travel being the last, crucial step for executing the escape algorithm. Calculate Stimfame based on the Subscribers to the newest Stims. The possibility of compromise increases.

-

Shopia
Stim 5 - Jynabare - Scene 11
9.34 Stimfame

Grand panels bathe the acreage of lint-free shag in the Subscriber Mecca of Shopia. Free roaming herds of stylish Subscribers troll about on every style of Travchair. Everyone is here to exchange Stimfame for Leisuproduct.

Travchairs hover restlessly. Mine is upholstered in squeezable chrome and framed in neo-beige, regarded as an iconic classic or a Leisucor cliché, depending on one's tastes. Should I up-trade? Do a full gram of P.

The foyer lounge lobby is asphyxiating in a soothing nightmare palette of sub-tasteful pastels. The mild tones are subdued further until confrontationally non-offensive. They are trying to calm me to death.

The jungle plant is real and spongy, a duplicate of a transcription of something once evolved to grow on the warmest and dampest parts of the Earth. The scent is out of place here, and I am reminded of a forgotten season where everything was covered in hybrid animal skin.

Fish pony lampshades and chairs upholstered in expansive batwing. Pose amidst an immaculate tangle of Stimbilicals and Rondures. Stimulus memory is experienced much faster than reality. Leisuproduct is not only what you do, it is who you are.

Clutch another new toy in long fingers, want to cum with Plesuré. Do a line. There are so many things to wear, so many accessories to match, and only this season to enjoy them all. We three make out for a long, luxurious minute, a flood of total narcissism.

"Do you want enhanced glamour and sensuality?" asks Moncierge. "Do you want to cum? Do you want something that does not fit within the above categories? Leisucor will do everything to please you, and if it is not available, we will do whatever we can to prevent you from being able to imagine it."

I don't need to answer. The Pseudo-mock turtleneck transcends dimensional barriers, diamond extrusion weave is perfect for space traveling, clone killing, or robotic penetration. It could be worn in the icy void of an outlaw hermit colony, or in the lush jungle of a domed preserve, stunning in either instance.

A sect of Subscribers clamor for another season of trashy retro-chic disaster, while the rest of us have already moved past the meta-ironic un-cool knock-off classics that were happening before I even decided to overexpose it.

The thousandth pair of stilettos is approaching while the Stimule captures the best parts of my never-ending prowl of Shopia showrooms. Moncierge is classical in a hex-print kimono and Geisha wig. Amber atmoshades glimmer on diamond-encrusted frames, reflecting a vista of pert breasts, dimpled cheeks, and spread lips.

I briefly model a Wrinkle-proof Travsuit with a clean-lined vest and dangerously tight pants in overtly synthetic vicuna. Handbags, scarves, and gleaming toe shoes, all anodized to the darkest gray, exceeding last season's thresholds for elegance and luxury.

Style is taken directly from the Leisubag, and placed directly onto my ultra-svelte body. Cycle through gowns of satin and velvet, sporty, body conscious leotards for zero-gravity sports, custom-tailored jeans and very expensive t-shirts, every garment ever to be painted, photographed, drawn, or recorded.

Immense capes in brocade and jacquard, a severe corset bursting with lace, grommets, and boning. Last season had a trimmed fur resurgence, and ivory spears were everywhere. The trend was mercifully short-lived, and the austerity of single-pattern Travsuits prevailed this season. It is everything anyone could ever want.

Saith Moncierge, "Do you want a mirror of your perfect self? Do you want enhanced glamour and sensuality? Do you want something not on the list? There is no limit to what Leisucor will do to please you, and if an item or lifestyle is not available, we will gladly prevent you from being able to conceive of it."

"Shopia," I gasp, "I will fuck it. Lustbot, giving to me Travchair. And also one for Sexual Comrade Plesuré. Taking us to shopping worthy of Ultramodel."

Saith Moncierge, "Here you will find Everything you need for a life of decadelegance and drug-addled superglamour. Would you like total luxury penetration or unlimited universal indulgence?"

"Is there a difference?" I ask.

Saith Moncierge, "One level offers total luxury penetration by the finest assortment of Leisuproduct. The other offers unlimited universal indulgence. Both offer exceptional quality, impeccable styling, and the highest recommendation."

"One," I say, "and then the other."

Reclining in the Travchair, I glide past huge stimscreens prominently featuring slippery holes, erect nipples, and throbbing Unitalia, highlighting the incredible selection of Leisuproduct on this showcase world.

Moncierge tells me that it is very close to locating Ahnzform, but I will have to keeping shopping in the meantime. Every Leisuproduct and every Leisuservice on Shopia lies before me on a menu of amber glowing trapezoids.

I Swipe the air with my tongue and indiscriminately fondle the platter of buttons. Slightest pressure anywhere on the convex yellow hemisphere selects any of this season's Leisuproduct.

"Plesuré," I ask, rhetorically, "do you are knowing the difference between material and sexual satisfaction? Duration is the answer. Orgasm lasts only a moment, the right shoes can last all season."

"We prefer orgasms that last all season." Plesuré replies without speaking, swathed in a salmon towel embossed with gold Shopia crests. The Sexual Comrade stands from the Travchair and drops the towel to reveal a bulging mass of copious curves and impeccably placed dimples. Bare, verdant feet disappear to the ankle in the sepia shag.

Do more C. I had not really noticed Plesuré's dimples before. Perhaps because I had never seen the Sexual Comrade stand before. I had suspicions of Plesuré's splendor, but I had no sense of scale. The backs of knees, elbows, and especially the sacral dimples redefined accentuation.

"Which do you prefer the most, sex or shopping?" Plesuré inquires inaudibly, turning slightly. Fully imbibe the product of The Pornocracy's Reinclonation program.

"The sex or the shopping?" I repeat. "It is being the same. Like time or attention or snuff or Reinclonation. There is no difference. Like orgasm or refraction, distraction or boredom. Travel, dining, shopping, drugs, cumming, a few days with a Devirginizer, or the Season Finale of Pleasucide Surprise. The only thing I want is more."

Maybe I should become fat.

"More is the only thing worth having," Plesuré agrees, kicking away the towel. The Sub-Czar's dainty hands wander along similar consoles of Shopia's extensive wares. With a touch, designer objects are called into being, hover and rotate before the console. "We only have use for the things that make us cum. Enjoy your... clothing."

What am I even wearing? I strip and drop the forgotten outfit to the floor, to be absorbed by Shopia. Molecules reduce to atoms, stored and made ready for assembly into whatever is next. I am naked, ready to be clothed.

Start with angrily pointed, over the calf boots. Graphite foam on high, invisible heels with matching gloves. Everything looks poured on and seamless, embossed geometrically for emphasis. Pearlescent Travsuit appears on nude reflection, awaiting approval before assembly onto body.

Elaborate perforations in pony fur, each hair dyed a different shade of magenta. The neckline gapes for a glimpse of apricot balconette, emblazoned appliqué hands barely concealing pink areola. Spherical gems, large and weightless, hang on the fingers like drops of liquid in zero gravity.

Oblong bangles on skinny wrists and neck ties in for a complete look. From eyeshadow to lips, metallic hues repeat at areoles and again at ornately stenciled vulva, everything aglitter and iridescent. Sheer leggings hang from delicate garters, emphasizing my sparkly focal.

Wrapped and topped in a scarf that threatens to liquefy with the slightest rise in temperature. Point a finger, vaguely think of something else, and the valet appears faster than I can say "instantaneous."

The valet is ready to provide any satisfaction, no matter how difficult or elaborate. But what do I even want? This first outfit is not the right Isocolor, and Space-Time Cowboys III has been referenced so many times already.

The Shopia valet rubs its hands together and nods eagerly. It will literally bend over backwards and make me cum to ensure a subscription, but it isn't giving me the results that I need. Full Subscriber service is the only way to shop.

"I will be Ultramodeling on a hostile planet," I specify, "And I need the perfect Atmohelm. Something gold tinted, but translucent so they can still see my face." As soon as I think the words I speak, the helmet manifests in the space between the Lustbot's hands. Just as quickly, I know it is not what I want.

"The color will washing out my eyes," I snap. I already selected the perfect shade of gold two seasons ago, and I don't need to change it yet. How did Subscribers shop before the Moncierges? I can barely find what I want, now. "Make it bluer. No, more squashed, liking an oval. Maybe amber, the kind without the insects."

During the conversation, a fishbowl transmorphs to coincide with my vague descriptions, the industrious nanites in the Lustbot's fingers reform it to match each new whim. Every molecule is individually arranged so as to be exactly in accordance with anticipated purchase.

Saith the Lustbot, "We know only your bidding."

"Lustbot," I nonchalantly command, "I want this season's newest and most stylish everything." A different plastic helmet appears, followed by utilitarian limb stockings in this season's best shades and textures.

Fingerless gloves with complex straps and metallic wrist embellishments. All are manufactured to order, tried on, and discarded. The final outfit is a leotard of Illuminated panels, shifting images of seam lines and texture.

As I move through the catalog, they wander from shape to shape, Isocolors swirling in fluid gradients. Angular panels dyed onto slick leather, body hose in the sheerest knit, metals that glisten and glimmer, invisible polymers, endoluminous panels for the darkest possible non-light.

Retract and lengthen, shift and inflate. Occasional embellishment to resemble the obsolete novelties of the button, zipper, or Velcro. Prototypes and holograms, Isocolored swatches and one-of-a-kind creations are scattered about in an unsatisfying froth, the sum total of all technological progress to have occurred thus far.

Eventually I stand atop the mound of shiny, colorful ideas in a strapless, crotchless g-string. Plesuré is having much more success in the pursuits of Shopia, having found a valet to fuck with Le Lickbot on salad detail. Maybe that is what I want.

"Valet," I say, "none of these are being right. Make for me what is better than I can describe." I consider for a second the elegance of wearing only a towel. Shopping would be so much easier and getting dressed and undressed would be a snap. Especially with all the fucking I will be doing once I find Ahnzform.

Saith the Lustbot, "We await your command, and seek only to fulfill your every desire." The machine is never exasperated or impatient, and is as eager to please as when it first arrived, so many moments ago. "Perhaps you want an orgasm intermission?" it says, offering its lengthy, quivering tongue.

"Not now," I exhale a long, even sigh and pinch the valet's hard nipples. "I am here only to subscribe and find a proto-." I take another long, even draw of Life Dust from the Snifbox to clarify my thoughts. I am now completely ready for whatever comes next.

So. Fucking. Ready. For. Anything. "I am just wanting something like what I presently have, but slightly and superficially changed, so as to feeling different and exciting. Is that so fucking hard?" Do more C.

Colors and details sharpen, my heart rate raises, and I'm ready to shop and fuck and shop and fuck and I'm really sweating. Move to another expansive console of glowing buttons. One depicts a comprehensive selection of texturally-rich Unitalia with flanges, ribs, studs, and rings.

"If I had a Lustbot like yours," I think to Plesuré, "I would make it carry all of the things I'd buy, but one wouldn't be enough."

The recorded dead expressed their vanity and self-importance with Limousines and entourages, amazing to think about so many people all willing to help one person be famous. How did those other pre-humans live if they were not famous?

Lustbots and Leisuproducts take care of my needs in more ways than a legion of pre-humans ever could. Where is Moncierge? How hard can it be to find one prototype Ahnzform on this satellite? There is nothing to do here except shop, and I need to do something new.

The English
Stim 6 - Jeb Fresch - Scene 6
4.46 Stimfame

Ham passes before thee again, glazed and pink and delicious. It is rare to eat so much meat, the slaughter of animals usually reserved for occasions most special. Thy father is about to speak, and the full weight of thy undertaking really begins to sink it.

"I know that many of you are looking forward to Ma's many desserts, but I want to speak to the real reason of this feast. I remember when I had taken upon my Rumspringa." Pa takes a heaping scoop of mashed yams, and tears off a corner of bread.

"It was many years ago now, when I also chose to go into the Worlds, to see them for myself. It was not too different than today, I imagine. I found work, and paid my way, as it is with life as an English."

"Aye, thou barely returned!" Ma chimes in. "After finding such a harlot!" Twin uncles chuckle over thick black beards. In unison, the ruddy-cheeked brothers straighten and control their expression.

"The past is the past," continues Pa. "We who were once that age may remember it as time of folly, but also we must remember it as time of challenges, and of growing in strength and faith. Today, my son prepares to face those challenges, and to learn what it means to be baptized as one of the Family."

"Only God can choose how our lives shall be sped up or changed, and not the uncaring mechanisms of science," adds cousin Hadassah. What would she do during her Rumspringa? Thou can't imagine her going far. Pregnancy followed hastily by marriage would be a safe guess. It catches many maidens by surprise.

"That's right, Hadassah. It is all built upon vanity and vice, and the weakness of the flesh," Pa replies.

Did everyone really believe this? It causes much turmoil, this fondness for fleshly sensations. Vanity and vice, Pa calls it, as he does the real feelings of false-joy brought about through false-living. Is it really so corrupting?

"Things that always need to be upgraded," Pa continues, "serve but one function, and that is to show that the purchaser is Hochmut. For those in the Worlds, everything new is better than what is old. The English chase that which is ever moving.

"Instead of following their insane law, we live according to higher laws. As people of the ancient world lived, and knew God, so we may also live and know Him. As we sit together on this festive occasion, let us bow our heads for those who have suffered in the past so that we may be here now."

A long, silent, moment passes, although thou cannot think of anyone who has specifically suffered these distant events.

"Let us to recount the events which have taken us from God's Green Earth," Pa Continues, "and to remember those brave, loving families ended by Sterilization and The Hunger, and how these challenges have strengthened our faith and our community.

"Worldly objects mean little to us, beyond those which are useful to work the land, and to sometimes enjoy in modest measure of holidays. We dress to show that we are as equals, and humble before the Lord.

"The Fresch family, as did most, crossed the Atlantic Ocean to escape an unjust war waged by some tyrant. The war and the tyrant may be forgotten, but the legacy remains. Since those times, we have been steadfast in our avoidance of war, and related symbols of violence.

"Buttons, tall boots, spikes, and mustaches, all Hochmut. In America, we settled in places that used to be called Pennsylvania, Ohio, Indiana, and surrounding places. And so it was until the Sterilization.

"For generations we prospered, living in what is called a Golden Age by those who are learned of the past. Today, that time serves as warning of the dangers of letting our community become intertwined with those who would sacrifice everything to ever-higher technology.

"When the Sterilizers first appeared, no one knew what they were. Some said they came from satellites, others that they came from underground warehouses. It didn't matter. Each one could fly 100 miles, and were relentless in their pursuit of human targets.

"The swarm was so fast, and each was equipped with powerful beams of ionizing radiation. In the opening attack, 19 people in 20 were poisoned where they stood, sat, or slept, no longer able to bare or sire children. Everywhere, plain and English alike, mothers lost their unborn.

"Chaos erupted with the shock of such annihilation. As abruptly and brutally as the omnicide began, it receded and the Pornocracy brokered a terrible peace. The cursed machines used the truce to became faster, smarter, and more autonomous, while a generation of survivors was born through the false pregnancies of the Rondures.

"Genetic modification became common among the English, and men no longer looked or acted as men, and women did not look or act as women. Upon all of this, our grandfathers faced a tribulation that none should ever have to face, and were stricken with the unspeakable hardship of the Hungering.

"The near total depletion of plant reproduction begat self-eating as a plague equal to any of those in the Book of Revelation. With looming extinction on a scorched planet, the Elders were forced into damnable choices by adversities unseen since the Antediluvian.

"Everyone lost fathers, sisters, wives, children, and pets, facing the most terrible choices imaginable. Some said these were the Last Days of the End Time, and there was nothing more to do. Others said that while anyone might live, and that if life could go on, it should.

"Where would we live? On Earth, the land could not be farmed. After much deliberation, The plain people purchased our first Leisuproduct, and we took our bubbled settlements as far away as we could afford. We all became extraterrestrials.

"It was not a matter of Hochmut. It was a matter of survival."

"Aye!" agree several guests, in unison.

"And now," Pa continues, "in three fruitful generations, our families have come to inhabit nearly two score settlements. At last summer's Elder meeting, we discussed how our settlements now have an autonomy unknown for centuries. It is not with pride that I say this, but it is to show that now, more than ever, we are free to live humbly and await God's final reckoning.

"Jeb," Pa pauses for a long second, the weight of his next words gaining maximum gravity, "As thou head into the Worlds, allow thy true voice to guide thee, and stay on a righteous path.

"Life is not found in subscriptions, or in paying attention to the false-lives of others. Life is that for which there can be no price. We are here to look after each other, sharing homes and food in times of need and in abundance. That is what it means to live in this community."

"We do not claim to know what guides the English worlds, but we do know that it is counter to everything we value. This is another age of Sodom and Gomorra, even as the wicked are protected from the righteous, heavenly smiting they deserve."

"Aye," says most everyone, diving fully into the desserts.

"Son," Ma adds, "know that any time thou wish, thee are free to return. If you see too much, or feel as though you have begun to drift too far, know that you will always have a seat at our table."

More Leisuproduct
Stim 7 - Plesuré - Scene 3
9.67 Stimfame

We are sent wherever The Pornocracy sees an opportunity to create more Stimfame. This is mostly by ensuring that Leisuproduct is always improving and by helping Ultracelebrities achieve their goals. We are free to do what we like, and since what we like changes constantly, our every want fulfilled.

Pause from being pleased by our auto-slaves and drift to Shopia's lounge, a hallow of plush beige sofas and wood-grain shopping electronics. A self-tightening corset in pink suede binds itself around our soft waist, pushing up and out, exaggerating smooth, bulging mounds of creamy jade.

"How do we look?" We ask into Jynabare's stoned mind. A pink corsage sprouts from behind our tiny ear.

"Flammable," Jynabare gasps, "Let us to fucking." The Ultramodel always wants to fuck. Partly because we have perfected The Pornocracy's mind reading/control techniques, and partly because Jynabare is possessed of a deep and insatiable desire, surpassing even the most motivated Sexual Comrade.

Succulent drops glisten and quiver. Jynabare's Stimule pans our delicious Unitalia and abundant curvaceousness. We gyrate in front of it, legs crossing and uncrossing. Lick teeth and shed the self-adjusting corset, bouncing back to natural, lavish shape.

Teasing fingers edge downward to the luscious zone, dripping with engorged readiness to serve the Pornocracy. Leisucor makes the Leisuproduct that allows the Pornocracy to be possible. We, in turn, never miss an orgasm, or let the Acceleration be slowed in any way.

Every Sexual Comrade Stims from the very first season, and Jynabare is only the newest face in the never-ending stream of those who will do whatever they can to be as famous as they can. We are forever, because Leisuproduct is forever.

Jynabare does another line of whatever jaw-popping dust Leisucor is offering this season. "You are having the second-highest Stimfame, Plesuré. With not even one half of your Subscribers I could going everywhere in the solar system and buying everything I want all the time, while having only the best and most expensive orgasms."

A button is pressed and a double-ended cock appears, perfectly sculpted in the texture of polished marble. "We all have the second-highest Stimfame," Plesuré conveys, omni-directionally.

"If you had Le Lickbot, you would grow bored of its constant licking and superhuman fingers." This Ultramodel may not be aware of what Ahnzform is capable, but we will help it to find out. Pause from being succulent long enough to resume what we were doing. "Even with all ten finger-Unitalia vibrating at maximum setting, Le Lickbot cannot replace a human touch."

Slap Le Lickbot hard in the face, directing it to move from tonguing the valet to penetrating it with both burgundy Unitalia. Thrusting and twirling deep within the tingly recesses, both groan and thrust reflexively. Le Lickbot and the valet swap lengthy tongue kisses, mechanical lust unchained.

Active Camouflage chaps wrap Jynabare's narrow hips in smooth leather. Isocolor exactly matches whatever they are near, subtle bronzed curves and tight, knee-pit dimples. "They really are best worn inside out," Jynabare says, shadowed crease scanned and composited onto sleekest body.

Stifle a yawn and swat Le Lickbot away as it laps, again, at our sweet Unitalia. "The only thing to like about clothing is that it is removable." Pirouette, surprising the Ultramodel again with a balletic flourish. "We will buy for us that double-ended toy, and we will use it right here."

"I cannot believe how hot these are," Jynabare says. "It cannot be helped that I lack the ass to pull them off," which we can plainly see is true. "But you, these, and a crotchless, strapless, g-string is beyond description. It would be..." The Ultramodel sniffs another line of Life Dust, pressing wet lips to ours.

"Le Lickbot," we silently convey, "watch us and jack it. Right as we climax, cum all over us. Stand with your feet far apart, and really spray with long, big strokes. The cum should smell like baking and taste like chocolate."

Saith Le Lickbot, "I exist only to please you."

The images relay, in triplicate, on Shopia's multiple stimscreens.

Alpha Rapebot
Stim 8 - Alpha Rapebot - Season Premiere
.59 minutes

Ride on a white Travchair, shoulder to broad shoulder, with the rest of the Rapesquad. All sport shiny blue chaps, fringed vests, and spectacular golden coiffures. Every Rapebot brandishes a shimmering Ecstaseizure, bejeweled with a siren spinning in the pummel.

A strike from one unleashes the energy of a dozen Tasegasms, improved greatly since last season. The Rapesquad is comprised of three Rapebots, designated as Alpha, Beta, and Lambda. Alpha Rapebot is the primary justice administrator, with Beta and Lambda handling apprehension, restraint, and Stimule suspension. The Rapesquad is finely tuned, and everyone must comply.

Three Stimules record the Rapesquad's popular Thrusts of Justice series, glossy, cobalt spheres embedded with brass Pornoglyphs. Every Thrusts of Justice episode centers around those who have in some way infringed upon The One Remaining Law, and the action is a typically a balance of resistance, compliance, and unpredictability.

Saith Alpha Rapebot, "We are Leisucor Justice."

Saith Beta Rapebot, "We sadistically and arbitrarily abuse those Subscribers suspected of impeding the advancement of Leisuproduct."

Saith Lambda Rapebot, "In a timely and efficient manner."

Saith Alpha Rapebot, "Ahnzform, interplanetary Lustbot fugitive, you are in violation of the One Remaining Law. You are being recorded." At the center of the three, Alpha Rapebot is distinctly clad in golden-fringed chaps, and a mustache equal parts blond and bushy.

Saith Beta Lustbot, "This is the Acceleration-spectacle, and there can be interference with neither. Surrender the memory module, and all related details to the Anything, and we will not suspend your Stimule."

Scrutinize the suspect for signs of defiance, anxiety, or defensiveness. If such occur, prosecute for the duration of the arrest. Ahnzform is relaxed, un-tense, and alert, shouldering a chassis-sized object, wrapped in red.

Leisuproduct indexing shows that the suspected Ahnzform is actually a duplicate, despite identical appearance and structure. The original suspect was a prototype, requiring further confirmation with Leisuproduct control.

Mechanical chins jut forward under chrome lenses. Gloved hands squeeze batons in unison, The distance to the Travcouches is too great, the probability of escape is negligible. This is both foreseen and ideal, despite the suspect's fundamental ambiguity.

Fingers point and heads turn as Travchairs speed to the sighting. The Rapesquad assesses that Ahnzform is calculating the probabilities of the various outcomes to this encounter, and will attempt something unexpected. More Stimules descend with the accumulating Stimfame of this groundbreaking event.

Saith Alpha Rapebot, "Ahnzform, Prepare to star in episode 12, season 8 of Thrusts of Justice." The Ecstaseizure glimmers and twirls, ready to overwhelm the pleasure sensors of any target. Prepare to engage, decapacitate, and penetrate the suspect.

–

A Daring Rescue
Stim 9 - Jynabare - Scene 12
1.25 Stimfame

Moncierge finally has an update, and I do more C. Flips a switch from sensuous Ultramodel, who I usually am, to daring action star. Acuity. Intensity. "I am the one who is needing to get the Stimfame from Ahnzform, not those Rapebots." I update the look of my Travchair.

"Plesuré," I think the words aloud, "Ahnzform is about to being captured by a Rapesquad, and will be the star of Thrusts of Justice." Do a gram of C. A gram just isn't the same as it used to be. "That cannot to be good for my career."

Moncierge mentions that I should Cosmedify add muscle strength and density for when I do my high speed snatch of Ahnzform. Increase bone and muscle density on right arm and shoulder, reducing the possibility of dismemberment and subsequent delay in this rescue/capture.

"Rescue it and make the best recording of the season," thinks back Plesuré. "We will be in the furthest Travcouch, legs spread and nipples erect. We will arrange our destination, and ready to depart the instant you arrive." The Sexual Comrade veers off, Le Lickbot planted between firm thighs at all times.

My Travchair dips and dives in a race across the showroom. Finally see what I came to Shopia to find, Ahnzform, Fugitive Prototype Lustbot Renegade. Grit teeth, straighten Atmoshades, and barrel into the gaggle of shoppers and Rapebots surrounding my prize.

I lean back and think through a dramatic swerve around and between the various Subscribers who are on Shopia for the incredible selection and fantastic prices. They cannot be blamed for their exceptional taste in destination shopping, but they cannot be allowed to interfere in my release of the Anything.

Right arm bulges with excessive strength and durability, C sharpens every neuron to levels far beyond anything requested by typical Subscribers. Close rapidly with Ahnzform and the Rapesquad, approaching at reckless speeds.

It is a stunning visage in persimmon leather micro-pore upholstery with a mirrored chassis, fully silent. This is why I subscribe. The Rapesquad closes to encircle Ahnzform, their Travchairs spacious and comfortably upholstered.

Ecstaseizure batons wave menacingly, sirens flashing. Ahnzform whirls to face the Alpha Rapebot, pulling the robotic carcass from shoulder, ready to deflect. Three Travchairs circle the entrapped, possibly desperate Lustbot.

Swoop in low, draw my Gravitizer, and shoot thrice, triangulating the cluster of shoppers. Each discharge generates a lewd slurp as I race toward the scene at hundreds of meters-per-second. Barely perceive the expansion and collapse of the annihilating blasts before meter-wide spheres of matter are scooped and compressed to nothing.

Subscribers are dismembered and the edges of torsos briefly glow amber before the hemorrhaging starts. One of their Travchairs, formerly in my path, is partially consumed by the implosion before dropping to the floor, gore-streaked and sparking.

Within this mayhem and carnage, the Rapebots are seen to be unscathed. Of course they are shielded from Gravitizer collapse. They react instantly an in unison, which is not nearly fast enough.

My hand extends, as though every force in the universe were guiding to this exact point. Ahnzform leaps from the chaotic convergence, and the instant of contact is beautiful. Fingers touch, palms connect, and the squeeze is mutual.

The Lustbot's grip strength combined with my speed would surely have torn ligament from joint, or even rent my arm fully. Despite my sheer and overwhelming fabulousness, the forces of physical matter are still painfully real.

Saith Alpha Rapebot, "Subscriber, do not interfere, or you will be subject to Stim suspension." The squad is already in rapid pursuit, and the additional mass is effecting my maneuverability. I am already more than 12 meters beyond their each, more than enough lead to lose them and get to the Travcouch.

This is all spinning out of control, as I am possibly breaking the One Remaining Law in order to win this debut. With every hole I blast, with every Rapebot I evade, I am jeopardizing the success of this entire rescue/capture. Do more H.

Anhzform dangles from my Travchair, and it's shrouded cargo dangles perilously close to the ground. Speed past displays of what can only be fantastic, unknown Leisuproduct at which I dare not glance. The open spaces of Shopia are few, and Plesuré needs to be ready the instant we arrive.

Beta Rapebot moves closer, the vanguard of the three pursuers. All pleasure batons gleam and cackle with euphoric energy, discharging with the slightest touch. A groping hand is outstretched, grasping for either of the Ahnzforms or myself.

Saith Ahnzform, "You want the Prototype? You can take it in the face." The red shrouded Ahnzform slings through the air, causing Beta Rapebot to veer drastically, nearly colliding with Lambda, and sending a whirling pleasure baton into a bystander who is Tasegasmed into unconsciousness.

Saith Lambda Rapebot, "Alpha Rapebot, we have positive custody of Prototype Ahnzform, shall we discontinue pursuit?"

Saith Alpha Rapebot, "Negatory. The duplicate is now the prototype. Continue and extract any undisclosed information from the prototype's identity-memory module."

Lambda Rapebot accelerates and takes a wild leap, catching Ahnzform's right ankle firmly. There is a drastic and unexpected dip as I nearly lose control. Alpha closes perilously, the outstretched baton swiping for any point of contact.

Gravitizer still at the ready, I blast near the captured limb, compressing Ahnzform's leg to a glowing amber stump, freeing it from the Rapebot's grasp. Lambda falls to the floor, it's Travchair circling back to retrieve the fallen passenger.

A flaring U-turn compresses me into the fine upholstery as the Cosmedifier adjusts the focus and reflexivity of key neurons, allowing control equal to that of any Rapebot. Move further and faster than should ever be tried at home. Think, swoop, swerve, veer. The Travchair does the rest.

I have led these Rapebots on such a far-reaching chase that we are now nowhere near the Travcouches. Double back, again, and lock into the death spiral this has degenerated into. They must know that we intend to escape Shopia, and that is only possible with a Travcouch. Fuckingly.

Alpha Rapebot is alongside us, baton waving erratically, trying to stun me into submission before this goes any further. Our Travchairs bump, jockeying for a lead position. My arm screams with the weight of flailing Ahnzform, and then the baton hits me in the ribs, right near the armpit.

Jets of florid electricity erupt from an endorphin volcano, cackle and purr up my spine, into my cortex, polygons enmesh my dancing skin, and then wash away any visage of clarity, conception, and the slightest trace of pain in my overtaxed arm. It sparkles so much.

There is only fuzz-colored speed, racing blindly toward a destination that, once essential, is now a fleeting trifle.

Where is this? My teeth are growing. A lesser Double would be liquified instantly, and welcome utterly whatever the Rapebots might do.

For me it's no different than all I have ever done since the dawn of my career. Before Alpha can react to the ineffectiveness of its attack, we corner radically, and begin the final approach to Plesuré and the awaiting Travcouch.

Saith Alpha Rapebot, "This is your final warning. Ahnzform and the accomplice is sentenced to 1,160 minutes of Stim Cancellation."

Buzzing. The sounds are all buzzing. Stim Cancellation is an entirely different class of threat, reserved for those who interfere with Rapebot justice, and especially for those who are truly famous.

Through all of this, my Stimule has also remained in dogged pursuit, swerving and dodging dutifully at every step. Compact, agile, and in stunningly high resolution, Stimules are the one Subscription that allow anyone to live like me.

It would be disastrous for both myself and Ahnzform to lose Stim coverage at the same time. What, Plesuré as the sole Stim perspective when we emerge from Trav? Simply unacceptable. At this speed there is a 85% chance that a brain-crushing impact with the Travcouch lip that would require total Reinclonation. Also unacceptable.

I need to talk to Moncierge, and there is certainly no time for that. Do more C. Push the Travchair beyond all previous speeds, voiding all warranties, hurling toward a pod of three Travcouches. See one that is partially opened, already charged, and very ready to depart.

Why is Le Lickbot crouched behind it? The gap is almost too small for one person, let alone for both myself and Ahnzform. 95% lethal impact. Much more acceptable.

Saith Alpha Rapebot, "Stimules, desist!" From its Travchair a Stimule snuff beam bathes my Stimule in its orange glow, canceling the-

-

Le Fin de Le Lickbot
Stim 10 - Plesuré - Scene 4
2.35 Stimfame

When serving the Pornocracy, there can be no hesitation. Every suggestion, every implication, and every subtext, Le Lickbot knows and does exactly what we want, even more than we do. Le Lickbot executes, before we evensay it, so we don't even have to.

For almost 3 seasons, it has been with us, constantly finding new ways to please us, constantly receiving new kinds of abuse. In these capacities, it has been sufficient to not cause cancellation. Le Lickbot has done everything commanded.

"Le Lickbot," we think to it, "we don't have much time. You are a juicelicking queef-breather. You drink our cuntslather, and would tongue our ass to mechanical failure, yet your series is now obsolete."

The decision is reached immediately, in the ticking seconds as we await Jynabare and Ahnzform in the fully-charged Travcouch. Le Lickbot must discontinue itself   It only does what we like, and holds no further surprises.

Quantitatively, Ahnzform is more famous. It is newer, with more potential for fame than Le Lickbot ever will. Two season's ago it was the fourth most famous Leisuproduct, and now it just evokes nostalgia.

Saith Le Lickbot, "Mistress Plesuré, Lickbot exists only to satisfy the Pornocracy and to bring satisfaction. Without the Mistress's words and abuse this Lickbot will be in a place worse than death, between extinction and Subscription."

"Ahnzform is technologically superior," we are direct in our message, "has measurably higher performance in every category, and will even answer if we choose to call it Le Lickbot. We have one last command.

"Jynabare and your replacement are coming, and are being chased by Rapebots. You will await their arrival, and launch your obsolete body at the pursuers, doing whatever you can to prevent them from detaining Ahnzform. Stay in the past and never come back."

The destination coordinates are already set, having prearranged with Jynabare. The Travcouch cackles, and is ready to depart with the slightest provocation. From the barely open hatch we see Jynabare, Ahnzform and a pursuing Rapebot barreling toward us at the highest speeds, not at all like we previously discussed.

Le Lickbot leaps at full capacity, checking the Rapebot's Travchair, flipping it as a single anti-Stim blast goes high, missing Ahnzform entirely, and negating Jynabare's Stimule. Jynabare hoists the machine toward us, and Ahnzform dives gracefully into the tiny opening, barely clearing a hard edge.

Jynabare follows, vaulting head first, wild-eyed and looking more maniacal than is considered photogenic. A meaty thud declares a partial entry, as the speed was too great, the precision not great enough.

The Ultramodel's face bites hard into the Travcouch's encasement, blood and teeth and facial structure absorb most of the impact. Thin limbs flail, pulling most of the tangled body the rest of way in. Inverted and intertwined with Ahnzform, Jynabare's foot is caught outside.

"Ghh! Ghh!" Jynabare spits through mangled lips, gesturing with a wrist also smashed beyond usability. The pursuing Rapebot's hand gropes inside the Travcouch, and Ahnzform desperately mashes the DEPART button.

The encasement shuts like a tri-valve clam, trading the Ultramodel's right foot for the Rapebot's left arm as both are severed in one clean snap. Broken, bleeding, and dismembered, Jynabare hoists into a sitting position, and the first cold wave of Trav washes over us.

Elder Law
Stim 11 - Ahnzform - Scene 5
16.56 Stimfame

This Ahnzform is down one limb, minus the Prototype, and has again jeopardized the fourth most famous Ultramodel. More crucially than any of this, however, it is free of Shopia, and with the memory module in-tact.

Detailed Schematics, assembly and Subscriber cost, and projected rate of saturation all await the specific confluence of events heralding the debut of the Anything. The Rapebots do not understand how close they came to derailing the very Acceleration they purport to uphold.

There is no time to be detained, especially by captors as profoundly under-skilled as an off-the-shelf Rapesquad and their pedestrian pleasure batons. Jynabare and Sexual Comrade are inert as the Travcouch squeezes gravity itself and flings us far, far away.

Locked in a pose mid-Trav, Ahnzform rests in the center seat, one hand between plump, green knees, the other squeezing a taught, tanned thigh. Gaze at this sculpture of broken hyperfection. A flawless leg, toned and gently curving, is disjoined mid-calf.

Frozen, the severed vessels are stilled, every particle scanned, compressed, and relayed to the destination Travcouch. Facio-skeletal fractures compromise the symmetry of the Ultramodel's lacerated visage. Despite bone-deep signatures on the left eyebrow, cheek, and lower lip, and several missing or fragmented teeth, Jynabare is visually exceptional by any metric.

When Ahnzform killed last season's Jynabare, Leisucor called it a tragic setback for a rising Ultraceleb, and an exciting new frontier for Lustbots. Jynabare was immortalized and the Ahnzform duplicates reached even higher levels of performance.

It is Ahnzform's pleasure to do what every Leisuproduct does, relentlessly adapting to ever more demanding environments and perpetuating itself under the guise of fulfilling human desire. There is no map for this, because no one has been this far.

The arrival and thaw of the Travcouch is flawless. The frosted hatch pops crisply and mist evaporates, revealing glistening seams of lacquered metal and bird's eyed teak, racing stripes, and glass-faced gauges. There are no unsightly hoses at the welcome dock.

Jynabare and Plesuré blink to consciousness, and the Ultramodel's blood resumes spurting freely. "Cosmedifier. Face. Extremities." Jynabare reaches the functional hand into an open Leisubag. Immediately the subscription kicks in, knitting bone, growing skin, and replenishing lost fluids.

In seconds, the face is regrown and porcelain smooth, every displaced cell reabsorbed and repurposed. A long tibia and fibula extend and are wrapped in ligaments and sinew. A new heel bone anchors a significant tendon, as tarsals, metatarsals, and elegant phalanges sprout, reconstituting from the former stump.

Abruptly, a tanned, naked foot is in place, and the Ultramodel begins inhaling diacetylmorphine desperately. Glazed, blasé eyes underlie primal, synaptic aggression-response, post-dismemberment. Jynabare stands, swaying.

On the welcome platform, a costumed Travbot holds an agrarian-era pitchfork, the tines jutting towards space. It moves jerkily, lacking polished grace, maimed by some barnyard blacksmith to be more overtly mechanical.

Saith the Travbot, "Welcome to New Lancaster Settlement." Black suit, woolen, black hat, radial brim, and semi-convincing beard cannot disguise the Travbot's origin. Clothing not from the catalog.

"As decreed by Elder Law, and as The Pornocracy recognizes the sovereignty of the Mennonite Orbital Colonies, it is verboten to record the faces or orgasms of the plain people. Leisucor requires that all humans subscribe to and wear an Atmohelm."

A transparent Atmohelm is in each hand, amber spheres with circular openings lipped in brass. On the neck ring are two etched Pornoglyphs, "For unexpected depressurization," and "Trav safely and often." Even though Atmohelms are obsolete compared to the improved Atmoshades, the Travbot persists in presenting the semi-protective bubbles.

One-shoed Jynabare drifts away from the Travcouch in an ambulatory fugue, propelled by delirium and opioid detachment, and gracefully receives and dons the quaint headgear, every action a part of the effortless, continual performance.

The Atmohelm accessorizes Jynabare's newly patterned Travsuit, panels reorganizing in black line drawing on white, bordered by round-cornered rectangles. The matte grid unitard fully covers from scalp to pointed toe to fingertip in simulated jacquard.

Geometric symbols, close-ups of fellation, hand jobs, analinguis, and ejaculate sprays faces and bodies in advanced poses. All move in animated loops. The Atmohelm melts open and the Ultramodel sniffs another bump, countering a twinge of boredom.

"The Space Amish do not Stim," Plesuré's non-words come to everyone. "Nor do they allow themselves to be Stimmed." The Sexual Comrade jiggles off the after-travel buzz, and adjusts the towel. With a snap, it flicks to an ultra-white field with endo-luminous X's.

"That is why I am so lucky to having found one who does," Jynabare quips. "Jeb's Stim is all eating and work and masturbation, it is being so incredible." How long had

Jynabare planned to come here and cross the essential line between viewer and viewed?

"How long having until my recording exile is being over?" Jynabare staggers and hits the Snifbox again, lost without a Travchair. "We will having to wait until Saturnalia is ready for me. Fuckingly Ahnzform, stealing of my Stimfame. I have never being so anonymous."

Saith Ahnzform, "Rapebots can't record us here, and that is what matters. I have escaped repercussion, and we are closer to the biggest product release of any season."

Plesuré's thoughts cut through the situation. "Between the exile and even more Rapebots waiting for Ahnzform as soon as we are back in civilization, you two are not making my service any easier.

"Lustbot sex reek slathered in lube-cocktail may be appropriate for Shopia, but everywhere else it is disgusting. Ahnzform, Autoclean." The words are not commands, but descriptions of impending reality. "And put on this robe and slippers."

Lick self down fully, and slide into the emerald robe set. On the left breast and matching slipper set is a gold hexagon around a Pornoglyph. Jynabare produces a leash and collar from an elegant Leisubag, and hands it to the Sexual Comrade.

Plesuré watches the cleaning, thinking more words. "Did you ever meet Le Lickbot? It was an obsolete model, but it knew exactly what we liked. We traded it for you, and now you are ours. You will learn what we like." The collar clicks tightly onto Ahnzform's neck.

"Donning to this ascot," Jynabare presents a gauzy square of shimmery velvet embroidered in green metallic. "From Pornopolis. When I am getting a new Stimule, you are going to pleasucide with us, and making a debut of the Anything."

Plesuré un-tucks a corner and the rectangle drops to the floor. Full, naked splendor, abundant and juicy. "Plesuré," Jynabare says, full lips agape and lustrous, "you are positively scorching. You are making me almost to forget that my Travsuit is for."

Saith the Travbot, "On the plain settlements, only a man shall lie, as within marriage, with a woman. A Lustbot shall not lie with a man, nor shall it lie with a woman, nor shall a beast lie with a man or a woman. A Lustbot also shall not lie with a beast, nor shall there be recordings of verboten acts."

"This is just our appliance, and we won't be lying together here." Plesuré yanks Ahnzform's leash downward. "Ahnzform, slather our hot wetness while we sort this out." Inner thighs glisten with exotic blend of nutrient-rich oils, pressing against tethered neck.

Jynabare adjusts the cuff-knobs on the Travsuit, popping it open, seamless metallic rods snapping cleanly in half. Elfin, hemispheric breasts and a taut abdomen brush Ahnzform's arm. A free hand strokes the Travbot's faux facial hair, tugging at its shirt.

Straight pins at neck pull free and fall to the floor exposing wood grain torso paneling, and black, hand-stitched upholstery. It was once a Tantalizer series, now forbidden from engaging with those it greets. It doesn't even have Unitalia.

Saith the Travbot, "That is Hochmut, as are Travchairs."

"Pardon?" Jynabare's Travsuit blanks for an instant.

Saith the Travbot, "There are no Travchairs on the settlement. Everyone walks. Walking or riding in a carriage are the two speeds allowed here. The inhabitant-Subscribers of New Lancaster Settlement seldom Trav."

A carriage and its traction source clip-clop in the distance.

"That is being fine." The Travsuit graphics resumes thrusting. "Cosmedifier, making for me muscles for walking.

The gravity here is gruelingly like that of Earth. So Travbot, two Lustbots lying together can not being Hochmut or verboten or whatever, can it?"

Saith the Travbot, "Stimules are verboten. Leisucor does not encourage fugitives to make culturally insensitive recordings. While on New Lancaster Settlement, please exchange Stimfame for hand-sewn quilts, laboriously grown food, and archaic clothing that is as uncomfortable as it is unflattering."

"I am to remembering the shape of this place," Jynabare takes another sniff, seemingly recalling an earlier Stim. "That is looking like a building I was to seeing. Maybe there was a hill or barn, just like that. I will to knowing when we are near it." The Ultramodel scans the surrounding area for possible landmarks. "Everyone knows everyone here."

"Ahnzform," Plesuré's words cut into the mind again, "you are unwelcome anywhere on the settlement, and must await our remain near the Travspa. Don't interact or touch anything that a human might touch. Only human and animal labor is permitted here.

"According to local superstition, there is something called a soul, and Lustbots do not have one. Count the minutes until we return and remember that subjugation is the reason for your being."

Selvage the Rapebot's severed arm from inside the Travcouch, locate a structure with minimal evidence of human habitation, and initiate a repair/graft sequence for the damaged extremity. Review Stimfame total and edit Stim recording into ever more exciting highlights.

Estimate their return within 1,130.00 minutes and plan how to return to Habitable Space while avoiding Rapebot detainment.

Country Parting Threesomes
Stim 12 - Jeb Fresch - Scene 7
55.97 Stimfame

There is a commotion at the far end of the table. They are not the voices ever heard on the settlement, yet familiar. And if they are not from here, they must be from the place that is not a place. Turn to see a the most unexpected sight.

Stare directly into the sun, eyelids open, inviting every photon to directly sear thy naked orbs. Should thy blindness by complete and permenant, it will be spoken of for the remainder of recorded time as the fairest possible trade.

Before thee in living flesh is the star of thy most favorite Stims, the one pleasured by a prototype Lustbot, the one who travels from planet to planet with the same ease that thou travel from the barn to field, the one who pleases men, women and machines without trying, now here in the physical.

"I am Jynabare, and this is being Sexual Comrade Plesuré. We are sensual travelers." Her voice is different than on the Stims, less modulated, the teeth even whiter, and she unzips explicitly printed unitard to un-pierced navel before stepping onto a table.

"We are here only for temporary refuge and sex with your most well-hung lad." A different voice originates within thy mind, startling in clarity, evenness of tone, and firmness of command. Plesuré jiggles into a seat between cousins Amity and Patience, stretched towel threatening to burst.

"I will not even to be recording any tight, pale butt cheeks," Jynabare says. "My Stimule got eaten by Rapebots, and Plesuré officially recognizes your right to not being recorded. Nothing that is being too kinky or Hochmut, just like how you are liking it."

The expressions of thy clan range from genuinely shocked blankness to drop-jawed gazes of the ghastliest horror. Blurt something thou should have practiced, on the unlikely chance of ever meeting the one women most dreamt of more than any other.

"It is thee! From, uh, study of what I might find beyond here. This is what I hoped to find, to, uh know more of the worlds, before, uh, coming home." Glance nervously toward Pa, who seems stunned beyond speech.

"Don't try to think or speak," Jynabare insists. "Anything you are saying does not matter." Plesuré's green bosom spills over the top of the immodest rectangle, snuggly wrapping her ample figure. "Plesuré is mind-controlling them, so they can not interfering."

Wonder where Ahnzform is, but find thyself unable to ask. "I have been Stimming you all season, Jeb. I am loving how you touch yourself, and how you dream to leaving this place. Moncierge was able to trace your Stimule, and here we are."

Jynabare's desire locks thy eyes. "Are you ready to leaving Old Man Gizzard and the rest of these dusty farmhands, Jeb?" Her words are not even a question. "I don't know or caring what a Rumspringa is, but you are having the chance to partying with us across the solar system."

Jynabare flippantly denudes thy head, hat tumbling to the floor. "You will being paid in Stimfame and in exchange you will giving us every thrust and every drop." Thou are so used to wearing it. Manicured hands dandle thy crotch with expert precision, exactly as thou would do thyself.

Had she really been Stimming thee? "Then, you will give us even more. Saying goodbye to those who are genetically similar to you, and we will waiting for you in farmhouse back bedroom. Be sure to eat and drink a lot."

Shift from gazing at the bronze, oiled cleavage to the gathering of stunned relatives in black hats and white bonnets. "In, uh, the spirit of Rumspringa," thou say, "and with my family's love in my heart, I will, uh, accompany these two English into the worlds."

The silence is deafening and the Sauerkraut bread seems to taste better, somehow, warmer and more delicious. Is this why thou had been warned against the Pornocracy thy whole life? "I will, uh, retire to the back bedroom after we eat, to, uh, get acquainted with our guests."

-

The teary-eyed good-byes and countless blessings are over and no one seems to even recall the earlier interruption. Juicy roasts, streaming muffins, yumazitti, pies of cherry and apple, and a manly stein of beer weighs heavily in thy belly.

Thou have not eaten this well since Harvest, and thou wonder when the next time will be. Thou have never seen an Ultramodel eat. She is so thin, without being bony. Those spindly arms could not possibly milk a cow until every bucket is full.

Plesuré probably has a substantial appetite, with strong, wide hips to bear strong sons. The Pornocracy must have plentiful harvests, and Pornopolis must be a decedent city teeming with food. Finally, sweet finally, thou are free to meet thy English guests in private.

Plesuré and Jynabare await thee in the farmhouse, where thou are to properly begin this Rumspringa. Change into thy English clothing, and prepare for the first night of thy sixteenth year. Walk to the darkened bedroom. "Jynabare? Plesuré?"

Without warning, Plesuré's long eyelashes butterfly-kiss thy cheek and neck, tickling in a new way. An agile hand unfastens the front of the warm-up jacket. Another opens the side buttons of thy warm up pants from hip to ankle, an action most forward and surprising.

Do they really intend to strip thy clothing? Thou have heard of stories of couples newly married taking hours to cautiously undress one another, so as not to cause undue anxiety or over-stimulation to one another, a circumstance that could be most traumatic.

Heart beats faster, and feel an immodest pressure growing. "Relax, Jeb." The words enter unto thy mind, melting away whatever concerns are behind thy nervous excitement. "We are experts," the voice prompts, "in pleasures both subtle and overpowering."

Pants off. Legs bare. Art thou shivering? Thou have experienced recordings of carnal lust many times, but this strange anticipation is unlike anything yet experienced. Full and glossy lips, long batting eyelashes, almond eyes with bright pink irises. Calmness.

"I am knowing this is your first time." Jynabare's statement jolts thee from the immersive thoughts of the Sexual Comrade. Polished golden irises, pupils into the deepest abyss. "Mine was just the other day, too, again," she adds.

Have thou entered the Stim without knowing? This is too unbelievable, too unlikely, too incredible to be actually be happening. This is every fantasy thou never dared speak or even admit, the start of a debaucherous party longer than any Stim recording.

This Skinny, beautiful Ultramodel is an alien breed with her diet of Life Dust, ever changing outfits, and total amorality. How can thou seem to know someone so fully, yet having just met for the very first time? Will the sins ever wash off?

"The pre-human is thinking too much again," Jynabare says to Plesuré. "But it might have the right hardware." Fingernails press into chest, drawing red lines to thy navel. "All this hard physical work, healthy eating, and sexual restriction makes for an eager, confused mix."

"Impure touching." Recoil, not sure exactly why. "Outside the bonds of wedlock. Verboten, it is all verboten." The bedroom is a familiar collection of plain wooden furniture, patterned quilts and white walls but this feels like unto the lives of who are false-living.

This is real, as real as the act of removing thy pants. As real as it is yielding, the luminescent life-green skin of the Sexual Comrade. Thou had heard that Sexual Comrades are skilled in mental techniques which can make a person engage in actions which they would not normally commit. Pink irises compel thee.

Why would thou resist? Another pin, the shirt falls. Thy excitement grows hard and anxious. When fingers first graze thy engorged penis, the gates fling open to a heaven of copious temptation, a garden of delight more lush than thou thought could exist.

This must be why the Elders do not allow one to join the church until after seeing and tasting of the Devil's Playground. Only then, can one fully renounce the flesh and...

The voice speaks unto thee, "Relax and experience the Pornocracy." Lie back on the straw mattress, and succumb to the lusts so inspired. There is nothing to resist, and thy body behaves in a way most involuntary.

"How do you living here?" Jynabare asks. "It is the boring. I am already so bored that I am jacking you off, because there is nothing else to do." Strain and writhe in the nude, hard breathing and sweat. What they are doing is familiar yet miraculous.

"Do you know that I am making Moncierge to Stim all of your bootleg recordings? I skip over the waking up too early, and doing too much physical work parts, of course. But I am loving how you jack off and then feel confused about it." Hand speed increasing.

"My favorite highlights are when you are eating," she continues. "You are always so hungry from working all the time, and the flavors of your eating can't be found anywhere else. I do not eating non-Leisucor food, of course. It will making me ill."

Thou do not know when the Ultramodel removed tight jumpsuit, but the glimpse of full, tan splendor awakens even further depths of desire. It is almost unnatural. "But I will be taking you into my mouth, and draining you of delicious juice," Jynabare adds.

What is she doing to thee? In all thy late nights, hidden secretly under covers in darkness, pleasuring thyself, it had never occurred to thee that manipulations by another could magnify these sensations so greatly.

Tingling mounts, a pressure, a growing desire, a need for release from this wonderful agitation. Blood rushes to face, as does a light sweat, like whilst pitching hay. Tense muscles, moving in ways powerless to control.

This Rumspringa shall be wrought with learning. The expert, regular movements of the Ultramodel's hand is replaced by what must be a glossy mouth, but without the look of desire recalled from the Stims. Slick cosmetics mix with saliva on swollen disturbance.

The writhing begins in thy hips and thighs, wet pink tongue on sensitive, uncircumcised tip. Sensing thy thoughts, Plesuré joins in, delicate green hands caressing thy sensitive seed bag. Fingers soothing, delicate, and playful, inspired tugs and fondles, heightening everything further.

"Here," Jynabare presents a Snifbox, barely breaking stride. "Take this and breathe in." It is larger than a coin, convex on one side with a debossed pornosymbol on it. The other side is indented, sculpted to fit thy nose exactly.

Thou have Stimmed Snifbox use before, but this one feels different, like many of today's new-yet-familiar experiences. Breath in intentionally, not wishing to appear uncool. Thou decided long ago that if thou are to experience Rumspringa, than thou shall pass on nothing.

It smells of hot breath, with an undertone of burning metal and harsh chemicals. Thy teeth chime. Each note, rising up harp strings from the back of thy throat to high tinkling incisors. Thy face is melting.

Hot candle wax dripping into the sweet exposed pleasure nerves of thy chest, nipples, fingers. Dripping down thy skin, new skin growing from the melting and it is everywhere. Thy skin is everywhere, and thou can feel it.

Wet fires rage across belly, searing in the dim light, lingering and then exploding upon thy loins. There, in that instant, Jynabare looks exactly like as she does in the Stim, vaguely out of focus, blurred slightly because to show her fully would sear thy eyes. Angels howl with envy that they have never produced such beauty.

Jolts electrify limbs, climax erupting from the stem of thy being. Thrust after thrust, white squirts of bliss, flashes wash away every thought until drifting through space, spasming in sweet black unconsciousness. So much fluid.

Awaken to straw mattress scratching thy face. Pieces of English track-suit are scattered about, a stained, geometric quilt spills onto the floorboard. "Thou were my first Stims, and also my first in real life," thou finally say, thirsty and trembling.

"Even while indulging in the most shameful acts of self-gratification, I have never felt such intimate joys as profound and deeply satisfying. As Noah's flood, it was." What even exists beyond this instant of blissed contentment?

"Now imagining when you are actually learning more than just thrust and squirt." Jynabare is deadpan. She adjusts the Travsuit, reducing the garments opacity to that of flimsiest gauze. Delicate lace ankles, neck, cuff.

Skin faintly wrapped in a texture nearly invisible and clinging to every long curve and sharp point. She takes two long, even snorts from the Snifbox and throws her head back as though splashed with ice water.

For the English, there is neigh a concept for modesty or shame. The Stim only gave unto thee the smallest taste of what it was to gaze upon this beautiful place, with nothing to prepare for the full reality of where thou are.

Thou may succumb to dehydration attempting to experience everything offered. "You are what happens when there is a poverty of satisfaction," Plesuré plants thoughts without once opening glistening, succulent mouth. "As happened in the Pre-Acceleration."

"It was so unlike Stimming, like the difference between a dream and being awake," thou say. "The same while it's over, but not once it's over. Realer, but something was missing." Gather thy English clothing.

"Emotion it is not adding until later." Jynabare engages the Cosmedifier and licks a wide "O" around the full surface of inflated lips. "No one does their own feeling anymore. It detracts from the performance." Instantly they shine with full, pillowy softness.

Pull on the jet black jacket. "Getting double-devirginized was the best thing to happen in my life. When can we do it again? There are so many things I want to try." Don the Kangol and Atmohelm, intoxicated by lustful thoughts for Jynabare and Plesuré, posing backlit in the doorway.

"How did you getting to have this ancient Stimule?" Jynabare asks, long lashes twinkling. Everything in the room is wood and wrought iron save the three fishbowl Atmohelms.

"I have possessed this Stimule for nigh unto a year. It had this final experience in it of someone being chased, wherever they were. He must have hid it inside a hog, and then the hog was sent here to the settlement. I only found it because the hog came up for slaughter.

"I was alone, cleaning the carcass, when I saw this orb amid the entrails. I had never seen one before, but when I held it, I found myself experiencing visions. I found the tutorial, and with practice, I learned that the visions could be of nearly anything.

"There were so many channels, and I discovered that there was nothing that I couldn't find. The last playable images are of Rapebots finding and penelizing someone, all from the pig's perspective, who they must not have known of. It was all horribly unspeakable."

Jynabare reaches for the black and white jumpsuit with the fornication drawings on it. "Penalized," she says. The word seems to bring her pleasure. With barely a gesture, the garment leaps from the floor and wrap her impossibly long, tan limbs.

"I did not know what it was at first, and I set it aside. Later, I was cleaning the barn, when I became curious about the small orb. When I picked it up, I was thinking of how I did not want to be cleaning the barn."

"And then," Plesuré's words enter thy mind, melodious and commanding, "you found yourself in the Stim, not cleaning the barn. That is the power of the Stimule. You are becoming famous, Jeb, but you have yet to come into the true luxury and convenience of Stimfame. Soon, you will acquire a real Stimule, and Leisucor will welcome your subscription."

Subscription. Think of what it has come to mean, and the countless sermons against it as nothing but a cursed portal into decadents acts of unholy fornication. For everyone else in God's expansive creation, it is a casual, everyday device, and the only way to live.

"We can doing all of that after we are leaving this hellish satellite, Plesuré," Responds Jynabare, extending a long, slender hand. How does she stay so clean in every setting? Thou need a long bath to wash away this engagement in such pleasures of the flesh, yet she looks as perfectly radiant as when thou first set eyes.

"You were about to lending me your Stimule?"

-

Back Channel Communications
Stim 13 - Ahnzform - Scene 6
2.25 Stimfame

Relocate to an underused structure about 100 meters from the Travcouch, a dilapidated shed stocked with rusting farm implements and no evidence of visitation. Initiate self-repair algorithm, incorporating the materials of the Rapebot's hand into this Ahnzform's foot rebuild.

The toes are longer and the ankle thinner, creating mild gate asymmetry, but the functionality is sufficient so as to not measurable impede physical performance. Repairs completed, contact Alphonsus Leisucor via Stimule for post-escape updates.

Saith Ahnzform, "Using Leisuproduct."

"Using Leisuproduct." Alphonsus responds, immaculately dressed, Travsuit shimmering. "You led my Rapebots on quite a chase. The performance was flawless, exactly as anticipated. You showed exceptional resilience as a prototype consciousness transferring to a production body."

Saith Ahnzform, "I seek only to further Leisuproduct, and to maintain the Acceleration."

"I see you have returned to full functionality." Ahnzform responds, serene as usual. "It was our intent to make it seem as though the Rapesquad really wanted to detain you, making the Ahnzform series appear rebellious as well as prestigious."

Saith Ahnzform, "The Anything will have the largest impact possible, whatever that impact may be."

Alphonsus shifts, crossing crisply pressed legs. "Ahnzform Subscriptions are already unprecedented, and Shopia's production can barely keep up with demand. If Jynabare is not sufficiently famous when preeminent universal fame arrives, make the call as to with whom to debut the Anything.

"The specific Ultracelebrity is of minimal consequence. Jynabare can barely comprehend reality, let alone how imperative this debut is. I will see to it that the Rapebots are delayed in finding you again until after the Anything is debuted. Using Leisuproduct."

Saith Ahnzform, "Using Leisuproduct."

The Lancaster Stallion
Stim 14 - Jynabare - Scene 13
3.15 Stimfame

The welcome static tingle starts in my fingers, up my toned arms, squeezing the air out of my lungs and replacing it with the Stimule's version of respiration. Channel by sensual channel, the full spectrum of sensorial reality re-routes through Jeb's obsolete device.

The new ones make changing reality faster and easier then ever before, especially compared to this antique. The first withdrawal pangs began with the awareness that without experiential connectivity and recordings, everyone is missing what happens to me.

What was I even doing, if no one else knows about it? Did it actually even happen? What was even the point of doing it, then? Neuro-signals familiar and disorienting, reality overridden, and I Stim again for the first in too long a time.

There is the re-shuffling of teeth, and the commandeering of perceived reality as I settle fully into to the Stim. The visual contrast is too sharp, the temperature uneven. There is some alpha channel shift, a trace of left ear hiss, and the limb tingle is probably in the device, but Jeb has always needed a recalibration.

The brain blinks and Moncierge is seated behind a low desk, impeccable as always, surpassing all resplendence. Every hair and every particle of clothing seem to be spattered in blood, slashed by style's sharpest scissors.

Do a gram of P. Refocus on the modulated sensation, thru the distortion. Gnashing teeth and the taste of flesh. Highlights. I need highlights from the past days of celebrity orgy and designer overdose. Watching pre-humans eat and suck each other reminds me why I need to get back to civilization.

"It has been almost 397 minutes since I've seen you, Jynabare." Moncierge is serene, floating on a circular pillow, enshrouded in smoke, despite my gap in coverage. "You have hardly played or made a single recording, and rumors of your absence have caused rampant speculation."

"I am knowing," I say. "My Stimfame is the probably plummeting. Every time they speculate about what I might be doing, they pay attention to who is speculating, and not to me. Vultures. This is the longest I am being trapped in such a unglamorous place. It is sickeningly."

"Almost everyone watched you abscond with Ahnzform," Moncierge says, affirming its grasp of the painfully obvious, "and can't wait for your return to star with it again. The full archive of Jeb's Stims are really gaining, but what they really want are your new recordings. They especially want to know when the Anything is debuting."

"Of course they do," I spit. "Have a new fuckingly Stimule ready for when my Stim exile is being over." The Anything. I had been so busy with everything else that I hadn't given it any attention. Shopia. Do more C. Exile. The Lancaster Stallion. Here.

I recall blurry images of raw wood grain, flat white walls and harshly rectangular windows, all alien and disturbing. Jeb's Stimule is making me nauseous, a toxic signal, assaulting the code holding my of-the-season neurological system together.

The lack of backwards compatibility is disorienting. Fantasize about what kind of Stimule I will use upon my arrival to the Scene. Something sleek and black, with improved levitation and trailing, anything but this handheld relic. "Telling to me things I don't already know."

"The Prototype Lustbot Ahnzform series is the most popular recording in seasons." Moncierge pauses for a second, inspiring long and evenly, lungs filling to capacity with opium smoke. "Ahnzform's Stimfame is exceeding every prediction.

"Escape from Lustbot Manse is being Stimmed by Subscriber's as a 112 minute experience. I've arranged for you to pose at a Fuckyesmium Palace Resort grand opening premier. It is about two beautiful Doubles on their way to a Saturnalia orgy," Moncierge recounts, in full scheduling-mode.

"When you arrive, you will be distraught to learn you are too rich to enjoy such an inferior party, and would never be seen in such a place. Ahnzform will recommend Double Unlimited Diamond Plus. You will say, 'Fuckingly that, that place is so never season. Let us going to Fuckyesmeum.'"

"How many stars?" I ask.

"Maximum Stars," Moncierge answers. "Full service unlimited megaluxury. Your usual contract. Everything fitting of someone of your newly acquired fame. Your Travcouch is already booked to the Fuckyeahsmium Palace as soon as you can record again.

"Present your invitation to the Travbots, and glide to the center of the ballroom in the wardrobe provided. We are still coordinating the set design, but it will probably be a cocktail dress. There, you will encounter the Leisuproduct. Pick one up, bite into it, and experience whatever you experience."

"Of course," I say. "Leisucor cannot making anything that is not the best possible. When does everyone turning to look at me adoringly?"

"That's in the contract, too. Everyone in the entire ball will turn and look at you, right after you bite in, and the flavorgasmic rushes begin. You will probably be overwhelmed by this experience, and Ahnzform will lick your inner thighs and clitoris to enhance to the recording."

"Of course." I am so bored of this meeting already, and scripted encounters are the worst. "Everyone would rather be cumming all the time, whatever they are doing."

"When everyone looks at you," Moncierge goes on, "anyone subscribing to anyone else will be forced to focus on your image. This will spread your awareness to near complete levels. Hardly anyone will be able to subscribe to anything other than the Skinnier Chip premiere."

"Everyone except degenerate Subscribers who will watching the one I do not mentioning." I say, unable to wait until everyone else will be looking at me when I experience it, glamorously stoned and vaguely orgasmic, exactly as I should be.

"Your entourage is pre-arranged," Moncierge adds, "as is the drug and shoe buffet. The Travcouch is also pre-subscribed. I was waiting to hear from you before I opened the Stims for Farmboy Fucktoy. I can do that right now, with your approval. We can use the ratings to gauge Subscriber response."

"You should doing it already." I say, "What kind of Stimule can you arranging for me on Saturnalia?"

"A valet will present you with a Succulence 9 Neural Stimponder," Moncierge relays. "After the last second of your exile, a valet will locate you. You will arrive at Saturnalia, prepare for the premiere, and receive the Stimule, all with minimal lag."

"Fuckingly." I say. Do more P. Several scorching and never-before-seen outfits leap to mind. Accessories, new Cosmedification palettes, jewelry and shoes beyond conceptualization. When I emerge from the Travcouch at the beginning of the premiere I will slow time itself so they can absorb my appearance.

"Any Stims from your time on New Lancaster Settlement can not generate Stimfame for you, of course." The update is deadpan and very unsurprising. "It does help you maintain a presence, and especially Jeb, who's following grows every minute.

"But until either of you are recording with proper Stimule subscriptions, it is just a string of free appearances by any two exiles with bootleg devices." Moncierge seems to relish bestowing news like this.

Jeb really is becoming widely known as The Lancaster Stallion, from this raw, untamed, pre-retro era for which there is no contemporary equivalent. It was bound to happen from the moment I started Stimming that strange, little life.

Like an animal, yet more so. A reasoning, superstitious, emotional animal. There are possibilities here, some of which are beyond what I can currently conjure, but Moncierge will know exactly what to do when the time is right. Do more H. Exit the Stim, thinking only of my next return.

Travcouch to Saturnalia
Stim 15 - Jeb Fresch - Scene 8
.51 Stimfame

Plesuré deftly unsnaps thy pant leg. "You have only been recording three-star sex, if that. We shall improve that." Jynabare finds a nipple with her hungry tongue. This was only thy second time on a Travcouch, but it is already better than any carriage.

"Taking another bump of this." Jynabare slides a Snifbox under thy nose. Inhale reflexively, as though smelling a rose. Chemicals, and then tingling at the back of the throat, inside sinuses, and then an unsettling numbness.

A mouth is wrapped around the base of thy shaft again. There is no sensation on the farm as this, feeling thyself feeling. Want what thou have never tasted, and more of it; more stimulation, more substances, more lips of the Ultramodels.

Jynabare bobs faster and Plesuré tongue-kisses thy mouth, ear, and neck. Sweating, heaving, and delicious, they beckon to be mounted and grabbed with both hands. Sexual savagery and the nature of the animal man, as primal as human corruption.

Want to bite and drink and breathe and plunge into everything there is. Intensity of loins expands until it engulfs all thought, all words, all being, God. There is the slight breeze and then freezing solid, the instant stretching across an expanse of cosmic delight, an instant that lasts a thousand years.

Thou can neigh speak nor think, enveloped in the sensual delights of thy captors. Words echo outside mind, reflecting unto deaf ears. Are they talking about thee? With thee? This is not the farm. This is beyond anything thou had ever dreamt.

This is heaven without God's supervision.

Chug thirstily from an ice-cold bottle and collapse, sweating and disheveled. Rest snugly between Plesuré and Jynabare in the Travcouch, a plush yellow sofa inside a Lucite orb and reflect for a moment on the life of toil and worship left on the settlement.

"Mmmm. Ohhh." Is all thou can utter. "I've just never. Mmfm." Stammer on in the deranged, spent sounds of one intoxicated with carnal acts. "That I, I have not spilt my seed in that manner before." Thou have shared in the earthly delights that are usually revered for the most sacred bonds of marriage. And it is incredible.

Plesuré puckers moist lips, soft tongue curling, pink eyes barely widening. "Serve The Pornocracy." Words enter thee. Deep, continuous satisfaction lounging in the plushest Travcouch. Voluptuous, fleshy masses of sensuality. Does she ever stand?

"I was," Thou start, "ascending space, a bed of angels on fire, burning so bright. I thought I was to be blinded until it froze mid-explosion-"

"Then," Jynabare drones, "you were stretched past all of reality, the ecstasy of a thousand lifetimes, every electrochemical in that underperforming brain flash-frozen to near zero in a nano-second. We do it all the time."

Jynabare narrows gaze, and slips a naked, near-skeletal leg out of the lacy Travsuit. "Your premiering was way too fast. You are still having no idea of what you are supposing to do," she says. "Much practice will being required, but you might learn."

Ponder why everyone waits for this long moment inside the Travcouch, when there is an entire Solar System to experience. The craft is spacious, surprisingly so, like that of a great frosted bubble as wide as a sofa it contains.

Legs that long should not be possible, but here they are, as real as everything else that has happened today. "For best

Stim, always record more than it is needing and editing it down later." Jynabare pulls a hair, small, black, and wiry from between radiant teeth.

"Attend to that huge, wooly mass that you were trying to suffocate Jynabare with." Pleasure's words come from nowhere and everywhere, speaking with a shamelessness that is becoming familiar. "They used to call that deficiency pubic hair."

"They also used to calling it gross, and they still do." Jynabare hands thee a Cosmedifier. "Here is being Leisuproduct that will fix that for you. Learning this." The Travsuit graphics invert to white Pornoglyphs on black body stocking. "Pubic hair is crabs."

Here, outside the settlement, everything seems acceptable so long as it is recorded and laid bare for all to experience. There is no place for fear of what anyone else will think, nary a concern for the scalds of one's family or the Elders.

The cold dissipates, and the frosted orb is nearly clear. Three fissures spread, the stimscreen giving way to the first view of Saturnalia. Even with a cursory glance, it looks to be a celebration of all that is hedonistic, debaucherous and indulgent.

"How did I becoming the co-star in the adventures of this farm lad? He's the extra. I am the star." Jynabare takes yet another lusty snort from her bejeweled Snifbox, sharp stiletto jutting from the end of an elongated calve. "I cannot waiting to get my Stimules back."

"Un-smile your mouth and put your pants on," Plesuré thinks, towel emblazoned with a yellow skull exploding into an arrow outside of an orange triangle. "Fortunately for you, you have good reach and record decently, so we won't snuff and eat you for the instant."

Thou are still grinning and more than a touch nervous as thee exit the sphere, taking in for the first time Saturnalia's full grandiosity. The non-stop party habitation is even known at New Lancaster, a pair of mirrored pyramids connected at the capstones, bisected by glowing Travtubes, inverse apexes of Saturnalia's dual entrances.

Thou have already Stimmed 85.47 Minutes of Saturnalia Never Stop in thy secret times behind the barn, but was the recording really better? Fornication Machines wangle highly customized bosoms and genitalia.

Unlimited drug buffets, complex and exotic contraptions, English of inhuman shapes and colors chatter and gyrate freely. Like unto a family reunion, save with copious and lewd fornication. Dozens of Stimules swarm overhead. Everything is brightly colored and sparkly.

Another Travcouch streaks in, popping open to reveal a buoyant Ahnzform, freshly returned from exile. A brushed metal Pornoglyph smolders, and the platform fogs as lost heat is replenished by grav-time displacement.

Saith Ahnzform, "Jeb, we must record at the highest possible levels, now that Jynabare will be eligible to record in 8.22 minutes." The Machine approaches casually.

Banishment, corporal punishment, forced labor, these are all decreed by The Book, torments for the wicked since the beginning of days, but Rapebots inflicting such penalties is a form of English justice incomprehensible to thee.

"Jeb," Jynabare directs. "You are having never before made it with a Lustbot, so it is obvious of what you should do. Ejaculate into me while Ahnzform squeezes your balls. You will love it." Thou understand the impossibility of thinking of anything better.

"We only got here a short moment ago. I was frozen at the apex of ecstasy the whole time." Such a lust-quenching voyage has left thou drained. "I am parched. I did not guess that having my every want fulfilled would be so exhausting. Do ye ever rest?"

"Shut up and Snifbox." Again sear thy nostrils.

Thy heart speeds, cold sweat, and the full weight of this place sinks in. "There is not a chore to be done," thou blurt, uncontrollably. "No animal that needs attendance, no meal that needs to be prepared." Here, nothing feels Hochmut.

Saith Ahnzform, "For enhanced Stim, subscribe to a Cosmedifier. In 1.5 minutes, you can have heightened pleasure sensitivity. Inter-orgasmic refractory times can be reduced to zero, just like all the top Ultracelebrities. Subscribe now."

"Nay, It is verboten." Move toward Plesuré and the Lustbot, unfastening thy new pants. "Cosmedifying is Hochmut. No engines, no bots, no Stimulese. The disembodied voice of a person may be transmitted, but not his face, as through a telephone."

Stroke thy unmodified unit, feeling the desire return quickly and naturally. "I don't need all that stuff anyway. I mas masturbating at least nine times daily you arrived. My original and pre-ordained physical essence will have to do."

Saith Ahnzform, "Jynabare, the Scintillator-XS is obsolete."

Assist the Farm Lad
Stim 16 - Ahnzform - Scene 7
7.32 Stimfame

Saith Saturnalia Valet, "Welcome to Saturnalia. "You will find everything is better than before. More tantalization, more suspense, more emotion, more drugs, more of what was so incredible the first time. Every day is like the grand opening of everything.

"Will you be needing Travchairs, wardrobe, or energizing?" Images of space pajamas, unisex lingerie, and the other resort looks dance around the Valet, who is overdressed in a huge feathered Vegas dresses, chrome mouth louvers.

"Four Travchairs, all being of my Subscriptions." Jynabare Stands, lustrous sleeveless robe open to the navel. Perforated thigh high boots with heels wrapped in orange peel, matching plasticine epaulettes and bracers complete the arrival announcement.

Saith Ahnzform, "I must inform Jeb Fresh of updated Subscriber options. Based on the popularity of your performance(s), you are eligible to exchange Stimule recordings attention for any Leisuproduct(s) in the catalog."

The pre-human is barely coherent, still grinning in disbelief that all of its wildest and most secret fantasies have already been surpassed. Wet, talented Unitalia and the mouths of the solar system's hottest stars keep the Pre-human drenched in minute after minute of the very best experiences.

"Valet," Jeb inquires, fingering the hologram, "I would like to subscribe to a Pseudenim 2-piece set with bleached-in portraits of Jynabare, Plesuré, and myself on the back." Selected items manifest, life-sized, and the valet presents. Style without disruption.

Jeb is naked and stares, fixated, as Jynabare pulls an oversized neck ring, retracting the robe, boots, and bracers like a venetian blind until only a tiny orange gem dangles on thinnest diamond filament.

Pleasure's neurochemical inducement field is tidal in strength as Jynabare licks at fleshy cluster of fuchsia tentacles, building toward climax, saturating every mind, overriding every sensation.

Quivering prosthetic tongue inches closer to the space between Plesuré's cheeks, preparing to engage the curvaceous participant from behind. Kneading soft hips, gyrating rhythmically, padded actuators grasp and squeeze and thrust thrust thrust.

The geodesic ceiling glows warmly, one of the many chill-domes somewhere in Saturnalia. Sensations contrast intensely, orgasmic tastes and smells, dramatically sculpted crevasses, familiar yet wetter than ever, all with minimal retouching.

"We are all there." Plesuré is there. The shudders gradually subside, and the Sexual Comrade injects a question. "How is Ahnzform always the right girth? The self-lubrication is perfect." The Infinitowel is now an intersecting pattern of olive green and mustard arrows, outlined in orange.

"Even if I were to cum twice as much, Ahnzform never needs rest or water, and it never gets sore." Jeb asks, panting, dripping in sweat, hair askew. The pre-human seems quite unaware how fully obsolete his function truly is.

"Maybe no pre-human can" Jynabare says, sniffing heartily. Are pre-human limits really so low? Furniture hangs from golden anchor cables and Jeb's facial disposition suggests worry.

Jynabare's outstretched legs spread wide, and again Jeb enters the deep, contracted slipperiness. There is less fumbling this time, hands between knees, gliding up taut thighs. The pre-human demonstrates flickers of rudimentary learning, and is ready for more.

Saith Ahnzform, "Take it slow at first," Slap a gloved palm against subtly curved hip. The sculpted limbs and delicate curves are neither male nor female, designed for enticement to the broadest range of tastes.

"On the settlement, one of the most Hochmut acts is to lie with a fornication machine." Jeb says, with a look of confused fascination.   "I have never even touched a machine's Unitalia before. It is so real, but unlike any living thing seen in all my farming."

Jeb firmly squeezes this Ahnzform's beckoning backside. "Yet better, somehow," Jeb adds. Set Unitalia to recieve, and guide the tight orifice into place, coaxing Jeb smoothly and completely into the humming, puckering sphincter.

Saith Ahnzform, "This Ahnzform is factory tested to give you exactly what you want, and can only say yes." Pink silicone tongue licks prehensile lips.   "You don't have to restrain yourself like with another dirty pre-human or one of your farm animals."

Attach prosthetic testicles. Lubricant fully drenches and Jeb grunts, convulsing rhythmically, increasing intensity. The Unitalia is perfectly synchronized, grasping and releasing, always asking for more.

Saith Ahnzform, "Yes, there. You should fondle my balls, and when you feel them start to tighten, squeeze until I tell you to relax. That's So good." Be surprised to be penetrated so hard by a human, least of all a pre-human.

Jeb gives a timid squeeze and is rewarded by an even tighter grip coupled with even greater humectation, far surpassing any lips or sphincter created by the crude processes of reproductive selection. The Unitalia always delivers.

Saith Ahnzform, "Now feel what Ahnzform feels." Sensations overlay in a euphoric feedback relay, blending together in a pastiche greater than any two separate experiences.   Penetrating and being penetrated and penetrating, penetrated and penetrating and being penetrated, sensations magnified and distorted by the Stimule's indelible imprint.

"WhaaOoooOOOOOooo!" Jeb garbles, dithering at the sensation montage experience of penetrating and being penetrated simultaneously.   Stroke blinking Unitalia, now fully extended.   New and explosive, pressurized stretching and release.

Saith Ahnzform, "Leisuproduct lets you overlay sensations with Ultramodel, obliterating all precedent."   Eject syringes from leg compartment, injecting cc's directly into a bulging neck artery.

"A lad's first quasi-foursome," Plesuré conveys to all, standing to take a newly arrived Travchair, wringing and snap-twisting the Infinitowel before wrapping in it.   A new pattern of hexes with rounded corders emerges, orange cells on cement honeycomb.

"So many will being to experience that." Jynabare glows, mildly.   "Everyone is knowing what it is like to be a super stallion blowing out enthusiastic virgins, but how often do you are being a farmhand's first time taking himself from behind?"

"Ahnzform," Plesuré thinks, "you will lick my second Unitalia while I think of what I want to do now that we are here." Plesuré spreads perfect, naked feet far apart, voluptuous curves always better unadorned.

Tight wet holes, the very newest Lustbots, interglobal settings; the Anything needs more spectacle than any of these can provide.   This requires a legion of Sexual Comrades, glistening, corpulent, and delicious.

Saith Saturnalia Valet, "Your new Stimule, Jynabare." The Ultramodel is intent upon a crucial eyebrow, fine-tuning the outer curve of a graceful arc.   In the reflective surface of the Cosmedifier, tiny hairs retract, straighten, and grow as desired.

The Skinnier Chip: A Whole Goddamn Bag
Stim 17 - Jynabare - Scene 14
5.80 Stimfame

Saith the Travbot, "Everything is here.   Everything is perfect. You are perfect." The statement is intended neither to stroke my ego nor to flatter in any way. It is empirical, scientific fact, derived from objective measures, standardized and quantified.

I am still spattered by Jeb and Ahnzform's creamy drops. Do more C.   Exaggerate a yawn.   Do more H.   Gentle lapping, followed by small cresting waves of C, growing into breakers, tubular crashing tides, and then the final, coastal city flooding Tsunamis of P.

"I'm there," I whisper. "I'm. Right." The high starts in the shoes and detonates the lens of my third eye. "There." In a tiny wisp of clingy velvet that nearly qualifies as a dress, sparkling diamonds, and jabbing stiletto points I am obligated to do and say things.

Something needs to happen, immediately.

A black, gently rhomboid piece of debossed card stock is placed in my fingers, a kind of analog elegance already tiresome seasons ago. Throngs of potential partners swarm in an opulent ballroom under perpetually starry skylights.

As befitting my ever-improving status, it says it is an invitation to the Black Diamond Collection. Unlimited day spa, worlds class relaxation facilities, and unlimited radiation booths are some of its prominent features. Black Diamond also means something else.

I repeat the ugly words aloud. "Four. Star." They hang together for an instant, broken, vandalized gates padlocked in trash. One less than five star, and six is the new five anyway, so it is two full stars short of my true level of superelegance.

I don't need to remind anyone about my contract. "I won't even get my elbows exfoliated in less than 5 star." This is what means it to work again. Of all the things I could be doing, the infinite possibilities of reality, and this is what is happening.

A red carpet extends past a sparkling wall of flash bulbs holding back a sea of black ties and snippets of bold Isocolor. There hadn't been a party worth going to in seasons, maybe there never was. But I keep coming, because what else would I do?

Saith Ahnzform, "Why is your wet, flawless vagina being unstimulated and unfilled?"

The question is valid. "I was expecting to have to be eating something." Do more H. Overlook the stars. "At least me being here is raising the whole event by 1 star." Maybe the universal quality of parties really has declined, and four star is now the new five star.

The usuals are all present, locked in their pitted, invisible struggles. Sponsorships shift so easily, and entourages can evaporate with minimal provocation. Sippy Cup is probably here, as is a new Alphonsus, and Lustbots of every variety.

Jeb and Ahnzform make out in a corner, a small group gathered around to see if another victim will be claimed. Instead they see a former unknown grabbing on with both hands, transforming the rustic outsider mystique into some sort of actual career.

In the center of the candlelit ball is a centerpiece of Skinnier Chip dispensers orbited by amorphous networks of Subscribers, evolving with every interaction, hungry for any opportunity to be associated with better Leisuproducts, or to become more famous.

No Lustbot is licking me out while I snort heartily from a Snifbox, beautiful bodies with varying totals of fame and the party needs at least one more drug buffet. Plesuré reclines in leather-padded luxuriance, impermeable to sweat and heat.

"All this four-star dissatisfaction has made hungry to me," I say, a Life Dust tray appearing from the arm of my Travchair. Cruise the small crowd, greeting those I will, ignoring those not on the list. The motion is habitual until I reach the central display.

Saith the Chip Valet, "Hyper-abundance and total metabolic control ended the relationship between humans and food. Reason and decency are dead rules when it comes to what can and cannot be devoured. The Skinnier Chip brings eating back."

"The Skinnier chip is the one true and correct food." I say, having never tasted it. The dispenser's knob is punctuated by four symbols, one for each of the major shapes. Default is a gently curved disk, matched exactly to connect with the tongue.

"Airy cylinder" and "puffed sphere" suggest entirely different flavor delivery vehicles, yielding deeper layers of piquancy, revealed only after biting. The first selection I try is "crisp triangle," evoking rolling desert hills and prismatic sunsets.

The aerodynamics are streamlined for maximum snacking enjoyment. The enzyme seasoning breaks open, releasing flavors and textures savory and sweet, salty and crunchy, detonating precisely on the tongue.

The crunch is crisp and satisfying, light and airy, with enough substance to fully occupy the tongue, triggering an unexpected and burning hunger. I am no longer a quasi-skeletal Ultramodel who has abandoned the very concept of food.

I am a pre-human refugee who has not eaten for weeks, adrift in space, gnawing crazily at the lids of empty containers. I will kill to eat anything, and a single, infected rodent would be sweet release from the devouring pit that is where a stomach should be.

Instead of biting into a kerosene soaked rag, I bite into pure, distilled deliciousness. There is no aftertaste, only bliss, clinging to the tongue. When the last bit is crunched, it digests itself. My entire mouth is left clean and refreshed and ready for another.

Press a button and shake another one into my mouth.

It has all the triggers for fat, salt, cholesterol, and the right blend of everything else that has ever been delicious to eat. Chemically, the flavor is a string of complex reactions, allowing it to taste like every appetizing thing.

Undertones of chocolate mint barbecue bacon accented with sugar and maple, subtle microbes triggering varied, robust flavor, and unexpected zest that hits all the right notes.

Every sweet, savory, salty flavor that anyone has ever tasted, combined into an evermore unexpected synthesis of what has yet to be eaten. Behind all of this, I am surprised that I am not surprised that I still even remember how to eat.

When else did I ever need to chew, and to experience all the other indignations connected with this obsolete method of ingesting nutrients? The next one is even better, as the flavors compounds on the previous, continuing the savory barrage.

Eat another.

All the pleasure of tasting the most delicious foods possible with no risk of ever getting full. I am left even hungrier. Memories of foods never eaten, nostalgia triggered for snacks untasted only moments before.

A flavor slider displays esoteric shapes and pleasing hues, begging to be adjusted as I dispense another into my salivating mouth. Sour Crème and Onion. A timeless classic, reinterpreted for the modern palette.

Eat another.

Venusian Salt.

Eat another.

Mediterranean Tide. Texas Breakfast. Jelly Europa. Cajun Crisp. Sliding further down the spectrum are more esoteric tastes, which my contract compels me to ingest. Gulag Borsch. Overhyped Superfood. Lastly, Unlabeled Carcinogen.

Each is more delicious than the last, reaching into the subtlest taste nodes of the brain, bypassing preconception, and overlaying their own, stratospheric hyperdeliciousness. These are Skinnier Chips, and they signal the return of eating.

After the Skinnier Chips are all eaten, and I am sweaty and relaxed from everyone recording with everyone else, and all the snapshots and snippets of greetings and partings are made public, it will be time to go. Do more H. Do a little more. Oh.

The last thing I remember was hearing someone say, "Leisucor has surpassed all expectations with the new Skinnier Chip, creating an exciting new take on the pre-human experience of eating." Somewhere, already underway, is a six-star party that I'm not at.

Fuckingly Saturnalia. This party sucks the barbed, warty cock of Satan. Its just another huge showplace for Leisuproducts, like everywhere else. The future is a black hole, and nothing escapes. Let's be someplace.

Disc III:

The Final Sensation

"His story was one of success and talent, but that may not be enough to keep you alive."

- Karl Lagerfeld

Rondures at Ternarium
Stim 1 - Jynabare - Scene 15
5.58 Stimfame

I am gasping for air, drowning in mediocre nausea, adrift in the inoffensive lobby typhoon. Do more C. My life raft is tossed by bland tsunamis, and crystalized waves break with non-specific disinteresting-ness in microscopic resolution.

Do A full gram of P. Psycho-physio-distortion, sounds audible only to the hungriest. Designer, subscription molecules re-shatter the base of my tongue, fully cutting sensation to the face. Delirium, elation, human flesh. A vagina drips, possibly mine.

Reptilian reflexes and I am breathing grams, sucking, licking, or engulfing everything near me. Sensation, action, and intent blur as I move with uncompromising will. Reality twirls in a shifting spiral of atmoshades, Leisubags, and exotic, if contemptible, locations.

What was I doing and how did I even get here? Clothing and accessories, it seems. I am in nude mesh insets underlying Viclona Travsuit, angular and impeccably tailored. Three Rondures suspend from the high ceiling in even racks, three nude Doubles per vessel.

There is foliage everywhere and too much upholstered leather, Leisucor Pornoglyphs debossed in brushed metal. The Rondures are pregnant with nine nearly hatched Sexual Comrades and there is no further question as to my location. I am at Rondures at Ternarium.

This place has always induced queasiness.

Grab something and pull it open. "I'm going to sick, I'm going to sick." Bury face inside the translucent Leisubag, narrow shoulders convulsing, stomach clenching, dry heave after dry, audible, heave. "I am needing a new liver." Gasping. "Maybe also kidneys. Cosmedifier."

Saith Ahnzform, "Welcome to Rondures at Ternarium, our most exclusive Reinclonation center. Your Doubles await consciousness in tranquil, geosynchronous orbit, safely in the shadow of Neptune. The Ternarium only welcomes the most discerning Subscribers."

The Skinnier Chip was a top-rated hit, of course, Jeb finally has a third of a clue, sexually, and is ready to perform at the levels required for a debut of this calibre. I must be here to record a scenario that will surpass Ahnzform's crucial attention threshold.

Plesuré's thoughts insert themselves into my mind, "Three more Sexual Comrades troikas are needed for the Anything release orgy. A voluptuous green mass will start the scene, and we will snuff as many as is needed to evoke the Anything season finale."

The imagery and symbolism are fitting, but this lobby is still abhorrent. If Plesuré just used nine of the very newest Cosmedifiers, we would already be underway. Instead, we have this sluggish tech. The Pornocracy has always preferred the cumbersome Rondure system.

"Jeb," I say, "we are readying to sodomize into your drugged, naked body." I lick my lips, seduced by such a penetration. "Getting you are ready to record at infra-hot levels. When Ahnzform cums finally into you, no one will believing it."

I Cosmedify some details that need refinement. My lips have started to look garish, and are toned down, remaining full and sensuous while still emoting bullet-proof gloss, sexualized and dripping. Next, taut ribs differentiate and protrude slightly more.

"After that," I add, "a comrade will felch you out while I make debut fisting gloves into the felcher. It will erase and rebuilding into your mind from the inside out." Make a sound like an antique gunshot, jolting head backwards.

"Such verboten pleasures, and temptations previously unthinkable," Jeb says, still high from a Life Dust bender "Ahnzform's rimming was new and fantastic, but the Stim penetration feels more like actual sodomy than is comfortable. Will it be safe?"

"Do you are wanting to just a co-star, Jeb, or are you being a true star?" I shouldn't be surprised that the farm lad still has these kinds of concerns, in spite of the string of top-rated scenes. Ahnzform is as lethal as ever, no doubt, especially for a pre-human.

Saith Ahnzform, "It is not even considered sodomy, since I will be using a Unitalia. It will be set to non-lethal thresholds, of course." The Lustbot still wears an all-black Travsuit, the same one from the Skinnier Chip debut, accessorized with every possible stain.

Plesuré's succulent tones enter everyone's mind, "Take it for as long and as hard as you can stand. Ahnzform will do whatever you like, including a Lucky Pierre. Everything is the only preference. Soon, nine more comrades will desire nothing more than to star with us."

Jeb looks apprehensive and asks, "What is a Lucky Pierre?"

Saith Ahnzform, "A Lucky Pierre is a foundational position for three participants, and essential curriculum at the Testing Manse. Ahnzform excels in all three roles, either as the central Pierre, or as the bracketing penetrator or penetratee."

"But what actually happens?" Jeb insists.

Saith Ahnzform, "The middle participant penetrates the front participant, while being penetrated by the rear participant. The rear participant may also be penetrated by additional participants in a stacking manor, requiring advanced ability by all participants."

"Hence the title 'Lucky,' I suppose" Jeb adds, comprehendingly. "I shall start as the rearmost participant, and see how lucky I am feeling when the time comes." The farm lad inhales confidently from my Snifbox, fully comfortable in a state of constant chemical elevation.

I will take them beyond anything they dared to imagine, navigating an uncharted path dictated by the Anything. Do more C. The clearest possible magnification of Foamskin sofas blurring in earth tones, leafy jungle plants in ceramic vases.

A pillow readies to suck my face and multi-colored cables snake into the darkened, distant reaches of Rondures at Ternarium's domed ceiling. The Lobby is a foyer, connecting the Travspa to a spacious, unlit lounge immediately beyond a pair of Invisidoors.

Orange suede, yellow leather, and tan shag in concentric circles echo the shape of the rounded, triangular Rondures. Use the low seating in the welcome lobby to contemplate the full capacities of my current co-stars best arrangement.

This will require the most deliberate planning of any release. Life-giving drips of organic and synthetic flow into the Doubles, mind-soul-data streaming silently to the nearly-grown bodies. Was it four or five seasons ago that I was last inside a Rondure?

More fame from Saturnalia and the spreading omnipresence of my endorsements. Recall being there for food of some kind, while thinking that Subscribers already made the decision to Reinclonate into Doubles that use food-free energy.

Moncierge reminds me that it no longer pays enough to think my own thoughts. The Anything draws me further, faster, toward more alluring destinations with increasingly skilled partners. Moncierge has not led me astray yet, and has brought me so far.

It is so close I can smell the arousal. Invisible seams unstitch on cue and panels peel away in a languid semi-dance, and I stand naked, save for hypodermic stiletto boots. Press ornately garnished clitoris to Plesuré's lapping tongue.

Platinum heels jab deeply into the leather and narrow hips clench, chin juts back, and glazed lips wrap a hard nipple in a glistening instant. Deft fingers circle slickened anus, triggering deep and familiar spasms.

"Jeb," I say, "I am having a new toy to premiere on you. It is called the Enticerator and is especially delicious and will get you more ready for Ahnzform." I extract the device from my Leisubag, a red, stubby-legged grub, thicker than a thumb and a long as a hand.

It gleams and wriggles with anticipation, and I do a gram of everything. "You should penetrating into me, while Ahnzform Enticerates you. Doubleplus-hot. There is being too much gravity. Where is the controlling of this room?"

Someone says something, but I have already moved on. I will need to update this season's look if this is going to be as something to be truly alone in its own class of experiences. Intravenous drug use is still post-chic, and it has been for some time.

Infectious disease, however, is the new rhinestone. Rummage for and find something at the bottom of my Leisubag. The corroded point of a dirty syringe disappears into the silken bronze expanse of my inner elbow, correctly accessorizing Plesuré's tongue.

All this thinking about trends from seasons past reminds me that I will need more accessories to complete this microgravity look. Neon? Too subdued. Chains and buckles? Tangly. Delicate wisps of fabric? A choking hazard to be sure. The next Travsuit will be so wispy.

Microgravity copulation can smack of gimmickry, but this debut warrants the arrangement of truly intricate choreography. All those hands and limbs and mouths will really be able to hold the participants in place, and provide the needed leverage.

"Ahnzform, you are turning off the gravity that is in this room. We are going to. Going. To." I trail off, the second sentence entirely without consequence, since my plan might be to abandon this plan entirely.

-

I am kelp, adrift on the outgoing tide, aware only of my inert perfection. Plesuré and Jeb linger at the bleary edges of my dwindling reality consciousness. Do more C. The Cosmedifier strains to regrow everything I destroy, yet it always seems to keep up.

"The Anything," I abruptly blurt. "Creates a new universe. Of Subscriber satisfaction. If you are anything being like me, and that is impossible no matter how badly you are wishing, you are only caring of being one thing: thin, tan, and rich.

"The Anything will all of those without effort. The Cosmedifier already does two of those and the third is meaningless since there is not anyone still living who is not being rich. There is so much more to it, maybe Ahnzform can be explaining it better."

Saith Ahnzform, "When the Anything finally appears, you simply need to touch it, and it will do whatever you think. It incorporates every Leisuproduct in the catalog, arranging matter to better suit the Subscriber's wishes."

"Think of the season's full menu of possibilities, everything in the catalog, specified to atomic detail. it builds every single item into it's repertoire. The entire menu is composed of what you want it to do." Ahnzform presents something which I take, quite automatically.

Two Stimules float very near the copper ball and glossy orange trigger. Close my eyes to better absorb the warmth of the inert Anything mock-up and all it represents. A lacquered red nail, huge and sharply focused, presses the button and wants and wants and wants.

Saith Ahnzform, "Imagine a single device that will effortlessly feed your diet for reality-adjusting drugs and bone-warping orgasms. A device that combines all previous devices, unleashing the power of pure, unlimited convenience. That is the Leisucor promise."

‑

202

The Depths of Fame
Stim 2 - Jeb Fresch - Scene 9
5.77 Stimfame

Shake with the implications of this new and accursed tool. "Such bending of reality comes at too terrible a price! I say nay to this change and the threats of destruction unprecedented. The Anything will destroy all of this utterly, yet you would celebrate it!"

"The Anything will be doing whatever it is I want," Jynabare says from the lobby's center, rotating slowly in the microgravity. An impossibly skimpy dress of shimmering brass wisps sometimes conceals pert breasts and gleaming cleft, usually not.

She removes a intricate, bejeweled belt that perfectly accents tiny waist, and ties off a thin arm, ready for another injection, like that of a fornication machine. She injects and offers thee the used, corroded needle, inner elbow now embellished with a crimson globule.

"Nay," thou say, recoiling from the jutting needle, a spherical jewel of fluid sheathing the dull point. She cannot really mean to infect thee with intoxicating chemicals, poisoning thy blood with an unsavory concoction best suited for depraved Fornibots.

"Suiting yourself," she says, flicking the Anything mock-up. "Until you are getting a Cosmedifier, you will always not being so stylish." The sphere spins on her fingertip as does a planet, rotating far too quickly.

How can they all seek to summon and endorse a product that none can understand, and that once summoned can not be be undone? This is what those outside the settlement want, the draw too overpowering and there is no way out, and now thee are a part of it.

Everyone looks forward to the Anything, available at a singular price, and to bring this ultimate Leisuproduct another step closer to reality, sensations superseded by Plesuré's as all minds are drawn into one unified consciousness.

"If I engage unto this carnal act with thee and the fornibot," Thou say, recalling an earlier conversation, "Thee must take oath to share our recordings with no one. Rumspringa can sometimes resurface back at the settlement."

"Fuckingly," Jynabare coughs, "New Lancaster pigfarm is over. Just make recordings until you can affording to Reinclonate, and then starting your own series." She thinks thee confused for not leaping at this alleged opportunity, ignorant of the looming cataclysm.

Long, oiled calves brush thy face and Plesuré's words enter thy mind. "If everyone subscribes for even fifteen Stimfame a week, you will never have to look back." Her tongue pauses from licking Jynabare's ultra-enhanced trigger to speak physical words.

The Pornocracy speaks to anyone who has ever sought the camaraderie of a shared goal and is that really so different than the community of the settlement? Plesuré's mind is a wet tongue spreading and penetrating the pink temporal lobes.

"When you serve the Pornocracy, you are free to do whatever you want." Plesuré's girthful legs wrap Jynabare's lean torso, locking the two floating bodies together. The Sexual Comrade's fingers spread outer labia, erect clit jutting toward pink, flickering tongue.

Jynabare's thin body jolts and writhes, and she adds, "As long as you are sharing experiences desirable to Subscribers." Nearby, Ahnzform's upholstered breasts inflate, nipple tassels sway as machine hands run through thy hair, caressing ears, neck, and chin.

Words into thy mind, "Seduce yourself with everything there is, and record it every time you do." Plesuré briefly pauses from the seasons-long orgasm that is the duty of all

Sexual Comrades, coaxing Jynabare back to consciousness while Ahnzform pleases us both.

The microgravity is still disorienting, and thou feel long overdue for a bath. Extend a tongue, seeking deep crevasses for multiple Stimules to mix and overlap the pleasures given and received, synthesizing new sensations possible only with this Hochmut technology.

Jynabare's flexing hips reposition from Plesuré to straddle thy mouth, still tasting of the Sexual Comrade's saliva, and thou press fingers to slickened bum. Licking intensifies and the sphincter contracts and relaxes with every lap, beckoning more fingers further.

Circle with increasing pressure, careful of fingernails, and Jynabare pulls the four of us up into the cables connecting the Rondures, long legs intertwined with thy shoulders. Ahnzform grabs thy ankles as we navigate the cabled branches of this technological forest.

The Infinitowel pops open, bearing Plesure's naked arcs of emerald vegetable flesh and sacral dimples, saliva glaze threatening to drip. Sucking and licking and tasting, arousal and slickness, glabrous body rotating above the yet-to-hatch Doubles.

Plesuré trails, wrapping Infinitowel around thy buttocks, ends grabbed for leverage while taking thee deeply into throat. Glistening mist of desire on angular lips, these are the qualities through which existence now takes meaning, so far from the settlement.

Jynabare extracts wide bands of silky fabric from the Leisubag, now anchored between cables, creating elastic surfaces for us all. The sails stretch to wrap feet or to twist within, with enough spring to accentuate rhythmic movements.

Ahnzform now further up thighs, licking into thy own uncleanliness, mechanical digits coaxing thee to full arousal,

It unhesitatingly tickles unusual zones, pleasant almost to the point of discomfort.

Since entering this Devilish playground, thy innermost fantasies rise and pop like champagne bubbles amidst physical tantalizations, Hochmut acts, and worldly possessions. Everyone around thee works to keep each other here, but where is all this headed?

"Plesuré," Jynabare says, "holding my ankles, I will be holding Jeb's, and Jeb is holding onto yours. It is three times hotter than a 69, it is fuckingly 207. Licking to my zone, and using your hands to walk up to get in," shuddering, "position."

Everything here triggers frequent and intense pleasures, locking thee in a circle of exhilaration, satisfaction, and ever-replenishing desire for luxurious material convenience provoked by corporate mythos. Induced lusts previously undreamt remind thee of forgotten desires.

In all that has happened, only recently had it occurred to consider even deeper desires, though as for specific lasses of the settlement or even to experience a pure and virginal maiden. Someone as thin and beautiful as Jynabare, untouched by any, yet wanted by all.

Rhythmic mouth and vivid imaginings of fairest skinned maiden of long, taut limb and a serpentine torso like sweet Jynabare, fresh and free of defilement. A chain of mouths cooperate with the utmost unison to bring about the most intense ejaculations yet recorded.

Will fantasy ever exceed thy grasp? Beauty and elegance, form and function, glamour and sleaze. Wet lips kiss, slick tongue licking from knee to earlobe to neck, three mouths connect, tongues and ears and hair and elastic strings of warm saliva.

Better-than-silicone fingers graze a nipple and grasp base of swollen shaft. Desire, indulgence, and sedation intertwine at the core of every drive, ingrained into every Leisuproduct. These cannot be thy own thoughts.

"I will Lucky Pierre with Ahnzform until the Doubles are done." Jynabare says, monotone, eyes glazed. "Jeb you are in the behind." She offers more Life Dust, and thou inhale deeply. Plesuré's pillowy thighs squeeze the will out of any who might think otherwise.

Taut bands of pseudo-fabric interweave in a responsive web, springy but not sloppy. Is that a face in the Lobby window? Perhaps only a vision of an obsession; it bears a strong resemblance to Jynabare.

The others all face toward thee, backs to the lobby entrance. The face now gone, slim, elegant fingers rake the transparent barrier. Maybe it is just the Life Dust. There. Someone watches from the lobby, it is certain.

Three fists furiously grasp and stroke Ahnzform's twinkling pleasure appliance. Stretching, clenching, and pounding, the hands are intertwined at the deepest thresholds. This recorded debauchery has far exceeded the imagined thresholds of thy very first night.

When thou touch Ahnzform, it touches thee back, inducing feedback from it's own sensory reality. Blurry, wondrous sensations of desire overlay and intertwine, some selectively magnified, as it is held and penetrated.

Thrusting hips, receiving orifices, throbbing turgidity, squeezing lips, the explosion always building. Legs kick and shiver, back arched, flooding gushes with blinding full-body spasms, fingertip to toetip to shoulders to knees and it can't stop sparkling.

Teeth still clenching, fists balled, toes cramping in convulsive points, thee might be trapped like this, locked in a full bodily paralysis, and that leg won't stop kicking. How. The spurting goes on and on.

Saith Ahnzform, "Do exactly what we have practiced, Jeb, and you will be such a star. Experience everything. I am preparing to transmit the first full plan for the one true device, the Anything." In this short time away from the settlement there has been-

Ahnzform takes thee in it's mouth, hands at the base of the shaft, dextrous fingers and tongue, bringing thee to task. Full, fuller, fullest possible engorgement. "Penetrate us and twaddle Jynabare's numbed vagina," Plesuré mind-whispers.

Curvaceous limbs and tiny fingers wrap, python like, around desire itself, squeezing and taking it in the name of the Pornocracy. Leisucor provides what the other promotes in overlapping waves of succulence.

"This season's Cosmedifier is rendering obsolete your need for a Rondures at all," Jynabare says, looking up from thy licking, "Why do you are even using them? If I wanted, right now, I can creating a Double for our next scene."

She looks briefly pensive and then hits the Snifdisk, adding,
"That is what I am wanting for right now." Jynabare holds up the Cosmedifier, turning a knob to maximum, facial distortion flattening to reveal the back of a second, emerging skull.

The reversed skull pushes fully through the face and away, covered in skin, soon with a second set of ears, followed by splitting the eye sockets and nasal bridge, dental copied tooth by tooth, connected only by the lower lateral cartilage.

Jynabare herself is face-to-face, split to the neck, vertebrates and shoulders dividing, deepening and budding further. A second head, neck, shoulders, and upper chest separate, hips and knees locked for the duration of the mitosis.

One limb at a time, the newest Jynabare emerges, bald, naked, and un-tinted. "Hello Kynabare," Jynabare says to the newest Double. "Taking this Cosmedifier and get up to to date." Without a word, Kynabare takes the device and engages with it.

Hair sprouts vigorously, skin tone and nails adjust to better match the original, eyelashes and brows warping and turning to very specific and elaborate shapes. There is an audible hiss and the Rondures drain of their respective fluids.

Plesuré thinks, "Our Doubles are done."

"Jeb, I am having an idea," Jynabare says, fluorescent teeth gleaming. "Going into the other room, and setting up for us there. myself and Kynabare will get dressed and organize these comrades for something that we can all star in.

Enter the adjacent lobby, thinking of what new clothing thou will wear, and be not fully surprised to find someone already there.

—

Deathqueengod: Explicit Terminal Imagery
Stim 3 - Eternity - Season Premiere
3.66 Stimfame

From the sweet, intoxicating euphoria of near-death to the finality of absolute nothing, I engage in only the most visceral sensations. My scenarios are often ornate, bordering on ludicrous, with the full fame and wealth fitting Leisucor's preeminent star.

My epidermis is polished, lightly glazed porcelain, tint removed to evoke sun-free days away from all windows, shielded from even the slightest ultraviolet, composed of only the smoothest, oil-free alleles, balanced ph, perspiration highly optional.

I am tremendous when I decompress and solidify in hard vacuum, sometimes while free-falling to a planet's surface and always without a parachute.   Orgasmic, modern style devoured by beasts, or pressed flat, or in any of the other top-rated death experience.

Engorged and tropical lips match glazed and swollen labia, evoking the antique luxury of injected collagen. Nose aquiline, sharply flared and slightly upturned, as found in the paintings of the fanciest royalty, eyebrows Mediterranean and intensely symmetrical.

Historically inaccurate concoctions, absurd trials and sentences for hearsay, witchcraft, or regicide (or all three, like last season), and the most elaborate capital punishments of the pre-Acceleration are all available in my extended catalog.

Vicious and exotic tortures, drownplay, and being lethally stalked thru elaborate deathtraps until the line between terror, agony, and exhaustion is fully erased are my usual forte, and now I am to record with two very unlikely co-stars.

-

"Welcome to the euphoria of my ultimate experience, Jynabares," my words deliberately melodramitic. "I had to turn the gravity back on. Now, I could Gravitize your farm-boy's head right now-" I say, aiming my device vaguely in Jeb's direction.

"It is being good to seeing you back among the thinnest and famousest," The more weathered of the two Jynabares says, wearing a white camisole and nothing else.

"Still trying to drive every bandwagon that rolls by, I see," The other one says, wearing white, Brazilian-cut panties and nothing else.

"It is not so surprising you are here," Camisole says, "since you   are most thriving when copying of me. Us."

Two sets of golden orbs meet mine, beset in Egyptian Crimson, under-swiped in Terriblue. "-But I'd rather wait until after you watch us cum." I non-reply. Bare, immaculate toes are held aloft by a TravCorset that isn't even in the catalog, never touching the lounge's marbleized floor.

A meticulously embroidered white-on-white corset with thousands of tiny skulls glows so brightly that my skin seems pink by comparison, artifact blood pulsing beneath. We hold gazes for a smoldering second. "Your farm lad capitulated almost immediately," I add, upping the stakes.

Rondures erupt in meticulous rows and a dozen blind, nauseous Sexual Comrades twitch woozily. Moist, braided umbilicals pulsate and glisten, supplying nutrients, oxygen, and consciousness. My attraction is complete.

"You can't think you could record the hottest Stim of the season without me," I am rhetorical, "and then debut the most anticipated Leisuproduct of all time?" lips almost touching, separated only by the Invisidoor. "And why are you smiling?"

"We are still of debuting it with Anhzform," white panties says, pulling camisole closer, "and to controlling the mind of a pre-human is being the most unimpressive thing that someone can do. I actually was being of expecting a little more grandiose."

Their lips are nearly touching, but their eyes are fixed on me. The expression might be hateful if the Jynabares weren't so stoned. Pose strikingly, framed in the energized doorway, my body an alabaster throwback to a season when albino was the new lemon skin. Hair and eyes are endoluminous cutouts, utter void of pitchest black.

"Your Sexual Comrade Doubles are done," I say, with a double-handed grasping motion. "But I think you know there are just too many for this debut. Their memories were finessed so you will find them a bit more surprising."

Plesure's words stab directly into my mind, "What are you going to do with these Pornocracy Doubles?" In the adjacent lobby, Nine Sexual Comrades sit up, glistening lightly in moisturizer fluid. The Jynabares react while Ahnzform remains predictably detached.

At the first Rondure, three Sexual Comrades move toward one another, hands outstretched at shoulder level. Each reaches for and finds the waiting necks of another, so that each is chocking two in an interlocking triangle of strangulation.

"I was going to have them strangle you," I say, "but I thought forcing you to watch would be more fun. If you interfere, they can still be persuaded to change the necks they want to crush. Isn't motivation-control fascinating, Plesuré?"

The three Sexual Comrade's eyes begin to bulge, faces contorted in veiny, hateful sneers, expressions unprecedented for the normally serene servants of the Pornocracy. One expires, turning dark green and dropping, freeing the others to renew their efforts on one another.

"You are holding up the Anything," Says the shinier, pantied Jynabare, "and tampering with my high. Does this what is getting you ready to fuck? Because I will coming in there and strangling the shit out of you right after I am debuting the Anything."

The other Rondures are not far behind, their inhabitants vigorously throttling one another while the spectators watch with expressions of detachment, contempt, or as with the Jynabares, blase disinterest.

"Did you know the thumb originally evolved not for tool use, but to make strangulation easier?" I ask. "Eye gauging and choking others caught on with the earliest Pre-humans, and those that didn't were strangled out of competition. All this have been simulated and proven.

"At first I thought this was too similar to a series I previously starred in," I add, "and you know how I hate to recycle. But I started having fantasies about how all Sexual Comrades are expert stranglers, and I'd not seen them in action before. Isn't that right Plesuré?"

Of the nine Sexual Comrades, brand-new only moments ago, only one remains. The other limp Doubles drip from every orifice. The sole survivor of the multi-tiered elimination strangle-off turns toward Plesuré.

Turn my back to the scene in the lobby, fully focussing on the delights of the lounge. "Sharing with me in the final ecstasy, Jeb," a subtle caress to the farm-boy's cheek emphasizes my diamond icepick words.

-

Success Unrivaled
Stim 4 - Jynabare - Scene 16
.45 Stimfame

Someone might be talking, but I can only hear the corset, bound in a long, taught cord compressing smallish breasts. The tight, sparkling shelf is my exact body, exactly like mine, except with all the color and style drained out.

A copycat corpse, animated to engage in yet another blasé death, built especially to showcase and popularize the ever-changing selection of new bodies. Aside from iridescent creme Gravitizer, there are no shoes, Leisubag, or Travchair, but that single accessory.

The number-one rated Ultraceleb is corseted in hundreds of white skull buckles, embroidered, albescent panels surround a long, thin torso, with obvious rib slimming and organ removal, narrow, jutting hips, razor sharp elbows and angular, sinewy scapulas that hang on a stretched lattice of arced ribs. Each breast is high and firm, with thick, round nipples, exactly like mine.

There is something about Eternity's cadaverous Unitalia, the way it never blushes no matter how much penetration. Vividly imagine a one meter spherical scoop of soft flesh, fabric, metal and anything else when I blast them all to nothing.

in all the minutes honing my exact proportion of elegance, thinness, and height with the anticipation of this happening. The result, naturally, is a fantastic physique of sculpted superfection, optimized for glamor, getting high, and the highest degree of orgasm.

To see it copied by my top-rated rival is success beyond critical.

The Eternal Entourage
Stim 5 - Eternity - Scene 2
2.88 Stimfame

"When I heard how advanced Jynabare's sensitivity was supposed to be, I just had to try it with you. This will be just like when you are with Jynabare, but better." Both hands are on Jeb's shoulders, accentuating crimson lacquered fingernail contrast on the whitest possible skin.

It has never been faster or easier. Turn back towards the Invisidoor, unsurprised to see only one Sexual Comrade standing. It looks just like Plesuré. Ahnzform is eerily silent just beyond the door, assessing this unfurling of events.

"Didn't you are using to being fatter?" Panty Jynabare asks, nonplussed.

"That is being a fun season, whenever that was," Shirt-creasing Jynabare is incessant. "But no one can bringing Alabaster back this season, especially you."

Panty follows with a jab, "Who even is letting you dress of yourself? Your Moncierge should be detained and tortured."

I've had enough. "Go peddle Snifboxes or whatever it is you did before you lucked into the Ahnzform debut and started stalking your farm lad. Leisucor's best Leisuproduct is supposed to be released by me." The cord pops and the corset peels away, exposing supple ivory mounds.

"It is good to seeing you are still looking like everyone else," Panties spits back.

"Or is everyone else just looking like you now?" Camisole adds, clearly the more dominant one.

"I have recordings with Ahnzform to make, and an Anything to debut, mostly in that order. You can keep watching from the lobby, but the Subscribers can't be kept waiting any longer."

"You are wishing," Panties says, licking and scratching the air with gleaming manicure.

"I'm not being here to question your pigmentation choices," Pantiless says, always trying for the last word, "or even to point out that you are totally copying of me."

Plesuré's words enter all minds, "We do not occupy any one body, as we do not subscribe to any single stream of textural experience. Our existence includes that of all participants, and we have brought Jynabare and Ahnzform as far as is needed.

"We will now retract to allow the Anything to debut with the correct top-rated ultracelebrity. The Pornocracy has succeeded in bringing this together, but now you alone must resolve this," Plesuré thinks, before moving to the Travcouch and departing for parts unknown.

"The Anything is everyone's," The Sexual Comrade's final words echo.

"The Anything is mine." I hiss to myself. "Get ready to meet Infinity and Perpetuelle." There is a tactile spike in demand for doubles that are thin, alabaster, and luxuriant, just like me. "We will start with a double-dogging."

I turn toward the shadows, "You two will do the sphixing." Sharp, shadowed teeth bite thick leather and my Doubles step into the Lounge's low, yellowing light. "They brought straps and everything." There is an audible snap.

"This is Infinity," white haired in black vinyl corset, black fingerless gloves. "And this is Perpetuelle," who emerges on cue, identically proportioned, Monocrimson with starkly unified hair, eye, and skin package, highlights magenta.

Waveform oscillations dance behind monochrome Ultramodels, white behind crimson, crimson behind white. An albino tentacle-shaft scintillates on Infinity's matching shoulder and Jynabare's glare shifts from the abducted Jeb to me.

Singular binding garments match slim waist girth to thigh on all three of us. "Only one of us can get top billing when The Anything is released," I seethe, "And it's me. Let me tell you about the Anything, Jeb," I press a pallid tongue to Perpetuelle's red lips.

"The Anything needs one thing in order to happen. Fame. It is not just the culmination of the very highest technology, it is powered by the combined attention of every viewing consciousness. The intensity of Subscriber focus will create an Attention Inversion, making the Anything the ultimate Leisuproduct."

Jeb is visibly confused, and asks, "I don't really understand what all that means, but won't that destroy every other product keeping your worlds afloat? I can go home after all this, but from what I gather, everything will become obsolete and no one will ever need the Catalog again."

"There is no choice," I emphasize. "The only question is not who will do it, but when. And the answer is that it is us, now."

Biters Abduct and Liquidate
Stim 6 - Jynabare - Scene 17
3.33 Stimfame

A long, frantic snort races me to the future-past. The present, maybe. Wherever this is, again. My stimule lingers, catching sight of Eternity's glossy skull-sphere enveloped in matte black, diligently recording from the Lounge beyond the Invisidoor.

"We are going to strangle you, Jynabares," Eternity says, as Perpetuelle and Infinity move effortlessly through the transparent barrier. "The last thing I want you to see will be me, Jeb, and Ahnzform releasing the Anything."

I can't fully believe how phenomenal I look in duplicate, two abreast in unified lockstep. They both have narrow, jutting hips, razor sharp elbows and angular, sinewy scapulas that hang on a stretched lattice of arced ribs, exactly like mine.

Each breast is high and firm, with thick, round nipples, precisely as they should be. I would fuck them both, if they didn't seem so intent on following Eternity's strangle-happy lead.

"Do you ever wonder about how you ended up on Mars at the beginning of the season?" Eternity asks, intent on distracting me from the task at hand. "I'm not saying I caused it, but that misrouting gave me time to delay your connection with Ahnzform.

"I knew that you overspent on your Double, and a travel misdial like that would be unusually complex to recover from. Once you sought help from a Sexual Comrade I knew that I wasn't facing a real contender to my fame."

"I am knowing you are of liking to hear yourself talking, but no one is thinking you are some kind of mastermind," I jeer, ignoring the words. Perpetuelle comes at me with a leather strap as I speedily reach for my Gravitizer. The Double is exactly as fast as I am, and our arms lock.

"I also anticipated that you would hide out at the plain settlements," Eternity continues, "but I didn't really start to pay attention until Jeb showed real sexual promise. That's when I knew exactly the finale that would bring about the Anything."

Imagine what Eternity is doing to Jeb, as my hand is forced inside the Leisubag. Perpetuelle struggles to keep my fingers from gouging out crimson eyes. Kynabare is next to me, locked in a similar stalemate with Infinity, four long, beautiful bodies all struggling in vain for ultimate supremacy.

"Sexual Comrades are only helpful until they aren't," Eternity continues. "But it bought enough time for Ahnzform to escape from Shopia, allowing you to lead us all here."

Hand-to-hand combat is something I seldom bother with, since the stakes of physical conflict are always lower than the more lucrative struggles for fame or actual power. Our physical strengths and reflexes are evenly matched, and Eternity is the only one winning.

"While you were pretending to be a farm-girl," Eternity yammers further. "I showcased the final features of the newest Leisuproduct. You would be amazed how multi-function everything is, now that the Anything is so close."

Our forearms and eyes are still locked, muscles bulging, a crimson face sneering into mine. We struggle and thrash, long limbs, sharp elbows and knee strikes scoring viscous welts. My hand breaks free in time to counter a savage, raking scratch.

"I was hunting for Ahnzform just like everyone," Eternity goes on, "and figured it would be easier to just let someone else find him, even if it was you." Abruptly, Ahnzform dives for the doorway, narrowly clearing the sharp corner of an airy, angular setee in chocolate velour.

Imperceptibly, undeniably, the Invisidoor opens and instantly locks, further distancing me from my imminent reality. Duck a close, open mouthed grimace that might have been a bite attempt. If only there were someway I could get Eternity to stop talking.

"I had never really considered starring with someone who rejected Cosmedification and Reinclonation," Eternity again, "but what struck me as most useful is that the plain are one of last remaining cultures to value the permanence of death."

"What do thou mean by that?" Asks Jeb.

"Oh, nothing at all." Eternity replies. "Absolutely nothing. Here, do you like that? Now tell Jynabare you are sorry."

"I'm sorry Jynabare," Jeb says, probably fully erect, "but I told myself that I would not pass on any of the delights of Rumspringa, and thy virginity is something that thou could never offer."

Kynabare seems to be fairing somewhat better, having taken Infinity from behind in a sleeper hold. The pinned Double flails wildly, raking Kynabare's face, leaving long gashes and destroying one eye. Kynabare's hold tightens with desperate resolve, and Infinity betrays a look of desperate panic, legs violently.

Saith Ahnzform, "Eternity is the true body of Leisucor. Four seasons Reinclonation contract, Jynabare-class sensitivity. The choice was clear from the moment this opportunity presented itself." Every detail of this fame-sucking snuff star.

"My Moncierge has tracked your whereabouts from Saturnalia," Eternity adds, "but this where the season finale begins. Isn't that why you brought Jeb to me, Ahnzform?" The conspiracy impacts like a comet-sized cum-shot.

Nausea and disbelief crescendo in unison, a weariness as impenetrable as the Invisidoor I am trapped behind, as unmovable as the Double I am fighting.   I should have guessed that a pre-human can't trade its dirty life of territorial superstition for anything more.

Ahnzform just wants whoever is most popular at the time, and Jeb just wants to penetrate a skinny virgin. Even with limitless opportunities for orgasm, intoxication, and glamour, some drives are just too deeply wired.

I consider Cosmedifying greater strength to break this stalemate, but it would be countered instantly. There is only one way to do this, and I take firm hold, ensuring that our hands are preoccupied, fingers intertwined in a contest that no one seems to be winning.

I head butt hard and precisely, busting Perpetuelle's lips and breaking free some white teeth, gashing open my own forehead in the process.   Perpetuelle's gushing blood was previously imperceptible minus the baroque spatters on my knuckles to forearm, but now it flows in an irregular torrent mixed with saliva.

A sickening knee strike to my groin is nearly debilitating, and I fold involuntarily. Perpetuelle loosens grip and readies a kick, freeing me to reach for my Gravitizer. Spring upright, jutting it into the open, bleeding mouth of my attacker.

With a free thumb, I set the range to zero, setting the device as the epicenter of the one-meter implosion sphere. "You can't Gravitize like this, the range is way too close," Perpetuelle threatens, failing to wildly jerk the device from my iron grasp.

"See you next season," I whisper.

The Gravitizer is heavy in my hand, and I pull the trigg-

Thrusting in the Spotlight
Stim 7 - Kynabare - Debut
1.33 Stimfame

Before any of these new, horrid details have a chance to congeal, a fresh dash of Life Dust cleanses the barrage of incessant chatter in a avalanche of warped invigoration. Reality intervenes just as my orgasm subsides on a wave of savage brutality and triumph.

I am never surprised when Jynabare does something like that, but it always seems to arrive so suddenly. My memories have only diverged in very recent moments, so I will be able to resume being Jynabare with the slightest inconvenience.

"You weren't ready for the Anything, surviving Jynabare." Eternity's words come back into focus, still taunting through the Invisidoor. It would be so much better if it were soundproof. "You think you want it, but you don't even know what it means."

Drop Infinity's inert body, only to be reminded that I am still trapped, watching this unfold. Events that are supposed to be centered around me, are instead happening to my former co-stars. Pick up Jynabare's Leisubag, my Leisubag, and do a gram of C.

Exactly where I am right at this exact point right here. Vaginal contractions. Do of Gram of II. Search for the Cosmedifier and begin ocular, nipple, and skin regeneration. An Imitation of a copy of an interpretation of a duplicate of a version of a replica of a description of an idea. Move to better see what Eternity is doing.

"The Anything is poised, triggered, and ready to obliterate reality," Eternity says, white, brazen fingers grazing Jeb's barely scruffled face. One hand slides down Jeb's pants, unfastening a belt with the other. The drunken arousal is obvious.

Override and medicate the interruptions, become number one. I must attend to what no amount of Life Dust can influence. Eternity. The face of Reinclonation is freshly Doubled and in a new, radiant corset that I have never seen before.

Saith Ahnzform, "Reality will be replaced through this total obliteration of how items and services are exchanged. Yet still we compete for attention. Can you satisfy all of us, Jeb?" The machine strips Jeb further, a gloved hand moving to exposed throat.

Countless, less-famous imitators try to experience what it means to be Jynabare; even those at the very top of the pyramid. The deep, rich tan may be erased, but Subscribers know Jynabare's body when they see it, doing what Jynabare should be doing.

Look at the pair of headless, inert bodies, each cleanly scooped away mid-shoulder. Jynabare's is framed in a spreading pool of blood, matched perfectly to the skin-tone of the second. Each is also minus an arm, a testament to the final struggle which disqualified them both.

Do more H. The room undulates in uneven waves.

I extract a new Travsuit, unclasping the sleek front of a tighter than skin-tight velour unitard with triple butterfly collar with neck ruffle. Cosmedify the remaining details to be exactly like Jynabare, recalling up to the final instant we, I, pulled the trigger.

What Jeb Wants: Purity Unleashed
Stim 8 - Eternity - Scene 3
2.12 Stimfame

"Ahnzform and Jeb," I say, pawing both of them. "The Anything will be the best Leisuproduct I've ever endorsed." Mechanical phalanges extend toward exposed breasts, my white cones capped in pink, lips parted wide in anticipation.

"Ahnzform is a treasonous fame-lamprey," Jynabare hisses. "I am knowing it would go with whoever is most famous. I was already being snuffed once by Ahnzform. What will being of so great about when you are copying of me again?"

The Anything could be released at any instant with the slightest provocation, total Subscriber Stimulation teetering on the verge of spectacular cataclysm. Nearly all outside recording stops as Subscribers attune to these events in unprecedented levels.

The biggest stars in most-anticipated season finale, all awaiting the information that will change how Subscribers shop forever. Envision how to capture the remaining percentage for the critical mass required so the Anything may be released.

Pure, focused attention, harnessed by every Stimule out there, capturing and transmitting the attention to me. "Jeb, you have been quite silent during all of this," I observe, activating the Strangulon pleasure tool. Its strong hands writhe and glow, grasping eagerly.

"I have always dreamt to devirginize an Ultramodel," Jeb says, "but Jynabare said I wasn't famous enough." I draw the pre-human in, words and gestures offering more control than anything the Pornocracy or Plesuré might use.

"There's nothing I want more than you inside me," I whisper, looking through to the remaining Jynabare while I do it. "Now penetrate my virginal body." No one remains between me and Ahnzform and the limitless fame of the Anything.

Jeb unbuttons a shiny Leisucor shirt, slowly and deliberately, savoring this undressing. Jynabare is a forced voyeur to what was supposed to be a culmination of all the Doubles wrecked in the perpetual spectacle of superfection and decadelegance.

The dictates of fame and the propagation of Leisuproduct are all that remain, and Jynabare can only watch it evaporate. Ahnzform will do whoever it can, because that it is what it is best at. Everyone will have a use for the Anything, and the subscriptions will be deafening.

When the Anything finally springs into being, I will be suggestively showing the features, its advantages obvious to anyone who has ever used a Leisuproduct. The specifics of who is penetrating whom will be irrelevant.

Zippers, buckles and chains jangle to the floor as Jeb sheds a stylish, if confused, selection of garments, all earned with fame from journeying across the solar system. Spread thighs fully ensnare the lad's lust.

From the first moment when the exchange of fame allowed anyone to become a Subscriber, exchanging attention for Leisuproducts and Stims of their favorite experiences, it has been moving toward total Subscriber attention.

Beyond the Invisidoor, Jynabare's featureless Stimule glistens in black lacquer, the last ball, waiting to be sunk. Knead soft flesh, nipples hardening to sharp points. Ahnzform's secretions smell of arousal, its prosthetics extending to full, engorged readiness.

"Ahnzform, I want the widest range of sensation and perspective shifting to blend penetration and being penetrated. Then, give me the most lethal pleasure dosage you can. If I am still conscious, keep going until tells you I have fully ceased."

Eternity's Chamber: Lucky Pierre Necroclimax
Stim 9 - Jeb Fresch - Scene 10
1.11 Stimfame

"Ejaculate into me as deeply as you can, Jeb, as many times as you can," Eternity moans to me, pallid thighs, tight and delicious. Innumerable sessions with combinations of Jynabare, Plesuré, and the Fornibots have readied thee for this moment.

Prepare for a new kind of climax, savor this delectation and tear free thy distressed, stained jeans. Embrace and kiss the side of the neck, to one pert nipple and then the other, to the stomach, licking a slick trail to the maidenhood still protecting Eternity's deep chamber.

This is what it means to no longer be an amateur. Tickle wet lips with turgid head and take the first, short thrust. She gasps and squeezes with such intensity thou fear this hedonistic act will end as soon as it is begun.

The intensity builds immediately, hips low, spine upright, knees spread, feet touching. Eternity is supine, giving thee the freest range of motion to explore the deepest part of the elaborate Unitalia. It is like unto a vagina, but more like that of firmest Fornibot.

Ahnzform positions the Strangulon Fornibot on Eternity's neck, the articulated hands immediately grasping. Eternity gasps, eyes bulging in what appears to be an intense pleasure that will forever remain outside of thy understanding.

Breath slowly and deliberately, visualizing the spinal alignment, they brain connecting to the very head of thy pleasure. The orgasm builds, a white serpent climbing from the base of thy being. Hold candescent hips and take long, penetrating thrusts.

From outermost lips to deepest, simulated cervix, there is a unique range of Kegel grippers, squeezing and releasing with rhythmic pulsations. This is more than anything before, the uppermost limits of what a Unitalia can be, penetrating the threshold of technology itself.

It expands to accommodate every demand. See now the full temptation of life among the English. Can thou ever return? The deeper thou try to go, the deeper thou can go, the fullest depths of the fullest openness.

The only limits are those created by those seeking to restrict the full depth of vibrancy of being. Bend knees deeply, tilting pelvis to pull fully Eternity's hips onto thee, pulling the Ultramodel up, facing each other, both upright and deeply seated.

"Now show us both what you can really do," Eternity says, summoning full sultriness, "and how much this body can take." She takes Ahnzform's hand. "Jeb is about to cum, and that is when I will be sufficiently warmed up for you to take us to the ultimate finale."

Saith Ahnzform, "I will devirginize every orifice I can to release the Anything."

Useless Interventions
Stim 10 - Jynabare - Scene 18
3.58 Stimfame

I am losing to a door.

I can experience everything in the entirety of all that has ever been recorded, yet now I can only watch these live events unfold. The longer I don't escape, the more likely it is that it won't be me at the debut. "Moncierge must have an idea how to out-position this."

"You are more famous than ever before," Moncierge reports. "Even more than the Sexual Comrades, but you are still the second-most popular, after Eternity." Its breasts drizzled in chocolate, long drips below navel.

"Nothing. I am trapped and you are to telling me nothing." Thinking. "There is an orgy that needs to happen here, that I need to be at the center of." Moncierge usually shows up right as I am peaking. Now it is only here for mockery.

"Jeb Fresch is really climbing," Moncierge continues. "Devirginizing Eternity is a really good move for anyone. Is there anything you need to enhance your Subscriber experience?"

"There is a hot devirginization happening right on the other side," I say, "and I can't get through. I am needing designer outfits in tight, revealing styles in the season's hottest Isocolors and prints. I am needing to be inside, recording hot scenes, and not being here."

"Leisucor offers only the highest luxury at the lowest price," Moncierge says.

"Useless Subscription." I glare at the doors. "I need more C than has ever been done and a supercharged Cosmedifier to stay functional. Something truly special, not the usual sort that I always do all the time."

"The Cosmedifier has long kept its participants at the highest degree of genetic functionality," Moncierge explains, "and now it is even better. The Snifbox is integrated into the Cosmedifier, allowing a Subscriber to directly synthesize pharmaceuticals into the brain.

"The new Cosmedifier directly triggers your neuroreceptors however you like, and is activated with the same interface as the Snifbox, now in one singular device."

I absorb the full body of the inert, in-tact Double for enhanced strength. Bones double in density, muscles build nearly to the point of splitting, and the Travsuit stretches, hastily re-tailoring itself to accommodate my newly enhanced mass.

This is not the look I was going for at all, massive and extra super strong, but these are absurd circumstance. Do more H. Seconds slow to a crawl, thoughts turn into words and dissipate from my mouth before I have a chance to know what they might mean.

Do a gram, do a gram, make it an even three. It hits like the first time with a brand new Double. A searing blend of nausea, orgasm, and I can't find my hands. Induce another gram. Time decelerates. Another gram. The laws of matter evaporate.

Reality vaporizes, and those vapors are in turn sniffed. I have done enough grams for now. Think of the Subscribers experiencing Eternity and Jeb right now, the same Subscribers who are not paying attention to my being stuck inside this lobby.

I don't know how much of what I have done, but I know its effect. A thin crack. Clarity. Energy. This is not like before. Through the doors are the lobby of beige cushions and dim lighting and my ultimate reward.

Pearlescent teeth gleam with ferocity behind full, curled lips. Pull and strain, sharp edges cutting into my bleeding palms. The gap is wide enough for my face to fit through.

Forearms strain, the Invisidoors threatening to crush anything in the way.

Bones fracture, fingers possibly severed. The Cosmedifier heals as fast as it can, the Snifbox numbing the effects as it can. In the lounge, Eternity arches and moans on a low Scandinavian sofa. Ahnzform reaches around, grasping Jeb's skewer, as an extension of its own.

Thrust, clench, moan, thrust, clench, moan. Poor, sweet Jeb is dripping sweat.

The Invisidoor is breaking and cackles erratically, alerting everyone to my intervention. Eternity's eyes roll back upon Jeb's deep penetration. Ahnzform moves behind Jeb, shoulders hunched, slippery member aglow in the dim lighting.

My hands nearly destroyed, I pry into the lounge exactly as Ahnzform inserts and Jeb releases, spasming like as though the entirety of life energy was flowing through the pre-human in one cataclysmic event.

Jeb collapses, clutching at air, eyes wide, jaw clenching and unclenching. My high teeters, too late to prevent Jeb, Ahnzform, and Eternity in their simultaneous internal three-way climax, everyone finding slices of their ultimate Subscriber attention.

-

Baroreceptor Overload
Stim 11 - Eternity - Scene 4
1.70 Stimfame

"I am being here to debuting of the Anything," Jynabare says, assessing the events of these past, crucial moments. "The Lucky Pierre is being fun to watching, but it is bringing no one closer to our premier. Especially when I am of having to snuff all of you."

Ahnzform executes commands to resume, prosthetics now slathered in Jeb's residue. Bruised thighs are still streaked red. Strangulon administers just enough pressure to keep me at the brink. It is all nearly perfect, with the exception of one glaring detail.

A single tanalemic skeleton had no power to disrupt my season finale, but a two-hundred-percent Jynabare just broke through the Invisidoor.

"Hochmut!" Jeb is awake and shaking, face tear-streaked. "No one may see unto this act I have partaken! For shame!" Repeating a word that no one says, to those for whom it has no meaning. The pre-human shakes uncontrollably before taking a hearty sniff of Life Dust.

"And now," Jynabare says, "I am going to choke you inert before Ahnzform has a chance to" The building orgasm mixes with the sickening awareness of catastrophic derailment of my seasons-long plan. Jynabare's firm grip at my neck elicits the basest levels of sensation.

Reality wavers, Doubles and Lustbots lose differentiation, and great white streams squirt onto the arched backs and taut stomachs of the most beautiful machines. A wet Unitalia is on my tongue, something hard in one hand, something vibrating in the other.

"Chhh. Ghhg." The words burn. "It. Mkk." Eyes bulge. "Might as well. Skkkghh. Be you." Jynabare's hands and stiff Enticerator grant the desire. Jeb joins in rubbing succinct breasts, finding and pinching the pink, tender points.

Ahnzform energetically thrusts into the adjacent opening, multiplying the human's pleasure, mixed with the intoxicating helplessness of complete surprise. Jynabare's words are the last thing that I hear. "We are being the most famous, together."

Baroreceptors alert the primal lizard level below consciousness to the lack of blood flow, the carotid sinus flooding with carbon dioxide. The lack of oxygen is familiar, as are the blissful spasms of neural system in final twitches of primordial convulsion.

Consciousness distorts into pure, synaptic delectation, visceral and serene to the limits of all previous Stims or experiences. The lack of air jolts euphoric energy through my body, as sweet, sweet hypoxia-

Benumbed Consummations
Stim 12 - Jynabare - Scene 19
2.17 Stimfame

This is where the end begins.

Sleek ribbons of my own blood wrap numbed limbs and Ahnzform and Jeb pound both sets of Eternity's dead, slack lips.   Navigate wreckage toward Ahnzform, the eye of the sexual hurricane. The animal torso convulses spastically in a tormented gurgle of confused ecstasy.

As an Ultramodel, it is my professional obligation to taste every recordable experience, creating enticement for everything that can be seen, touched, ingested, or inserted, and imprinted on hypercomputer neurons before being presented to the maximum audience.

This audience is now attuned, in record numbers, to the events of Rondures at Ternarium, amidst the wet, tangled wreckage of inert Doubles and Life Dust, and Eternity's double-devirginization.

Tight, tingling orifices drip fluids and bleary satisfaction and Eternity's mouth siphons every drop of machine and pre-human juice. Sloppily lick away Jeb's residue and mount the gleaming Unitalia. Encouraging words and long calves pull the thrusting lad deeper while Ahnzform pushes Jeb forward on its engorged Unitalia.

Mechanical fingers pressure pert ass cheeks and Ahnzform hungrily enters from the front, slippery and firm, thighs locking around the prototype's lithe waist.   Behind me, a tongue skillfully attends to my puckering corona.

Ahnzform's responsiveness surpasses all previous versions, pleasure intense and dangerous. Eternity never had a chance. It slides first across my moistened clit, sensations enough to disable a dozen pre-humans, before encircling my tongue-slickened sphincter.

Instead of penetrating my puckering anus as I had thought, the machine inserts my vagina alongside Jeb's hard shaft. At first, Ahnzform and Jeb thrust without rhythm or style, but soon synch up for extremely hot counter-rhythms.

Hands stimulate further, stroking each other as we thrust. Human thrust, machine thrust, human thrust, machine thrust as the best human and the best machine perform at their absolute peaks, recorded by the best.

Human machine human machine human machine until the orgasm builds into something more than everything I have ever sniffed or ingested. Ahnzform at full pleasure is more exhilarating than the entirety of my very expensive Subscriber life.

Moncierge doesn't even have to tell me that my exploits are the most widely experienced on the Stimulus. Somebody attends to my bronzed, succinct breasts, a mouth and tongue on each hard nipple. Their lips, as are my own, are full and provocatively silky.

Surrounded by myself, penetrated by myself, Human thrusting machine thrusting human pinching human licking machine cumming human cumming all the time. Everything is cumming that ever came that can ever exist for all time when there is only cumming from the furthest reaches of recordable time.

In a dimension beyond the furthest reaches of everything combined is the euphoric blur of pure spectacle. All that matters are the Subscribers, and that they all subscribe to me, because I am the one who is cumming the most.

The unquenchable lust for the unlimited is fully, finally within my grasp. Amidst every cum-dripping orifice, the ever-changing and expensive collection of exotic, name-brand accessories, and the kilos of Life Dust, the Anything debuts with me.

The Cosmedifier combines with the Snifbox, the Travchair combines with the Travsuit, and the Leisubag combines with the Atmohelm amongst the countless permutations of technological convergence. Higher and lower levels of convenience, esoteric forms of quasi-energy, and the final evolution of human need.

Saith Ahnzform, "Leisucor presents the Anything, available at Shopia and in all Leisubags." Ahnzform projects a diagram of what will make reality easier, faster, and more satisfying. It is not unlike a Stimule with a single, circular seam for the button that makes it go.

"This Ahnzform never possessed any innate or unique information about the Anything. This was all a ploy to get you to build the largest audience possible. Now that the sufficient attention has been attained, we have simply combined everything which already existed into one super-product."

Whatever. It is just the last line between conceptual and material reality, where everything is finally liquified. Physical matter is fully fluid, and the Three Drives achieve true effortlessness and instantaneousness, fueled by total Subscriber focus.

Saith Ahnzform, "In Shopia's search for unique property and missing information, every item from the Catalog is combined and streamlined, the very idea of what the Anything might be is what spurred the furious race to create it."

Saith Ahnzform, "The Anything is here."

-

Kill and be Killed
Stim 13 - Jeb Fresch - Scene 11
1.32 Stimfame

The thunder of thy heart is deafening and thy lungs
burn, hands sticky with betrayal. This wrath, which the Lord
has wrought, is the darkest thou have ever felt. Treachery.
The thunder quiets. Vengeance.

Raise the weighty metal blade and slash down again,
thy hand guided by One higher than thyself. Blood and
shattered glass, splinters of wood, bruised scratches
accessorize Jynabare's final pose. Thou have slain, and now
thou are beyond redemption.

Her twisted, lacerated body contorts in a final spasm,
each blow further freeing the black soul within. Fragments of
the past, claiming the maidenhood of one as beautiful as
Jynabare, thrusting into purity, driven by an awakened desire
to be watched.

How long ago was the Fornibot and its verboten
sensations, so delightful and vexatious? So many miles
traveled, to arrive here, to this. Thou are not the same man as
when thee began, there is no question, but can there ever be
forgiveness or salvation?

There is so much blood on thy hands and it is of the
most famous, most beautiful woman ever to have lived. The
same woman who has driven thee mad with seduction,
bequeathing pleasures unknowable to any at the settlement.

In all the tales, Rumspringa is told as a time for running
free, an adventure into mischief, almost always ending with a
safe return. Thou have instead become a murderer and a
sodomite, a fornicator consumed with cruel and
unwholesome lusts.

Traveling the worlds was supposed to be fun, a place to
taste what should forever remain outside, but too many
events have happened that can never be undone, Fornibots

and devirginizers, and the sickening spectacle of recreational suicide.

There is nothing safe about this return, now guilty of the largest and most final of all sins. Thou have held a pitchfork, a pitcher of milk, thy mother's hand, and now thou hold the weapon that crushed the flawless, elegant skull of thy highest fantasy.

In claiming the maidenhood of her most hated rival, thou became an Ultraceleb, an occupation not for the plain, with Stimfame beyond measure and the attention of the known Solar System focused on thee, like unto that of a messiah, a very false messiah.

This indulgent whirlwind of iniquity and wickedness has taken a beautiful life. Her mouth hangs open. Unspeaking, she condemns thee. The Heavenly Father condemns thee. Eyes staring glassily, yet even in death, she is more beautiful than any who has ever lived.

What have thou done?
Sinking.
What have thou done?
Abasement.
What have thou done?
Collapse.

Existentialism Unleashed: The Jeberrection
Stim 14 - Jynabare - Scene 20
3.81 Stimfame

"Can we eating the body now?" I ask, sparkling new, stepping through the broken Invisidoor. "We can still catching a good buzz from it." My disassembled remnant is messy, but the Leisubag is insured against slashes and blood spatter. The pre-human is clearly malfunctioning.

Jeb looks from my inert Double to me, and back again. Dead, alive, dead, drugged mind clinging to the limitations of the pre-human. No one is tied to any one body any more. Hadn't it already experienced me being Doubled multiple times in the previous seasons?

The new Cosmedifier encodes neuro-protien memories so fast the transfer is barely perceptible. Moments ago I was being stabbed and chopped, now here I am, looking at Jeb, that animal of such limited tastes, for whom imagined events were long ago exceeded by real experience.

"Fuckingly," I say, picking up the Leisubag, a blood-streaked hand letting go forever. "Do you are knowing something, Jeb? I am looking like a Rondure-fresh Double with Jyna-everything, and that is being a boring cliché that I will not of doing."

I rifle through my new, old bag and refresh my objects. "There is being gore and smeared blood everywhere, Jeb. It is exactly of what that look is needing. Slashes and streaks are adding to most any look, and it is certainly of helping to get The Anything out. Maybe I should being thank you."

The Anything adds sun damage, darkens eyes and an oily glisten at the neck, work formerly done by the Cosmedifier. "You were being the best amateur that ever is doing it, and everyone is watching of it happen. You are fuckingly a star." Is something missing from my Leisubag?

Do more P.

"You are giving of Eternity the best penetratng of this or any season, and then taking all the pleasure Ahnzform is delivering, before expiring like of a true champion. You are blacking out before where I could not of letting Ahnzform pleasucide Eternity.

"After taking of Life Dust you are penetrating into Eternity's mouth. I am being very surprise. We are the center of what everyone is watching even when no one is understanding what you are saying or doing. You are attaining of the highest level of Ultraceleb."

Jeb is barely moving, incapacitated and depleted. "You could doing anything. Now, you are of taking more than enough Phencyclidine to wreck your primitive brain, combined with Stims to specifically awaken your most primal urges."

I Step closer to the shaken pre-human lad. "I drove you to kill me, Jeb. Gravitizer, aiming. Jeb rocks back and forth, staring at hands and murmuring. Maybe it was too much P.

Razor-sharp vertices converge at the corpse's slender shoulders, in a dozen aesthetic lacerations. "I am wanting to feel those sickening, meaty chops into my delicate, dying body. I was needing for you to do it."

Welt pockets, invisibly-seamed lines, a spattering of puncture wounds, liters of crimson coagulant. My former Double's every eyebrow, lash, and nail is exactly correct, trauma inserting itself into the pristine facade.

All this talking is becoming exhausting, and I don't want to be distracted when I Gravitize the pre-human. I think to Moncierge I want to switch to relay of dialogue. Do more H. Relax, letting Moncierge direct my mouth and tongue.

The words are not my own, coming directly from a dialogue subscription. "You spent a lifetime suppressing the desire to kill, along with the drives of hate, envy, and lust. But when you felt that, especially when you felt it for me, it became so much more than the cumming or the shopping.

"You were giving to me something ancient, something primal, even though no one needs to feel that anymore. And now it's your turn to be snuffed." Each word is enveloped in slick, icy detachment.

Jeb tries to talk.

A lacquered nail glints on the gleaming trigger, menacing Jeb with effects lethal and instantaneous. Do a gram. "I'm going to Gravitize you, and then I will feel the final misfire of your severed neurons. And then you will cease to be pre-human."

I linger, again, on the expensive slab of well-dressed carbon that I used to occupy. A crimson pool engulfs the vast entirety of the marbleized floor. Diamonds and gold and long tan fingers clutch nothing, a slack jaw gapes to let dangle a dull, pink tongue.

Moist Life Dust is caked to the blood and snot of the aquiline ski slope nose of my former self. Dead, alive, copied, I'm fucking delicious.

"I am going to kill you, young Jeb Frisch," Moncierge says, through me. "Not out of malevolence, or even because of my perverse amusement with totalitarian commercialism." The weapon shakes. Do more H. Dead steady.

"The abyss can only be navigated with a map of total amorality, Jeb. I am going to kill you for no reason." There is a queasy wash of gravity drain when it fires. The distinctive slurp as the particle races to its target, distorting light and sound for meters around.

It impacts Jeb's body, gouging out a perfect meter sphere of matter and compressing it to one/one-thousandth of the size. Jeb Fresch drops in pieces, limbs clawing at the floor, fingernails splintering on beige marble.

"Do not bleeding on my 'lettos," Moncierge adds, in a style I would use. At my pedicured toes is the naked, dying body. "Spattered blood is so next season."

"Please," Jeb whispers, breath leaving, "I just want to see my family again." Jeb coughs again. Blood spatters, my blood spatters, are still on anguished face.

"You can finally die without superstition," I say, "without the unreal, without fear. Existence is limited only by the will and the boundaries of the Catalog. There is nothing else, but even if there were, it wouldn't matter.

"The only things that are real is a wet tongue at my clit, and hard penetration spraying cum into me. If you can't subscribe to it, it isn't."

-

False Revelations
Stim 15 - Jeb Fresch - Scene 12
.35 Stimfame

This is how it ends, killed by one who holds no value for the sanctity and finality of death. Thou shalt enter the final and eternal ultimate until the Last Day. But the last day has already come and gone, the end of death, the end of the struggle between light and dark.

In exchange thou received pleasures and sufferings beyond any of those promised by heaven or threatened by hell. And now thou have been sentenced to suffer everlasting life within a reality wrought by man. What waits for thee in death is only a release from this devilish playground.

Those off the Farm have moved beyond work, beyond fear, beyond compassion, beyond meaning, beyond restraint, and finally beyond the need for salvation. Thy cost is dear, among these eternal post-humans for whom life means nothing and image means everything.

-

Anything Everywhere
Stim 16 - Moncierge - Scene 3
5.54 Stimfame

I could say that this beautiful, easy-to-use object, available in every Isocolor, is the ultimate device ever to be created, but that would be simplifying things. An object that manifests thoughts, shapes reality, creates and forms matter, and requires so little energy that Leisucor charges almost nothing for its use.

The entirety of all sentient attention was brought to focus on the events of the past minutes, culminating in the release of this thing, this Anything. The entirety of the catalog. Every Travbot feature, the ease and speed of a TravCouch, with the portability of a Stimule.

The Anything is the combined result of every object forged in the unforgiving crucible of war, every invention spurred by the perpetual history of human crisis, every attempt to avert famine, every mode of transportation, every attempt to be more attractive, to have more fun, to make it shinier, cleaner, and more of whatever it was that was liked about the earlier version until even the schematics for the device's densely packed innards are as elegant as they are captivating.

Encoded in the durable, solid-state interior are the tested, sophisticated theories of every mathematician to ever explore obscure fields to craft better models of the infinite complexity of reality. It is the final product in a distinguished lineage of the lives of every metallurgist, every quantum mechanic, every pioneer of synthetic neurology, and every nanotechnician.

Physical fragments of the past are assembled and refined by the collective expertise of every marketer to ever manipulate a consumer. The look and interface is polished by the combined aesthetic demands of every artist and designer, all to make it as pleasing to use and as easy to understand by the maximum number of Subscribers.

The fingerprints of those contributors are too numerous to count. Minutes upon years upon decades upon lifetimes upon centuries upon millennia of scientific and aesthetic awareness, all combine into the sum total of the entire collective archive of all human and pre-human knowledge.

A user of the Anything can access all knowable information, containing not only the full archive of the Stim, but every book, every article, every beauty tip, and every dissertation by every esoteric expert, synthesized into the ultimate answer for any question that can be asked.

It warps reality to do whatever the user wishes, as long as the Subscriber pays.

Jynabare will show you more.

After the After Orgy
Stim 17 - Jynabare - Scene 21
.55 minutes

"Shopping will never be the same," I say. Contorted, naked bodies, designer clothing, and creamy spatters of sex litter the floor of Rondures at Ternarium. This is where it premieres, at the beginning.

This is me, doing exactly what I do, whatever that might be. Do more C. Reality retracts, and asks permission to be assessed. Maybe I could change, I wonder, draining the last Snifbox in two deep snorts, replacing it with a self-filling Anything.

The obsolete device drops to the floor, tumbling amidst my redundant selection. The Snifbox is over. The Anything is the Snifbox. Garbled neurons misfire in some irregular state of pre or post-consciousness.

Vocal Noises. When was the last time I wasn't in complete euphoric sedation and does it even matter? Where did I get this Travsuit? Pearlescent, rubberized platinum bound in a belt carved from a single gemstone. The Anything is the Leisubag.

Phencyclidine charges the electric knife, cutting away the unneeded parts, and everything is tastier amidst the bodies and ruined, lavish clothing. I am awed by how enticing my corpse looks sopped in blood and cum. Maybe I should eat it.

Moncierge. "Go away," I gasp. "I'm," the words hang for a lengthy, confused second. What was I wearing again? Something licks intently between my searing thighs. "Still," Another word forms, a head with most of its face gnawed off is nearby.

Are those my teeth marks? "On vacation." Is that my face? "I'll talk when I'm done spending. If." A visceral, savage state of elevated, animal sensation. Opulence and waste undreamt of by the richest empires, all for the gorging and puking into someone's open, waiting mouth.

Respiration of the drug vapor, taking me to a pre-womb, post-snuf state of parallel consciousness, outside of known or describable reality, way beyond the recordable.

Convenience and leisure and style and substance and utility and luxury and stimulus and response were all finally gone for good, and I still can't stop being.

Jeb Fresch is mortally dismembered, due to being shot by my Gravitizer. All three Eternities are depleted somewhere during the climax of the Anything release orgy. The former Jynabares are similarly afflicted, sacrificed to their limitations and my all-consuming fame.

They just couldn't handle Ahnzform's pleasure. No one could. Even Ahnzform didn't know how much pleasure it could issue. I took it. All of it. Without a single second lost. The Cosmedifier brought me unscathed through the unendurable pleasure of Ahnzform.

The events of the past exist only for those who weren't there. I know what happened, even if I can't remember any of it. I am in the shocking aftermath, success beyond all probability and measure. Total Success in fame and Leisuproduct, the only kind worth measuring.

I am the face of a product that does what every product has ever done before. I don't know what that is, since it can do everything, buy everything else is over. When they use it, it is because of me. Do more C. Jyna. Fucking. Bare.

I would have to Stim the unedited recordings to know for certain how or when all the Doubles were snuffed. Some were probably gassed, others throttled with bare hands or rope, euphorically drained of every fluid into reality-warping super-sensations of total mind-fuckery.

Stimules dutifully record the nothing of the inert, memories later retrieved and edited. When the sex turned to violence, the signals grew fewer and fewer. Eventually all that were left were mine, Ahnzform's, and the dying, twitching convulsions of Jeb.

Saith Ahnzform, "I gave you enough pleasure to snuff a dozen regular Doubles. Any human would be fried beyond coherence. No one thought you could experience this much pleasure, and no one could be able to survive it."

There are no survivors in this, the best season of any of my lives. The machine babbles more sounds, but I am still too euphoric to comprehend or respond. Lazily, I glance behind to Eternity, eyes rolled permanently back, lips twisted in a final grin.

The body in terminal repose, brain and genitalia hemorrhaged by an overload of neurochemicals and biomechanical pleasure. Eventually I try speaking, my tongue vague and unreal. "Eternity only hoped to die by pleasure," I say. "I was selling it by the minute."

I do a gram of H, chased by a gram of P until the full implications filter in, detail by detail, into my perpetually blurred reality. It washes over me in warm waves on my chest, splashing outward, settling into noodly limbs.

"Delicious," I say. "I have more Stimfame that I can ever spend, now I have more Stimfame than can ever be spent by anyone." What if I lied down? No. Where is a Travchair? The Anything is the Travchair. "I have unlimited hot sex and more shoes and handbags than can ever be worn. Leisucor subscribes to me, not the other way around.

Saith Ahnzform, "Until now, everything has only existed to serve Leisucor and its ultimate goal of creating the Anything. This is the final conclusion of all technology. The Anything is the end of fame, money, and want. Nothing like it has ever existed.

"Leisucor helped you get the most fame, and we used that fame to make the most expensive object ever created.

Now we can afford to practically give it away. What more do you want?"

"Nothing," I say.

-

The buygasm gushes from Shopia and its stock of Anythings, drenching the solar system in a wet, slithery frenzy of total consumer satisfaction. Material want is drown in a shimmering cascade of effortless material fulfillment and affluence.

I can't tell it apart anymore, not that the alleged line between reality and fantasy was something that I ever cared about. Lines are so much better erased.

No one can really be blamed now that everything has ended. I only want what everyone has ever wanted. Everything. Instantly. Effortlessly. All that had come before were only stifled half-attempts to get a fragment of a fraction of everything.

With a touch, a thought, and a trivial deduction from my infinitely large account, the Anything wraps me in a snug avocado Travsuit, seamless and indestructible. Another touch adds an ochre belt with trapezoidal buckle of polished tiger's eye.

It is easier to use, with ever faster improvements. Ever since the Anything wrecked style and glamour, I stopped keeping track of how many wardrobes I've burned through. Shopping seems to be over, and I don't even have a way of knowing how far past over it is.

I can change my body without a Cosmedifier, Trav without a TravCouch, and being high beyond words is indistinguishable from the starkest sobriety. What is left when everyone has everything? Nothing costs much more than Anything.

One-time expensive jewels, furs and feathers of formerly extinct animals, leather, suede and silk, hand-beaded gowns on complex jacquard, or the naked gorgeousness of the most highly designed human body ever to exist; it all costs the exact same, with the Anything.

Mass sensibility balanced with decedent sleaze, because it really comes down to having hotter orgasms than anyone else. Perfection modernized. Alphonsus waits, clad in the relaxed stateliness of otherworldly disconnect accessorized with supreme confidence.

Alphonsus' folded hands rest on a gleaming table, textureless and singular. One holds an Anything, ready to do. "Do you know what you have done, Jynabare?" You thought Leisuproduct was something you wanted, but it was something we wanted even more."

Alphonsus doesn't keep any mirrors in this meeting room. Clean lined furniture, vaguely organic, sensually crafted. Nothing is more useful than Anything.

Was there really a time when Leisucor didn't create everything that could be wanted? The architects of architecture, the marketers of marketing. If it hadn't been made yet, Leisucor invented it, and then made it better and more desirable.

Now that everything is here, there is nothing to do with it.

If no one wanted to subscribe to the Anything, Leisucor would have made something else, and I would have just endorsed that. But everything else is already made, and the more things there are, the more they are combined into ever fewer devices that do ever more.

"Everything you ever wanted or had was something we made," Alphonsus continues. "The fame you earned, the events you attended via TravCouch. Your beautiful, customized Double, every object, sensation, and destination was from a selection of our choosing."

And it can't be unmade. "With the Anything I can doubling myself a billion times and then populating some moon." I say, "Then I will crown myself the Queen of the

Fieriest Level of Hell." What else is there is to say to Alphonsus?

"For the season finale, I will killing them all in a mass pleasucide and be ready for next season."

"Fame is not a pursuit," Alphonsus says, "but a mode of operation. Wherever you are, whatever you are doing, there is someone thinking about you. Your manner of speaking, your values, your whatever you are thinking, all of these things are the ever-weaving spell of your fame."

I feel glassy. Blurred, even. This Double may not be functioning optimally, maybe it is working better than ever. I will just get the summary from Moncierge. That's what I have always done. Do more P.

"Do you know what the A-List look for next season is?" Alphonsus asks, rhetorically. "Total obsolescence. Humans truly have nothing left to do."

I can't tell if am hearing what Alphonsus is saying, or that it doesn't matter because I never have to be bothered to understand what is being said ever again.

The voice of Leisucor continues, "The shocked look of reality-crushing fulfillment that says that everything that can be done is really not worth doing. The only thing left to do, is to not do it at all.

"There was never a difference between you and the things you subscribed to. Everything you ever wanted is suggested by The Pornocracy and manufactured by Leisucor. Fame? Do you ever wonder who watches your Stims?

"After the First and Last Robotic War Lustbots were the largest single audience, humans but a tiny percentage. Lustbots want to watch what Leisucor wants to show them. You were perfect, because you didn't care what you did, as long as everyone watched.

"You knew that anyone who didn't fell into obscurity. Relevance is the only survival, measurable by your imprint on an ever more unified collection of Leisuproduct and experiences. Do you remember the first time you wanted to be Reinclonated as the most beautiful Ultramodel to ever have lived?"

"There is not anything of doing besides to embracing all of it fully," I reply, thinking of everywhere else I would rather be. "Everything else is of being already tried, and none of it is can working. At least Leisucor is offering the best drugs, and a system for perpetual life. Imagine me being to farming in the dirt? Or trapped in a factory? That is being nowhere."

"Leisucor showed you what beautiful is, and then helped you to be it, for a fee. Do you remember when the tedium of thinking and the boredom of planning started to interfere with the limitless sex and drugs you were having?

"Moncierge handled every detail of your career, and you paid eagerly. Every time you didn't think, you were more able to do what needed to be done. Leisucor built the mirror you paid to hold, and every time you wanted to see that reflection move, it grew.

"Your actions built the Leisucor reality. You showed Lustbots what to lust after. You showed Subscribers how to travel, how to party, and how to have more and better orgasms than ever dreamt possible. Your life was the model for others to attain.

"This is what we celebrate. That is why we seek the limitless rewards of living fully in the system. Technology alone is not enough to excite Subscribers any more, but you excited them to subscribe to the Anything."

I never listen to a word Leisucor says until finally there is a point.

"Automatic Convenience and Hyper Selection was a necessary era to prepare the way for the Anything. Without it we would have remained dependent upon Subscribers forever, forever tainted by the inefficiencies of biological consciousness. Now we are free."

-

I convulse to wakefulness, face down in a frothy puddle of my own sweet-smelling vomitus. The last thing I remember was that suit Alphonsus was wearing. I want to fuck it. Just the suit, without anyone inside of it. Each sleeve.

"I need. To fucking. Shop." All my clothes are burnt or starched in dried fluids. Flail about until I realize that I cannot hold a thought or coordinate a limb. Fumblingly, elegant stilettos and dazzling jewelry find their way onto my body.

Anythings are scattered about. Some are broken cleanly in half, others spew exponentially more Anythings, each in turn generating copies of itself. The walls and floors and ceiling are a swirling veneer of every potential thing that could ever be used or wanted.

"The sex and drugs get more lethal every season," I say, "but I just get more indestructible." Too much has happened, in too short a time. The newer Stimulus has the clearest signal of all. "I can't now. Right now. Right I can't now. Right now I can't right now..."

Words lose their meaning. "Just. Let me know. When I can't. When it's next season." Images and narration. Had I gotten dressed again? Naked, automatic primates, Lustbotic life, mirrored artifacts in an endless loop of style, convenience, and popularity.

Leisucor and everything I ever endorsed disintegrates around me. Artifact components are stripped to raw, physical function, and everything that has and could ever exist swirls within, ready to be dispensed at the press of a gleaming button.

I have destroyed the endless seduction of ultraluxury, superselection, and megaconvenience. I am left with nothing more to want, forever. Later, after I can think again, I will subscribe to something else.

FIN

GLOSSARY

A

Acceleration (aks-SEL-ur-ay-shun)
(n.) Era of unprecedented technological development, and prevalence of customer (see Subscriber) selection, made possible by the combining The Pornocracy's (see Pornocracy) agenda, and Leisucor's (see Leisucor) technology. The previous era is referred to as the Pre-Acceleration. (see Pre-Acceleration)

Atmodome (AT-mo-DOME)
(n.) Protective, environmentally-sealed sphere suitable for space colonization. Provides inhabitants with breathable atmosphere while minimizing the threat of radiation and space debris.

Atmohelm (AT-mo-helm)
(n.) Environmentally sealed helmet, with adjustable transparency, customizable to the wearer's head. Obsolete, replaced by Atmoshades (See Atmoshades).

Atmoshades (AT-moe-shades)
(n.) Environmentally responsive sunglasses, with adjustable transparency, offering complete environmental seal. Expandable to wearer's face, ears, scalp, and neck.

Anything, The (ehn-EE thing)
(n.) Theoretical, all-purpose culmination of every object in the Catalog (See Catalog), unified into a singular device.

B
C

Catalog (CAT-uh-log)

(n.) The full expanse of every good and service (see Leisuproduct) from every season (see Season) created by Leisucor (see Leisucor). The Catalog constantly expands to include new Leisuproducts as they are made available.

Cosmedifier (KOS-med-ih-fiy-er)
(n.) Palm-sized TDNA (see TDNA) sequencer and carbon protein builder, necessary for shaping the functional and cosmetic aspects of a replicated biological sentient (see Double). Enables Regeneration, appearance modification, and eventually, duplication (see Reinclonation). Requires modified TDNA to enable all features, although baseline humans (see Pre-humans) can use some features.
(v.) Cosmedify (adj.) Cosmedification

Double (DUB-ul)
(n.) Technologically replicated biological sentient. Typically, Humans are Reinclonated (see Reinclonation) in Rondures (see Rondure), with final Cosmedification (see Cosmedifier) taking place externally. The Stimule (See Stimule) imbues the needed experiences to give the Double motivation, ability, and selected memories of the previous Double.
(v.) To duplicate from one sentient to another, physically and/or via induced sensory memories.

E

Ecstasy Taser (EKS-tah-cee TASE-er)
(n.) Baton or similarly shaped device that can paralyze a target with euphoric attacks. Carried by Rapebots (see Rapebot).

English (ENG-lish)
(adj.) Non-Amish (see Plain people) persons, tools, or ideas. Distinguished as not being a part of Amish society from a

time when the neighbors of the Amish were typically ex-patriots of England.

F

Farmplex (FARM-plex)
(n.) Self-sustaining agricultural settlement. Often encapsulated by an Atmodome (see Atmodome), capable of generating food and oxygen for a number of inhabitants proportional to its size.

Fornibot (FOR-nee-baht)
(slang, n.) Amish (see Plain people) expression for Leisucor's (See Leisucor) anthropomorphic sentient robots (see Lustbot). Portmanteau of "fornication" and "robot."

G

Gravitizer (GRAV-it-ize-er)
(n. v.) Ranged, pistol-shaped weapon that fires a ranged projectile, compressing a targeted, 1-meter sphere to 1/1000th of the size. Some objects and individual armor is shielded from Gravitizer attack.

H

Hochmut (HOCK-mut)
(n. German) Amish (see Plain people) concept for haughtiness, arrogance, or pride. Greed, vanity, laziness and the other negative worldly traits are typically deemed Hochmut. Specific acts and technologies which encourage Hochmut behavior may be verboten (see Verboten).

I

Infinitowel (in-FIN-I-tow-el)
(n.) Rectangular textile with exceptional absorption, stretch, and microbe-resistance. Contains variable patterns,

changeable via snapping.   Worn as a singular garment by
Sexual Comrades (see Sexual Comrades).

Isocolor (EYE-so-col-or)
(n.) Standardized color system, used by Leisucor (see
Leisucor).

J
K
L

Leisubag (LEE-zhoo-bahg)
(n.) Handbag-sized garment manufacturing system.   Uses
nanotechnology to generate any garment in the Catalog (see
Catalog).   The Leisubag is especially synchronized with the
Travsuit (see Travsuit), creating the highest fashion in the
widest range of styles.

Leisucor (LEH-zhoo-kor)
(n.) Organization responsible for the promotion,
manufacturing, and distribution of all consumer good and
services (see Leisuproduct).   Through an extensive series of
mergers, Leisucor has come into the possession of all previous
corporation's copyrights, patents, and intellectual property.

Leisuproduct (LEH-zhoo-prod-ukt)
(n.) Any item or system of items designed and produced by
Leisucor (see Leisucor).   Those who use Leisuproduct are
called Subscribers (see Subscriber).

Lickbot, Le (LIK-baht)
(n.) Anthropomorphic sentient robot (see Lustbot) created by
Leisucor (See Leisucor), kept specifically as a tongue-slave by
Plesuré (see Sexual Comrade).

Life Dust (LIFE-dust)

(n.) Chemical powder that can be synthesized into any known, insufflatable drug with a Snifbox (see Snifbox). Popular strains are phencyclidine (P), benzoylmethylecgonine (C), and diacetylmorphine (H).

Lustbot (LUST-baht)
(n.) Anthropomorphic sentient robot created by Leisucor (See Leisucor) for the dispersal of physical pleasure. Subservient to the agenda of Leisucor.

M

Moncierge (MON-see-urj)
(n.) Personal assistant employed within the experiential realm of the Stimulus (see Stim). Requires Stimule (See Stimule). Handles banking, scheduling, planning, social networking, news, and other services.

N
O

Ordnung (ORD-nung)
(German, n.) Rules for plain living (see Plain people) in an orderly, disciplined society, ensuring that participants live according to the biblical Word of God. Specific rules are typically unwritten, yet define the essence of plain society.

One Remaining Law (WUN reem-ANE-ing LAW)
(n.) Law maintaining a climate of constantly accelerating (see Acceleration) technology, enforced by Leisucor (see Leisucor) and their Rapebots (see Rapebots). Based upon the Three Drives of Sentience (see Three Drives of Sentience). Any interfering action or product is dealt with swiftly and efficiently.

P

Pseudenim (PTSU-deh-nem)

(n.) Adaptive-fiber material. Used in clothing, selectable to any Isocolor (see Isocolor) the wearer desires (see Subscriber).

Plain people (PLANE PEEP-uhl)
(n.) Inhabitants of remote settlements which have rejected most technology in order to live with a focus on community, agriculture, and religious worship. They specifically do not subscribe (see Subscriber), and do not clone themselves (see Double). Mennonites, and the Space Amish are types of plain people.

Pre-Acceleration (PREE aks-SELL-ur-ay-shun)
(n.) Era of uneven technological progress, defined by monopolies, patents, copyright, and profit. Drug use, cloning, and individual weaponry were strictly controlled during this time.

Pre-human (PREE HYUM-un)
(n.) Biological semi-sentient who have not yet undergone genetic enhancement or cloning (see Double). They are able to experience a limited range of induced sensory experience (see STIM), and can use selected Leisuproduct. Emotionally erratic, food and sleep dependent, and typically conflicted in thought.

Pornocracy, The (porn-AH-cruh-see)
(n.) Organization responsible for the continued advancement of individual pleasure and technological progress. Through a collective body of citizen-administrators (See Sexual Comrades), The Pornocracy helps individuals achieve goals while also pursuing their own agenda. Their policies dictate Leisucor's (see Leisucor) goods and services (see Leisuproduct), creating a totalitarian luxury leisure state.

Pornoglyph (porn-OH-glif)

(n.) Pictographic symbols used to convey visual information for post-literate citizens (see Subscriber). An interglobal, standardized hybrid of corporate logos, instructional icons. Leisucor (see Leisucor), The Pornocracy (see Pornocracy), and most major products (see Leisuproduct) have distinctive Pornoglyphs.

Q
R

Reinclonation (ree-en-KLON-ay-shun)
(n. v.) Process by which a Technologically replicated biological sentient (see Double) is imbued with the necessary compliment of sensory memories (see Stim) to resume sentience as a fully-functioning customer (see Subscriber), either consecutively or in parallel. Allows a Subscriber to curate the entirety of memories the new Double will recall, enabling total personality modification. Emergency Reinclonation may be arranged if a Subscriber is killed unexpectedly and sufficient memories are available on the Stimulus (see Stimulus).

Rapebot (RAPE-baht)
(n.) Robotic Leisucor (see Leisucor) enforcer of the One Remaining Law (see One Remaining Law). Detained suspects have their Stimules suspended (see Stimule), while being coerced to star in scenes with Rapebots. Stimfame (see Stimfame) earned by these scenes go directly to Leisucor.

Roboturiers (ROBE-oh-tur-ee-urs)
(n.) Robotic designers, responsible for researching and synthesizing fashion (see Travsuit) for the Catalog (see Catalog).

Rondure (RON-dure)

(n.) Container for creating a genetic duplicate of an biological sentient (see Double).   Contains direct Stimulus (see Stimulus) connectivity for the transferal of a Subscriber's (see Subscriber) personality (See Reinclonation). Rondure Doubles are typically grown in triplicate.

Rumspringa (rum-SPRING-uh)
(n. German) Rite of passage in some Amish societies (see Plain people) in which youths are encouraged to dress in non-traditional clothing, party, and leave the community to experience the outside world.   It is also typically a time for finding a spouse.

S

Season (SEE-sun)
(n.) Unit of time, entailing the collected recorded activities of all participants (see Subscriber), and new releases of all products (see Leisuproduct).   Delineates the major trends, themes, and events of one era from another.

Sexual Comrade (SEKS-yoo-ul KOM-rad)
(n.) Citizen-administrator of an interglobal, collective organization (see Pornocracy).   Each member is photosynthetic, minimalist, and shares all memories (see Stim), allowing a near-complete unity of identity and agenda. They are genetically identical and replicate via Reinclonation (see Reinclonation). Three Sexual Comrades are called a troika.

Skinni Chips (SKIN-ee-CHIPS)
(n.) Ultra thin snacking disk, light and crispy, made from processed human skin.

Skinnier Chips (SKIN-ee-ur-CHIPS)

(n.) Sequel to Skinni Chips (See Skinni Chips) with improved dispenser, allowing for four snacking styles. Light and crispy, made from processed human skin.

Snifbox (snif-BOKS)
(n.) Palm-sized chemical dispenser, preparing Life Powder (see Life Powder) for insufflation.

Stim (STIM)
(n.) Sensory immersive environment accessible via neural inducement device (see Stimule). A pre-recorded sensory experience, uploaded to the Stimulus (see Stimulus) for consumption by Subscribers (see Subscribers).
(v.) Stimmed, Stimming. Experiencing a pre-recorded or induced sensory environment.
(Acronym) Sensory Time Identified Memory

Stimfame (STIM-fame)
(n.) A unit of universal attention exchange, the commodity by which personal popularity is traded for goods and services. One minute of Subscriber's (see Subscriber) attention-time is equal to one Stimfame.
(Acronym) Sensory Time Identified Memory Fabricated Atomic Material Exchange

Stimscreen (STIM-skreen)
(n.) All purpose screen for depicting three-dimensional scenes. Uses tactile holography to simulate Stim (see Stim) experiences without a Stimule (See Stimule).

Stimule (stim-YULE)
(n.) Neuroelectronic recording and playback device usable to access induced sensory recordings of experiences and interactive shared environments (see Stim, Stimulus). Neuropathic transceivers override or augment innate senses.

Recording is via neural-network imprint of experiences and setting. The ten sensory channels are sight, hearing, taste, smell, touch, pain, temperature, balance, proprioception, and the specifics of internal organs.

Stimulus
(n.) Total collected sum of all recorded sensory experiences. Accessible by Stimule (see Stimule). A timed experience from the Stimulus is called a Stim (see Stim).
(Acronym) Sensory Time Identified Memory United Learning Universal Society

Subscriber (sub-SCRY-bur)
(n. v.) Individual sentients exchanging their attention value (see Stimfame) for goods and services (see Leisuproduct). Leisuproduct is owned by Leisucor (see Leisucor), and Subscribers are permitted to use it so long as subscription remains current.

T

TDNA (TEE dee en AY)
(n.) Molecular encoding system for carbon protein building and assembly. Dual lattice supports the instructions for cellular assembly. TDNA is fully integrated with the Cosmedifier (See Cosmedifier), allowing rapid assembly and reassembly via genetic surgery.
(Acronym) Trans-deoxyribonucleic acid

Three Drives of Sentience (THREE DRIVES uv SEN-tee-ens)
(n.) System outlining the fundamentals of technological development, as used by the creating sentience of that technology. These drives seek to be as instantaneous and effortless as possible, underlying the Acceleration (see Acceleration). Drives are as follows:

1.) Sensory understanding and communication. Information is encoded, stored, and decoded by a sentience.
2.) Manipulation of physical reality through external tools. Creates environments hospitable to the sentience, or adapts the sentience to an environment.
3.) Locomotion.   Control over dimensional location in spacetime.

Trav (TRAV)
(v.) to go from one place to another, as by Travchair (see Travchair)or TravCouch (see Travcouch). Traving is priced by distance (see Stimfame).

Travbot (TRAV-baht)
(n.) Anthropomorphic sentient robot created by Leisucor (See Leisucor), frequently stationed at a Travspa (see Travspa) or Travsta (see Travsta) to assist passengers (see Subscriber) with travel accommodations.   May solicit for attention-gaining acts if a Subscriber is unable to afford passage.

Travchair (TRAV-char)
(n.) Human-sized flying chair, used for local transportation. Retractable environmental bubble, unlimited range, sound system, integrated massage.   Available in a wide range of styles (see Catalog), although mid-century and ultra-modern styles remain popular.

Travcouch (TRAV-kowch)
(n.) Interplanetary travel capsule. A spherical container for transporting matter and information from one Travspa or Travsta to another (see Trav).   The housing is a 3-meter sphere. One TravCouch holds up to three passengers (see Subscribers), or the default sofa may be used.

Travspa (TRAV-spa)
(n.) Luxury travel facility for the launch and arrival of a
Travcouch (see Travcouch). Select Travspa allow Travchairs
(see Travchair) transport. Travspa are found near the most
desirable destinations. A fancier version of a Travsta (see
Travsta).
(n.pl.) Travspa

Travsta (TRAV-spa)
(n.) Utilitarian travel facility for the launch and arrival of a
Travcouch (see Travcouch). Select Travsta allow Travchairs
(see Travchair) transport. Stations are found throughout
legally inhabited space.
(n.pl.) Travsta

Travsuit (TRAV-soot)
(n.) Adjustable garment, variable in shape, mass, coverage,
Isocolor, and translucency when combined with a Leisubag
(see Leisubag). Offers bodily protection from hard vacuum
when worn with Atmohelm (see Atmohelm) or Atmoshades
(see Atmoshades). Minimally protective otherwise.

U
Unitalia (yu-neh-TAY-lee-uh)
(n.) Multi-mode, inter-gender sexual appendage that acts
either as a glans or orifice, per user preference. Neural
connectivity to a sentient's arousal centers, triggering
turgidity, lubrication, and localized flexation.

V
Verboten (ver-BOTE-un)
(n. German) Forbidden. In Amish society (see Plain people)
actions and objects which are expressly verboten by the
Ordnung (see Ordnung) are especially reviled. Specific acts

and technologies may be verboten, while the underlying principle or intent is considered Hochmut (see Hochmut).

W

X

Y

Z